MAISEY YATES

avenge me

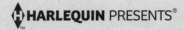

HARLEQUIN PRESENTS®

6.29 06/14

Recycling programs
for this product may
not exist in your area.

ISBN-13: 978-0-373-43037-6

AVENGE ME

Special thanks and acknowledgment are given to Maisey Yates for her contribution
to the *Fifth Avenue* trilogy.

Printed in U.S.A.

HARLEQUIN®
www.Harlequin.com

avenge me

Prologue

It was supposed to be an evening of bland conversation. That was what Alex, Hunter and he did every year. Drinks and bland conversation. The kind of conversation that skirted around anything of interest or meaning. That lay thick like graveyard dirt over the skeletons of the past.

Buried beneath talk of 401(k)s, football statistics and current events. So deep that it was easy to forget they were all dining over a coffin.

Unfortunately, the letter he had in his hand was the damned shovel.

It was going to unearth everything. He didn't think there would be a bland enough topic in existence to ever put the ghosts to rest again.

Austin looked at the two men sitting across from him. The men he'd once called his best friends. Men who had become little more than distant strangers over the past ten years.

Hunter was throwing out some sort of B.S. line about how much more action he'd get now that he'd been ousted from the NFL, and Alex was nodding along. All a bunch of shallow nothing, but then, what else would they talk about?

They were barely acquaintances now. Acquaintances who

met every year on the grimmest of anniversaries and never once spoke of why they'd gathered. Acquaintances who could barely look each other in the eye.

But then, that was what bland conversation did, he supposed. It kept bad memories at bay and old friends at a distance. A distance that wasn't an accident. Not in the least.

But they didn't have time for distance now. Didn't have time for circular talk that meant less than nothing. Not now. Not when he had the letter burning a hole straight through to his skin.

Austin reached into the interior pocket of his jacket and ran his fingers over the folded document. He pulled it out and put it on the table, white paper blending into the pristine white cloth.

Strange. He'd half expected it to leave a crimson stain.

"I'm afraid the usual dinner of denial and quiet regret will not be served tonight," he said.

"What the hell?" Hunter said, deadpan, not making a move for the letter, waiting for an explanation. Austin found that he didn't have the words.

It was Alex who picked it up and opened it. He skimmed it then handed it to Hunter. "What the hell is this?" he asked, reframing Hunter's question with more intensity.

"The truth. At least, I believe it is." Austin sat down, wrapping his fingers around the fork to his left and resting his thumb on the tines, gradually increasing the pressure until he nearly broke the skin. "My father, Jason Treffen, sainted advocate for women in the workplace, tireless defender of the downtrodden and harassed, did in fact cause a woman to commit suicide because of his unwanted advances. Because of his actions." He released his hold on the fork and let it drop onto the table. "I'm afraid of what he might have done to her. I mean…I knew it was bad. I knew…because of what she did. What she felt she had to do. But I didn't really believe that he'd touched her. Now…"

"This is why she did it." The statement came from Hunter. His voice was rough, his eyes unfocused. Alex's dark eyes were glued to Hunter, as if waiting to see what the other man might do.

Austin knew they were all thinking the same thing. Of the same night.

And the same woman.

Sarah.

"I think so," he said.

"Where did you get the info?" Alex asked.

"Anonymously provided. Naturally."

"Naturally," said Hunter.

"It didn't come to me," he said, his voice rough. "It came to the pro bono office. Publicly it's not very well connected with me, and I doubt whoever sent it knew that I would end up with it. Since I'm rarely in the office I might not have seen it…. But it was passed on to me by Travis Beringer, an old classmate of ours who volunteers at the place on occasion. It's from a woman asking for help. Because my damned father has been getting so much media attention. Since he and all his good works are about to be profiled on the largest talk show in the country. Given the nature of the contents, and knowing something about Sarah, Travis thought I should see it."

"And someone has evidence that he…that he drove Sarah to her death by harassing her? Assaulting her?" Hunter asked.

"It's not evidence. Not *real* evidence. It's wild accusation.

Assumption that what he did to her caused her to kill herself."

"You believe it, Austin?" Alex asked.

"Hell yeah." Not that he was happy about it. He'd been sick to his stomach since he'd gotten the damn thing two days ago. But he believed it.

The suspicion had always been there, along with the guilt. Along with a call that had gone unanswered and a voice mail he hadn't listened to until it was too late.

But there had been no proof. Still, it had been enough for him to cut ties with his father. For him to relegate his family to holiday visits. Lunches with his mother and sister at hotels rather than at the Treffen estate.

Now the suspicion was turning into certainty. Truth gnawed through his last remaining shreds of doubt. For two days now, he'd been replaying his last conversation with Sarah. Over and over again. The last time he ever saw her alive.

She'd looked so brittle. So sad and tired…

"This job is much more demanding than I ever could have imagined, Austin. I'm just so…tired. And I don't like the kinds of things I have to do."

"That's being a lawyer, honey," he said, laughing. "Sometimes you have to defend things that seem indefensible. But in the end, you trust the court system."

"I'm not sure I trust anything anymore."

"You'll get more jaded. You'll get used to it."

"I don't think I will. I need your help, Austin. It's about…it's about your father."

He hadn't bothered to listen. Not really. He'd been buzzing over his admittance into an incredible law program. Over his father's promise to secure him a position at his firm, to make him a partner. He'd been too intoxicated by all the power to care. To truly hear her. The weight behind her words. The sadness. No, he was too focused on himself. And why not? Life had always been there to serve him. He had it all; he had it easy.

His family name was everything, and he traded on it.

Like father like son and all.

Then Sarah had thrown herself off a building. And the rumors had begun. The first hint that Jason Treffen might not be the saint that others imagined him to be, but Austin hadn't listened. He had ignored it all for too long.

Until that final confrontation. When he'd walked away from his father's firm for good.

The family got more money than they deserved. She was taken care of. A misunderstanding.

All these excuses. So like the men his father had pretended to disdain for all those years. He was one of them. One of those men who assumed he could take whatever he wanted from women simply because he was a man. Because he held power over them.

And now this. So much more than he'd ever imagined. That he had harassed her so badly she'd killed herself.

But history gave him no reason to doubt it.

"And he's still getting his *This Is Your Life* B.S. all over the news?" Hunter asked.

"Yes. Yes, he is."

"Well. Screw that."

"I agree," said Alex.

"I do, too, but what the hell do we do about it?"

"You're the lawyer, Austin. It seems like you should be

able to think of something. Something legal and shit," Hunter said.

"That's the problem. I have nothing legal. Nothing that will stand up in court."

Alex leaned in. "Then we'll have to find something."

"For what purpose?"

Hunter looked down at his knuckles, and Austin's eyes followed his line of sight and noticed the faint purple bruises that colored the skin there. Hunter tightened his hand into a fist. "If he had anything to do with Sarah's death, and I think we've all suspected it, always, then I'll do whatever I have to do in order to bring him down." He looked back up, his eyes meeting Austin's. "I mean it. I'll end him. Run him off the top of a building. Just like he did to her."

The violence in Hunter's tone left little doubt in Austin's mind that his friend wasn't speaking figuratively.

Part of him rejected the thought. Because no matter how evil, Jason was his father. Because his blood was in Austin's veins. The same blood that kept his heart pumping. It was hard to hate it entirely, even when he should.

"To the bloody end, then?" Austin asked. "Even if it means destroying my family?"

Alex put his palms flat on the table. Spread the paper out flat. "She killed herself, Austin. Because of him. How many more women has he touched like he did her? How many more? If we don't stop it, it keeps going." He looked up at Austin. "And then we're just as guilty. Then we're no different."

No different.

Austin had privately feared that very thing for a long time.

But it wouldn't be true. He'd make sure it ended up not being true.

"Well, then," Austin said, standing. "Let's end it."

Chapter One

Treffen Christmas Ball Set To Be As Glittering As Ever!

With a national honor for his good works on the horizon, celebrated women's advocate Jason Treffen is preparing to host his annual Holiday Ball. Though once overshadowed by a tragedy that occurred during the festivities a decade ago, Treffen has never canceled the event, and Manhattan's elite all clamor for an invitation. It's even rumored that Jason's son, New York's other premier attorney, will be in attendance.

The younger Treffen has skipped the event since the unpleasantness ten years ago, which seemed to have caused a rift between father and son—the only tarnish on an otherwise glossy legacy. Could this finally be the reconciliation that the public has long hoped to see?

Reconciliation. There was no chance for it, and yet his father had bought into his reason for coming to the office Christmas party without blinking. But then, the public had bought it as well, so why wouldn't his father?

He really hated these types of events. Because they were

reminders. This one especially. Ten years ago was the last time he'd been to a Treffen Christmas party. His father enjoyed the holidays, not because of any sort of religious fervor or sense of merriment, but because it gave him a chance to do what he loved best.

Showing off his wealth, his excess. Making a show of his name, his fortune. His goodwill. There was a silent auction happening tonight, the proceeds of which would go to benefit a shelter for battered women.

The irony burned. Because if Austin's suspicions were correct, very few people had left more emotionally battered women in their wake than Jason Treffen.

Of course, the media would never believe it. Jason was so high-profile. On every late-night news show, commenting on sexual harassment and abuse cases in the news. Spitting fire and brimstone on any man who dared to harm a woman. On misogynists and their power games.

But Austin knew Jason was the wolf condemning foxes for being predators.

Still, here he was, wrapped up in his brilliant, shining lie. People fawning over him, his achievements, his goodness.

And this year was no different. The largest of his three holiday parties, this one included past clients, current clients and anyone who was anyone in New York's social circle.

Everything was pristine, glittering, dipped in his father's wealth and left to sparkle before the magpies who were attracted to it all without having any idea just how tarnished it was underneath.

The same as it had always been. The same as it had been ten years ago.

Oh, yes, Austin well remembered the last time he'd been

to this party. It had ended with a dear friend throwing herself to her death. And it had been his own father's fault.

No, he wasn't here for reconciliation. He was here for blood. But before he could have his revenge, he would have to get closer to his old man again. Keep your enemies close, and all that.

He wondered what Jason's reaction would be. Hell, he might kill the fatted calf. The prodigal son, returned to the old law firm.

That was the reaction he dreaded most, though it was the one he should want.

What he really wanted was alcohol.

He walked over to the bar and leaned on the counter. "Scotch. Neat." The whole bottle would be nice.

The bartender poured a measured amount and Austin knocked it back then set the glass back down. "More."

He took another hit and let the burn wash through him. He'd never thought of himself as the kind of man who needed liquid courage. And maybe it wasn't courage he needed, not really. He needed to blunt the memories. Of what it had been like to be in this building with Christmas carols playing when, suddenly, screams had risen over the band.

When people had gone running. To the balcony. To the street. He'd stopped at the window, frozen, transfixed by the broken figure below.

And he had known. In his gut, without having to be told, who it was.

He hadn't had the strength to go down. Hadn't been able to face seeing her like that. With no life in her. Her skin cold. Her body crushed. Nothing of Sarah there anymore except for her shell.

He hadn't been able to face it then. He could scarcely stand to recall what little he'd seen now. This was where the alcohol came into play. Blessed alcohol. It helped hold back some of the cold.

Ten years ago, at this very party, his life had been going perfectly.

Two weeks until Christmas, an end-of-term party that had been filled with toasts and slaps on the back. And then he'd come to the Treffen party. He'd stood next to his father, a proud Treffen, basking in the promise of a partnership in the prestigious firm, in the position he'd gotten in law school because of that name. The name that had opened every door to him for all of his life. That had seen him educated in the finest private schools, had given to him the very best connections.

A name he now had to see was destroyed.

His father's. And his along with it, because it would be inextricably linked.

That was how it worked. That was how the media worked. It was how society worked.

The silver spoon that had gotten him through life would damn well choke him now. It only seemed fair, really.

Everything felt out of control. For the first time, things felt well and truly beyond him.

Which called for another drink.

He tapped the top of his tumbler and the bartender filled it again. Austin held it up and looked through the faceted glass and amber liquid. And he saw her.

Nothing more than an impressionistic vision at first. Obscured by the glass and the unsteady golden line.

Even then, he could tell she was beautiful.

He lowered his drink and stared past the crowd of people at the woman. Dark hair twisted into a neat bun, her skin pale, flawless, her lips a deep crimson.

It was her hair that had him truly transfixed. He wondered how long it was. What it would be like to unwind it. Wrap it around his hand and draw her to him.

Damn. That was the alcohol. He had more control than that. He knew better than to let his mind wander down dark alleys. Every so often, in the privacy of his own room, he indulged in a bout of shameful, illicit fantasy. But never with a woman.

Never.

He wasn't the type of man to treat women that way. Because he knew better than to ever let the monster out of its cage.

And he knew there was a monster in him. In his blood, wrapped around his genes. He was a Treffen, and to most of the world, that meant something good.

He knew that name should only ever be synonymous with evil.

And once he, Hunter and Alex had their way, it would be.

He would go down with the ship. It was unavoidable. He was a Treffen, after all. In name, and in every other way that counted.

But right now, he was just a man, transfixed by a woman.

He set the glass back down on the bar and started across the room before he could think his next action through. He wanted to meet her.

She was something new in this stale, horrific memory. She hadn't been there that night. She was a stranger. Separate from all of the insidious darkness that surrounded this building. That surrounded his family.

She looked up for a moment, her eyes meeting his. They were electric blue, a shocking contrast with her dark hair. It made him wonder if her hair or eyes were artificial. It was so unusual. So enticing.

She turned away and headed toward the other side of the room, her stride purposeful. Then Austin saw just whom she was headed toward.

His father. Jason Treffen.

She smiled, crimson lips parting and revealing straight white teeth. She looked down, then back up, the move demure and flirtatious. It made his blood boil. Just imagining the bastard's hands on her…

He started toward them, then stopped. Reconciliation. Oh, yes, that was the name of the game tonight. He was supposed to be reconciling with the bastard, not introducing his face to the marble floors.

But he did not like the smile his father gave to the woman in return. He didn't like the way she ducked her head again, like a child expecting a pat.

Maybe she was already one of his creatures.

He breathed in deeply, rage pouring through him. He couldn't handle this. It was too much on a night like tonight. At the party where Sarah had died.

Why had he left his drink back at the counter? He needed more alcohol.

The woman turned away from his father and he saw something pass across her face. Anger. Sadness. Grief. He recognized the emotions because they echoed inside of him.

Because they were with him, always. Amplified now as the truth about Jason's treachery became clearer.

Files and files of women who were being paid for vague "services." Interior design. Catering. Event planning.

Austin was still turning over the implications.

None of the possibilities made him happy. Except for the possibility that his father had used the design services of a couple of young women more than six times in a fiscal year. But he highly doubted that was the case.

Highly.

It was taken care of. They were compensated.

That last conversation played again in his mind.

He closed his eyes for a moment and tried to get his head together. He was drowning in air. His tie strangling him. Icy fingers wrapping around his neck.

Sarah's, maybe. He deserved it. God knew he did.

He pictured the dark-haired beauty again, scanned the crowd for her and couldn't see her. Where was she now? Was she waiting to meet his father? Would she end up as a name on one of Jason Treffen's invoices? Payment for services rendered.

No. Not if he could do anything to stop it.

He'd let it happen once. He'd be damned if he ever let it happen again.

He started back across the room and swung by the bar, grabbing his scotch and knocking it back.

Hell, he was damned either way. But she didn't have to be.

Katy Michaels sent up a silent prayer and hoped that, for once, someone was listening. She didn't want to get caught, not now. All she wanted to do was verify that the invoices existed.

She was armed with a tip and a key from Jason Treffen's front desk attendant, Stephanie, a bright young girl with brown eyes that had permanent shadows beneath them.

Just looking at her made Katy's skin crawl.

Her eyes reminded her of Sarah's eyes. Haunted. Tired. Hollow, as if the hope had been carved out of her and an endless black hole was left behind instead.

She went into the office and stared down at the dark wood file cabinets. What an asshole. With his defunct filing system, all old and stately. It was like a big middle finger to everyone, to her, to the women he hurt, that he didn't even bother to keep this information in cryptic folders. That he kept records at all.

Had to get his damned tax write-off. Even when he was paying for sex.

He was lucky she was pursuing legal action rather than going Batman on his ass and seeking a little vigilante justice.

"I am the night," she muttered, going toward the third cabinet to the left, as instructed, and putting the key in the lock. She turned it and it gave, a small click in the silence of the room.

She pulled the drawer open and went for the folder marked "special services," then she opened it and rifled through. It was one year. Just one year and it was filled with names.

Sarah's name would have been in it ten years ago. So many women.

"Binders full of them," she said, trying to smile at her own frail joke as she snapped a shot of the first invoice with her phone's scanner. Humor was all she had left to get her through this crap. She'd taken her other crutches away from herself.

Her parents' drug use. Her sister's death. Raising a younger brother—Trey—who was angry at the world. And it was much better to laugh when she was beating back her own demons with a stick.

And she definitely had her own.

Scanning invoice after invoice that represented a woman who had been abused by Jason Treffen.

She had to laugh or curl into a ball and give up on humanity. Or go back down the deep dark rabbit holes she used to hide in. Soothe her pain in the other ways she knew how to soothe it.

No. She wasn't going back there. Not again.

She scanned every doc, then put them back in the folder, and back in the drawer, which she locked. Then she stuck her phone back in her handbag and made her way out of Jason's office, dropping the key beneath a little potted flower on Stephanie's desk, as she'd requested.

Katy let out a long breath and started walking back down the empty corridor, back to the party.

Back toward Jason Treffen.

Talking to that scumbag had just about made her lose her mind. It had taken everything in her not to grab his glass from his hand and pour it over his head. Then break the glass on his face.

She considered the man as good as her sister's murderer, so she was short on charitable feelings where he was concerned.

The door to the ballroom opened and she froze, trying to affect an "I'm just coming back from the bathroom" demeanor. Whatever the hell that was.

Oh. Her breath left her in a rush, a current of electricity washing over her skin.

It was him.

The man who'd been drinking scotch. The man whose eyes were like an endless black hole, drawing her in, a force she couldn't deny or control.

The man who had looked at her for a moment.

Someone looking at her wasn't really that significant. It happened every day. Except when this man had looked at her, she'd felt as if she were grounded to the spot. She'd felt like he had looked and *seen* her.

Seen everything. More than that, she'd looked back and she'd seen him.

Had seen a grief in him. An anger.

It had been, in some ways, like looking into a mirror.

And in just a second, it had been over. She'd gone to find Jason, to put herself in his vicinity. Just because she'd promised herself she would. Because she'd promised herself she would look him dead in the eye one day, knowing she was going to destroy him, while he didn't have a clue.

And so she had.

But it had been a sacrifice, because she'd had to look away from the man. It was a moment that summed up her entire life, really. Deny, deny, repress. Push on through. Don't let the pain touch you. Don't let the pleasure touch you, either.

"It's you," he said, his voice deep, smooth. Like really good chocolate.

"Yes, it's me. I was…in the bathroom." *Oh, nice, Katy. That was very good.*

He arched a brow. "Fascinating."

"Not so much, I know."

"I'll let it slide because I was hoping to run into you."

"Were you?"

"Yes," he said, walking closer to her, his eyes burning into hers.

She'd never seen anything like his eyes. They were so intense she couldn't look away.

And his body...perfectly showcased by his custom-made suit. Broad shoulders, trim waist and slim hips. Very expensive shoes.

Then there was his face. He was arresting. Dark brows, chiseled jaw, Roman nose. His lips were perfection. She couldn't remember ever being fascinated by a man's lips before. Even the men's mouths she'd come into direct physical contact with hadn't *fascinated* her.

His mouth was shaped perfectly. She found herself utterly obsessed by the thought of tracing his top lip with her tongue. Of letting the tip of it slide into the little V just beneath his nose.

Jeez. She needed help. A good night's sleep. Something. This wasn't normal. Not for her.

"Wh-why were you hoping to run into me?" she asked.

"Because you're the most beautiful woman here. Why wouldn't I want to see you?"

"I call B.S.," she said. "There are models here."

"So? You were the one who caught my attention."

"You're a flirt."

"That's the thing—I'm not really. So if I'm doing a poor job of it, it's only because I lack practice." He put his hands in his pockets, a wicked half smile curling that sinful mouth.

"Again, I call bull."

"Again, you're wrong."

"You're drunk."

"A little."

"Honest," she said. "But I have to get back."

She started to walk past him and he took her arm, stopped her progress. Her breath left her lungs in a rush, his grip shockingly tight. She looked up and met cold, dark eyes. "To who?" he asked, his voice gentle, an opposing force to the hold he had on her.

Her heart was thundering hard. But it wasn't with fear. There was something about his grip, so tight, so certain, that made her feel...

She blinked. Oh, no, she was not getting turned on by a strange man in the corridor of a party she was technically coordinating.

But there was something about that grip. Commanding. Hard. It spoke to every secret fantasy that lived in the dark shadows inside of her. The parts of her that didn't want a sweet kiss at midnight from Prince Charming. The parts that had always craved things she'd never quite understood.

The parts of herself that had looked at every man she'd even tried to date and found them lacking.

But not him. He wouldn't be lacking. Something shivered inside of her, a whisper.

He would know what you wanted.

"None of your business," she growled.

"Jason Treffen?" he asked, a tinge of bitterness to his tone. "Why?"

"I saw you speaking with him earlier."

"Guilty," she said. "Now will you let go of me?"

"Will you stay for a moment?"

"What if I say no?"

His gaze flickered over her. "I'm not sure."

Part of her wanted to dare him. Wanted to say no. Wanted

to see if the grip would tighten. If he would take the control. "I'll stay for a moment."

He released his hold on her. "Good. Then I'll work on being more interesting than whatever's in that party."

"Oooh," she said, affecting a regretful smile, "they have cocktail shrimp."

"I'm losing out to shellfish?"

"It's prime. I hear they brought all the seafood from Maine."

"Well, I'm not from Maine, so I'm not sure I can compete."

"Where are you from?" she asked.

"Upstate."

"Hmm. Vague."

He lifted one shoulder. "Where are *you* from?"

"Originally? Somewhere in the Eastern Seaboard."

"Also vague," he said.

"Vague is okay. We're just talking in the hall."

"Are we?" he asked. He put his hand back on her arm, his fingertips hot against her skin.

She'd never really flirted much, either. Her last date had been long enough ago that she didn't want to count. And her sex life? That was nonexistent. A younger brother and parents who were usually passed out somewhere made a sex life impossible. Plus, dating someone implied letting someone in. Bringing them into that hellhole she called a life.

Anyway, there was no man she found overly appealing in that deadbeat town. All she'd ever wanted to do was leave it behind.

And since she'd left, she'd been working. Tirelessly toward the moment she'd just had. Toward getting herself in a position where she could be in this social circle. Toward looking Jason Treffen in the eye. Gathering evidence against him.

Suddenly she felt exhausted. She felt every missed opportunity in her life, every emotion she'd dulled or ruthlessly cut from herself, every moment she'd sacrificed, including that moment of eye contact in the ballroom with this man, so that she could have this revenge.

So that she could see justice done.

And suddenly, she didn't want to go back into the ballroom. She wanted to stay in the hall, with him. With the man who carried a matching darkness inside of him. A man who she knew, instinctively, would want what she did.

She felt like he was the one. The one to tear the lid off all those fantasies that she kept down deep. Like he was the first one to offer real, serious temptation.

"Maybe it's more than that," she said. "If we're being honest, I'm not especially up on the flirting game, either."

"I find that hard to believe."

"Why?"

"Why did you find it hard to believe I wasn't?"

"Because you're so forward."

He shifted his weight, drew closer to her. "Oh, don't mistake me. I might not be a flirt, but when I want something, I get it. When I want someone," he said, lifting his hand and drawing it over her cheek, "I make sure I have her."

She should hate this. She should shove him back. She should tell him to go to hell with all his proprietary male garbage. But she didn't.

Because she didn't hate it.

Because this wasn't the game she'd been taught to loathe so much. This wasn't the thing that Sarah had been caught up in. There was no artifice here. There was an edge of honesty to this man's words. A rawness.

This was her fantasy. This was why no other man had ever tempted her. Why she'd never gone out of her way to pursue more than a kiss.

"And you want me?" she asked.

"Yes," he said.

"Damn. You *are* drunk."

"I am," he said, "but not so much that I don't know what I want. Who I want."

"We don't know each other," she said.

"I know. But in some ways, doesn't that make it better?"

She shrugged. "I don't know. I've never…" She started to say she'd never been with a man, one she knew or not, but she let it trail off. A twenty-six-year-old virgin was a bit of a joke and she wasn't exactly in the mood to confess that.

Besides, it might scare him off. And she hadn't decided if she wanted to do that or not.

One thing was for sure: she didn't want him to think that because she'd never been with a man, she needed some sort of gentle, soothing seduction.

That was the last thing she wanted. She wanted those strong hands on her. Rough. In control.

"Me neither," he said.

"You haven't what?" she asked. Because he wasn't a virgin. That was for sure.

"I don't do this kind of thing. Pick up women I meet in corridors. I have relationships. I take a woman out to dinner at least three times before I make a move toward the bedroom."

"That's very courteous of you."

"Isn't it?"

"And what about right now?"

"Right now? I'm thinking I don't want to take you out to dinner three times. I want to take you against the wall. Now."

His words hit those dark places inside of her. Called to needs she had that she'd never given voice to. Something in her sensed that he could give her what she wanted. Sensed that he would know what it was she wanted, everything she'd never given voice to. Things she'd never even let herself think.

"That would be..." Incredible. And she didn't know why she was sure about that, only that she was. "Well, it would be a bad idea because anyone could walk by."

"Danger doesn't get you off?" he asked, leaning in, his lips a whisper from hers.

Apparently, a certain kind of danger did get her off. But not the idea of getting caught having sex for the first time in a hallway. No, that didn't turn her on so much.

Lies.

"Danger, maybe," she said, choosing her words carefully. "Voyeurism, not so much."

"Not really my thing, either, I have to confess. But...I haven't even kissed you yet and I'm not sure I can wait to get you to a hotel room."

"You're very sure of yourself."

"Not of myself. Of this. You have to feel it, too. You have to."

She did. She nodded slowly. "I think anyone who came within three feet of us would be able to feel it."

Like the heavy lid of a well had just been moved and she

suddenly had access to all of these things she'd kept in the deep darkness of her soul. Things she'd been hiding from.

Maybe it was him. Maybe it was just because her world felt rocked. Because life seemed dirtier and uglier than it ever had, with those invoices scanned into her phone. With the weight of her reality, Sarah's reality, pressing down on her.

With the realization of what her life had become. An endless sea of numbness.

Maybe that was why this stranger suddenly seemed like the most important thing in the world. Maybe it was why he seemed to be rooting her to the earth.

Or maybe it was just lust. Base, dirty lust. Lust that had gone unpursued for the past twenty-six years. Lust that wanted something her body had decided only he could give.

But then, in the end she wasn't sure the reason mattered.

"Probably," he said.

"Why don't you kiss me?" she asked, desperate for something she'd at least done before. "Just to test it. We could be wrong, you know. We could kiss and decide it's really not worth the trouble."

He touched her lip with his thumb and she shivered. "If I kiss you now, I guarantee you, you will find yourself shoved up against a hard surface or bent over a piece of furniture with your dress over your hips and your panties at your ankles. Is that what you want?"

Yes. Heaven help her, yes.

For your first time? Really?

Why not? He knew what he was doing. If he told her what to do she was damn sure it would feel good.

He was what she wanted. What she craved.

"If I say yes," she said, "will you judge me?"

"No. But I might fuck you."

She swallowed hard, her throat suddenly dry. "Is that a promise?"

"Do you still want to go back inside and have cocktail shrimp?"

She thought of Jason Treffen. Of the party she was meant to be coordinating.

Well, it was late yet and everything was working just fine without her in there holding everyone's hand. Because she'd already done a lot of coordinating and so it was all going smoothly and...and they really didn't need her.

And she wanted. For the first time in longer than she could remember, she *wanted*. For her. Not for Trey. Not for Sarah.

"I've never wanted shrimp less in my life."

"I'm glad I have your attention."

"You do."

"Do you still want that kiss?"

Her heart started thundering harder. "I really do think that we should do...things...in private."

"What if I promise to behave?"

"Can you keep the promise?"

"One kiss," he said. "That's all you can have. No more."

"What if I want two?" she asked.

He cupped her chin, held her steady, his eyes intent on hers. "One," he repeated. "Or I walk away. You have to obey, or I stop now."

She nodded slowly. "One kiss."

"Good girl." He leaned in, his breath hot as it skimmed over her lips.

He didn't press his mouth to hers, not at first. He waited.

Waited until she thought she would die with how much she wanted it. With how much she wanted him.

And then he kissed her.

It was firm. Hot. He tasted like alcohol and spices, like something completely new and unfamiliar. She wanted more. Wanted to explore his mouth, drown in his flavor.

But before she could, he'd moved away.

He stood back, assessing her, his eyes so dark they were nearly black. "What do you think?" he asked.

"I don't know.... What do *you* think?"

"I think we need that hotel room. Now."

Chapter Two

Forget letting his mind wander down dark alleys. He was committed now. Not just his mind—his body and soul, as well.

One night. It wouldn't matter later.

He'd never see this woman again. And he could…he could grab ahold of something just for the night. For one night he could have the control back. Everything was falling apart. Falling away, and once he dropped the bomb on his family, once the scandal broke over the Treffen name, all the control would be gone. Wrenched from his hands.

This might make things feel all right, if only for a few hours.

To have someone at his command. To have something that was his.

He thought of the way she'd been talking to his father and a knot lodged in his throat. If she needed money…

Put some money on the dresser?

Well, why not? If she needed it. It would be better if it was him and not his father she was going to for security through sex. Because the other man couldn't have her. No one else could. *He* wanted her.

The things he wanted her for...

He closed his hand into a fist and tried to stave off the surge of lust that shot through his veins. He needed to get a grip.

Or not.

He was tired. Tired of always fighting everything. Everyone's demons and his own.

He took his phone out of his pocket and dialed a hotel downtown that a business acquaintance owned. He'd been telling the truth when he'd told her he wasn't a one-night-stand sort of man.

But he had his connections.

"I need a room for tonight," he said. "Account number four fifty-three. The penthouse suite." He didn't want this woman to know his connection to Jason, not if she was ignorant of it. And he didn't know why she should know who he was. Ten years he'd spent separate from Jason, and he wasn't the media whore his father was.

Austin preferred to keep his head down and do his work. He preferred to stay away from the spotlight. Passion, lust, greed, a desire for fame. It all corrupted.

He looked over his date for the night. Well, tonight he would be indulging two of those infamous corrupters.

And he couldn't find any regret for it.

"I have a guest," he said, the words heavy with meaning. "I shall need the appropriate amenities."

"Of course, sir. A code will be texted to your phone," the man on the other end said. "It will grant you admittance to your room. No need to check in at the desk. All supplies you might need for yourself and your guest will be waiting."

"Perfect," he said, hanging up. "We're set for the night. Unless you've changed your mind?"

He looked at her, blue eyes wide, a slight tremble in her full lower lip. That little bit of sass and confidence he'd seen in her earlier had waned a bit. She looked vulnerable. She made him feel a bit like a predator.

And damned if he couldn't muster up any remorse for that. Damned if it didn't make him a little bit harder.

She met his eyes. "No. I haven't changed my mind. Only… the shrimp. I didn't get any."

"I can order you shrimp. Room service."

"From Maine?"

"From any damn place you want."

The corner of her mouth twitched. "How can a girl say no to that?"

"I don't know, but if you're going to say no," he said, his voice rough, everything in him feeling rough, "do it now."

She looked down, and she seemed to be seriously considering it. He didn't think he could handle her refusal now. He was too far gone.

One kiss, and he was too far gone.

"I'm not going to say no."

He wrapped his arm around her waist and tugged her up against his body. And he didn't care if anyone else walked out into the hall. He didn't care about a damn thing except for the feeling of her breasts against his chest, the harsh, rapid pattern of her breathing bringing them up tighter against him, before giving him a brief reprieve, then repeating.

He felt as if he were on the edge of breaking completely. The world was splintering around him; his self-control was shattering inside of him.

He wanted to seize it. Take it back with both hands. Claim it. Over her bare body, and if that was wrong, he couldn't muster up the energy to care. Not now.

But she had to agree. Because now that he'd given himself permission to do this, to act on it…he wasn't sure how far it might go.

"Be sure," he said. "I am short on self-control tonight, if what I've said to you here wasn't enough of an indicator. I don't want to hurt you. But once we're in the hotel room? I'm in charge. I will have what I want. So while we're out here, you have the chance to tell me you don't want that. If you want a sweet night of making love, then, darling, you need to find another man. That's not what I want tonight. I don't want to hold you, and go slow and tender. Tonight? I want you hard. I want you fast. I want you every time I ask. I want you on your knees. Tonight, you're mine. If that's not what you want? Get another guy to go home with you. You won't have any trouble finding one. If that's okay with you…don't act like you weren't warned."

"You're in charge?" she asked, her voice unsteady.

"Yes."

"You'll tell me what to do?" she asked, the black in her eyes expanding, the blue turning to a little sliver of color.

"Yes. Because once we're in that suite, you're mine." He'd never said things like this to a woman in his life. He was polite. Courteous. Respectful.

Never once had he given in to that desire to ask a woman to get on her knees in front of him and do what she was told.

Never once had he spoken with such absolute honesty about what he wanted. Because he'd never been this honest with himself about what he wanted. Because he spent his life in denial of those ugly things, the twisted shadows in his soul, the dirty blood that he couldn't escape.

"Then let's go," she said.

"This is what you want?"

"Do I have to say it again?"

"Do I have to tell you what I want again?"

"Only if you want me to push you up against the wall and have you here and now," she said. "Because I've never had a man say anything like that to me before, and I have to tell you, it's the sexiest thing I've ever heard in my life."

"Then I suppose we better get to our room."

She swallowed hard, the motion of her throat fascinating. He wanted to press his lips to it. He wanted to scrape her skin with his teeth and listen to the sound she would make.

He wanted to feel her shiver beneath his touch.

"Yes," he said again. "We need to go. Now."

"You going to call us a car?"

"I have a car."

"Oh."

"I mean, a driver."

"That makes more sense. Kind of."

He held his hand out and she took it, delicate fingers curling around his. "I assume you want to get out without being seen?"

"I'd rather not parade back through the ballroom, now that you mention it."

"You don't want to advertise that you're leaving with me?"

"Not so much. Can we keep it clandestine? That's pretty sexy, really."

"You're ashamed," he said.

A slash of color faded into her cheeks. "Maybe a little."

"Because you want me so much."

"Yes."

"And that's bad to you, isn't it?"

"Yes," she said. "I think having sex with a stranger is pretty bad."

"But you sort of like the idea of being a bad girl, don't you?"

The color in her cheeks deepened. "Seriously, let's go."

"We're going to have fun," he said, tugging her down the empty hall. *Fun* was the wrong word for it, though. He could already sense that.

But it would be a release.

And he needed one. More than he'd realized.

When they got into the elevator and the doors closed, he felt the tension wrap around them like a cloak. Thick and heavy. He thought it might suffocate him. He could have her. Push the stop button and push her against the wall. Work it out in five minutes. Take the edge off the intense need.

But it wasn't what he wanted. Not really.

He wanted to make them both wait.

Wanted to have her to himself. A whole night. A night to play with his demons instead of shoving them down deep. He would feel worse if he didn't get the sense that she was doing the same. That she was about to perform an exorcism, using his body as holy water.

That suited him just fine.

But the wait didn't.

"These elevators are effing slow," she said, letting out a long breath as a five flashed across the light board at the top of the wall.

"They are a bit. I hadn't noticed until now."

"Me either. They seemed normal until tonight."

Four, three, two, L. *Thank God.*

The doors opened and he walked out ahead of her. He didn't touch her. Not again. Because it would be too tempting. It would be too much. He was on the edge as it was, and one more brush of her soft skin on his and he would lose it completely.

He picked up his phone. "Car. Up front. Now."

The lobby doors opened just as his black town car pulled up to the front of the building.

He opened the door and waited. "Get in," he said when she approached and paused.

She obeyed, lowering her head, the lights from the building shimmering over that hair, still contained in the tight bun. Heat burst through him, starting in his gut and spreading outward, pooling in his groin.

He got in and closed the door. "The Black Book Hotel," he said to his driver before leaning back in the seat and pressing a button that put up a black divider between them and the man in front.

They hadn't exchanged names. And that suited him just fine. He didn't need a name to know that tonight she was his. Though, she might feel differently.

"Did you want to exchange names?" he asked, not sure, if she did, if he would be honest or not.

"I sort of like it like this."

"Do you?"

"Not being me for the night? It works."

He'd been right about the demons. Maybe she had a husband or boyfriend. Or it was related to what she felt she owed

Jason. He didn't care. Didn't care if she loved someone else, as long as tonight, she didn't think of anyone else.

None of that would come between them tonight. Nothing existed tonight but the fantasy. But a few blessed moments of feeling like there was something in his life that wasn't beyond him.

"I'm going to kiss you again," he said. "Come here."

She was across the car from him, her seat belt buckled. She pressed the button slowly and then put her hands on the seat, crawling to him slowly, on her hands and knees.

Everything in him tightened to the point where he thought he might break. It was the practical way to move across the car; he knew that. But there was something about it that grabbed him by the throat and shook him hard.

His eyes dropped to her breasts, emphasized by the motion, pale and round, spilling over the top of her black dress. Her red lips were parted slightly and it was so easy to imagine them wrapped around his cock. And her hair loose, wrapped around his hand...

Not yet.

He captured her face and leaned in, kissing her firmly, his tongue sliding along the seam of her mouth, delving in deeply when she parted for him. A muffled sound escaped her and he captured it, kissing her harder.

Lust, need, fired through him. All heat and desire, the kind he'd never known had existed before. He'd tasted it. On the edge of dreams, with fantasy women, when he woke up, sweaty and wrapped in his sheets, slick with shame and release.

But never in reality. Because he'd always held a part of himself back. And he'd imagined he always would.

Not tonight.

He kept kissing her, their bodies separate, need roaring through him. He wanted to tug her up against him, to feel those delicious curves pressed against his body, but he was determined to wait.

Determined to prolong the torture because there was something about it—this lust that bordered on pain—that appealed to him in a way that was beyond description. Beyond comprehension.

It wasn't even his own deprivation that mattered. It was hers. She wanted more. And he wasn't allowing her to have it. He had her on the brink with just a kiss, and he knew it. And he had the power to deny her pleasure, and right now he was using that power.

The car stopped and he pulled away from her. "Ready?"

She nodded slowly.

"You get out first," he said.

She did, as she slid past him and opened the car door. She got out and stood on the sidewalk, waiting for him as people walked past, her breath a cloud in the cold air.

He got out, shutting the door behind him. "Walk ahead of me," he said. "I want to watch you."

She did, and he followed, his eyes on the elegant curve of her neck, the delicate line of her spine. And her ass. So round and perfect.

She went through the revolving door of the hotel and into the lobby, and he continued in behind her. He liked this. Liked the feeling that she was putting on a show, in public, meant only for him.

Her legs demanded at least an hour devoted to a fantasy starring them exclusively. Sky-high black pumps emphasized the length and the sleek muscles. The seams of her stockings—damn, he hoped they were stay-ups—centered so perfectly in the backs of her calves, a tease, a hint that she was some sort of sweet old-fashioned girl. Which made him want to do bad things to her even more.

He could picture her now, without the dress, stockings and shoes on, bent over a piece of furniture, just waiting for him to take her....

That was going to happen. At some point tonight, he would be sure that it did.

Another damned elevator.

She got inside and leaned back against the walls. The doors started to close and he had to jog to make it in time. He stuck his arm in between them, then slipped inside, letting the doors slide shut behind him.

"That was naughty," he said.

Her cheeks colored and she met his gaze. "Sorry."

"Are you?"

"Yes."

"Why did you do that?"

She lifted one shoulder. "I'm not sure."

"Are you going out of your way to misbehave?" he asked.

"Maybe."

"It's almost like you want some consequences," he said, his voice tight, making it almost impossible to breathe. He wasn't sure what he was saying anymore. He wasn't sure what he was thinking.

Except that it was hard to think with all of his blood just south of his belt.

But fantasies, erotic images, didn't require much thought. He could think of so many ways to punish her....

No. He had to have a limit.

"If I did?" she asked, sounding breathless. Excited. Aroused.

Damn. This woman was a lit match against a pool of gasoline inside of him. Sitting there, dormant and under control for so many years.

Yeah, he'd known it was there, but he'd done his best to ignore it.

But with her, he was on the verge of exploding. And it was too late to go back.

"I can give them to you, baby, but I'm not sure exactly what you expect."

"I'm not sure, either. Only that…you make me want things… I don't know what I want," she said, her eyes never leaving his. "You'll have to show me."

The elevator stopped and the doors opened. He took her hand in his again, her fingers icy now. Nerves. It made him feel like the asshole he very likely was.

He was a stranger. Much larger than her. And here he was, taking her back to a hotel to play power games that not even he knew the boundaries to.

He might just have a spot in hell next to his father yet. The kind of man who said he only wanted to protect women, while he used and manipulated them.

No. This isn't the same.

Isn't it?

He shut down that thought and held her more firmly, walking toward the room and checking his phone before keying in the code on the ornate door.

"Ladies first," he said.

Katy shivered as she walked into the hotel room. There was nothing restrained or modern about their surroundings.

It was like a vampire whorehouse. Black fleur-de-lis wallpaper gilded with ornate sconces. A sumptuous bed with deep purple velvet pillows and a black bedspread. Everything about it screamed dark seduction, which was appropriate, since that was what she was in the middle of.

And she didn't know what she'd been thinking. Not in the car when she'd crawled over to him, not in the elevator when she'd tried to… Had she been trying to make him angry?

No. Because she hadn't really thought it would make him angry. But she'd thought it might provoke a reaction.

Earn her the threat of punishment.

And there was something about it that she liked. Something about the edge of danger that was wrapped in gauzy sensuality that she found irresistible.

Something that made it feel real and present. It was a desire she'd always known she'd had, but had never, ever been brave enough to go and get.

Until him.

This moment, this man, was like coming up to the surface for air after years of being held underwater. And all she could do was gasp for breath. Take in everything she possibly could.

Because it wouldn't last. This feeling, this moment, wouldn't—couldn't—last.

He closed the door behind them, the sound so final. Strangely arousing. Because this was it. The point of no return.

And she didn't want to stop anyway.

She turned to face him, his eyes dark. In that moment, she felt she saw this man, this stranger, in a more honest light than she'd ever seen anyone else in her life.

Her parents were always lost in a drug haze. Sarah wrapped

up in her ambitions, working to make a life for them, away from the hellhole they lived in. Trey in the safety net of anger that kept him from having to feel just what a horrible life they had.

And as for her? She hid everything. Even from herself.

But this man was looking at her, stark and hungry, in pain. He was stripped bare, standing there in his custom suit. All the expensive fabric and elegant tailoring couldn't conceal the fact that he was a man on the edge.

And everything in her responded to that fact.

Maybe because it forced her into honesty. Because it made her have to break through the glass case she surrounded herself in. Keeping everyone and everything at a distance so that she could simply make it through life. So that she could make it through to the end without falling into the dark places she used to be.

Because she had no choice but to make it to the end.

To her revenge. To her justice.

Her entire life was lived for someone else. All of her desires sealed away safely.

Until now. Until this moment.

That was why she wanted it all. Every emotion in this one experience. Why she wanted it intense and dark and everything she'd ever wanted sex to be.

Because this was all she would get. This night. This man. And then it was back to living for other people.

Back inside her glass case.

Not tonight. Tonight she was simply going to follow his orders. And whatever it made her feel would be for her. Not anyone else.

Confessing ignorance. Asking for help. They were two

things she never did. Normally she would rather chew glass. But this…game. Whatever it was. This thing with him made it okay. It made it feel right. It made it feel okay.

More than that, it felt like a release in and of itself. The slow removal of a weight she hadn't known she'd been carrying.

"Stand against the wall," he said.

She did, because obeying him gave her a sort of illicit thrill. "Now what?"

"I want to see you without that dress."

"You don't want to kiss me first?" she asked, feeling nervous.

"No."

"But—"

"Take off your dress for me. Now."

She put her arm behind her back and gripped her zipper with shaking fingers, drawing it down slowly, her breathing harsh and unsteady, her heart thundering in her ears.

The bodice went slack, sliding down and revealing her breasts, covered by a black satin push-up bra that was doing her a whole lot of favors.

His nostrils flared, his jaw clenched tight as his hand drifted to the bulge at the front of his slacks. His fingers drifted along the ridge there and she had to squeeze her thighs together to try to assuage the answering ache between her legs.

"The rest," he said, his voice rough.

She pushed the dress down her hips on her exhalation, and let it pool at her feet. She kicked the dress aside, leaning against the wall. The velvet fleur-de-lis and satin that covered the wall was both warm and cool against her skin.

She lifted her hands to the front clasp of her bra.

"No," he said, his hand pausing over his clothed erection. "Leave it. Everything else stays for now."

He approached her slowly, a predator stalking his prey. His movements liquid and powerful. He extended his hand and brushed his thumb over her cheek.

"I think I first saw you two hours ago," he said. "It feels like I've been waiting for you for a lot longer than that."

"Forever, even," she said, her heart pounding hard, virginal nerves starting to get the better of her.

What had she gotten herself into? This was a situation, a man, way above her pay grade.

But he's the man you deserve. After waiting so long. After working so hard for everyone else. You haven't felt anything for so long. And he'll make you feel it all.

Her inner selfish heathen was determined to have her way tonight, and damn the consequences.

He moved to her, pressing his body against hers, her back firm against the wall. He leaned in, kissing her hard, his mouth savage, demanding. He cupped her face, blunt fingertips digging into her skin as he took possession of her with his lips, teeth and tongue.

She kissed him back, helpless to do anything but answer his every demand.

She'd never even conceived of a kiss like this. Filled with so much desperation. So much need.

The need to control, the need to submit. The need to possess and the need to yield.

It was everything, and it all blended together. His needs and hers. It was a perfect storm, and it was happening around them. In them.

He lowered his head, lips on her neck, her collarbone. He cupped her breasts, lowered his head and slid the flat of his tongue down between the valley of her breasts.

She arched into him, her shoulder blades still against the wall, a hoarse cry rising in her throat.

"How should I punish you?" he asked, scraping his teeth along the plump curve of her breast before soothing it with his tongue. "With pleasure? With pain? Or do you like both?" He bit her again, harder this time, the shaft of pure, undiluted lust it sent through her far more shocking than the sting he left behind.

"I like whatever you want to give me," she said, shocked by the huskiness in her tone. By the confidence in the statement.

"That's what I want to hear." He grabbed the cup of her bra and tugged it down. "You are beautiful." He rubbed his thumb over the tip of her nipple, drawing it into a point so tight it hurt in the best way possible.

Yes. She liked whatever he wanted to give.

And it made all of this so easy.

He tugged the other side of her bra down and squeezed her nipple between his thumb and forefinger, increasing the pressure until she had to bite her lip to keep from whimpering from the pain.

"You like it," he said, not a question.

She nodded.

"Good. I like it, too," he said. "I like that I can push it to the edge with you. That you want me enough that it all feels good. That's it, isn't it?"

A rush of warmth burst through her. "Yes."

"I bet I know what you want," he said.

"Do you?"

"You want to come."

His words sent a shaft of heat—embarrassed and aroused— through her. "Well, doesn't everyone?"

He chuckled, low and sexy. "I suppose. But that's what you want, isn't it?"

"Yes."

"Tell me."

"I want to..." She'd never said anything like this out loud before. "I want to c-come."

"Have I mentioned," he said, not addressing what she said at all, "that I was dying to see you in these stockings and heels?"

"No..."

"I was." He slid his finger along the lace top of her stay-ups. "So sexy. And these..." He moved his index finger to the top of her panties and dipped it beneath the thin black fabric. She could hardly breathe. Her body felt like it was going to burst into flame at any moment. "These are per-fect. But—" he slipped his hand down inside, his palm barely skimming the most intimate part of her as he pushed her underwear down her legs "—I don't think you'll need them for a while."

He cupped her then, sliding his fingers across her slick flesh, one pressing inside of her. She gripped his shoulders, her nails digging into his skin.

He rocked his palm against her clitoris as he pushed his finger in deep, sending a shock wave of sensation through her.

He dropped down to his knees and kissed her stomach, leaning in then and removing his hand, flicking his tongue over her clit while his finger worked in time with the strokes.

"Oh..." She laced her fingers through his hair and held

her to him, her head back against the wall as she warred between trying to figure out how she'd gotten here tonight, mostly naked, with a man on his knees in front of her, and just trying not to black out.

She held him tight to her, flexing her hips and chasing her release. She was close...so close...

"Enough," he said. "Not yet."

"No," she said, tightening her hold on his hair.

"You aren't in any position to give orders," he said, moving away from her and standing. She wanted to cry with frustration now.

"I need..."

"I know what you need," he said. He started to loosen his tie, undoing the knot and letting it drape over his shoulder. Then he shrugged his coat off. Undid his cuffs. It was maddening to watch. Each detail meticulous, far too slow and utterly arousing.

She didn't want to watch him do the world's slowest striptease. She wanted him to touch her again. Taste her again.

"We do need some rules," he said. "Because I want control, but I don't want to hurt you. Not really. If you need me to stop, you tell me to stop. Just say the word. Don't think it. Don't hope it. *Say* it. I want control, but not force. Do you promise to tell me to stop?" There was something in his eyes when he said that, something that tugged at her. And there was a strand of fear in his voice.

As if he were truly afraid she would let him go too far.

And she realized something. He wanted control, but only the control she would give him.

That was her power. He needed this from her, but she had

to be willing to give it. She had to trust him enough that she believed he would stop if she asked.

She nodded slowly. "Yes."

"Good," he said, the word rough. "Now, on the bed."

"What...now?"

"On the bed," he said. "Don't talk unless I tell you to. Get on the bed, in your high heels and stockings, and spread your legs for me."

She kept her eyes on his, because she had a feeling she wasn't permitted to look away, as she got onto the massive bed. She lay back, breathing difficult now as she put her feet as flat as she could.

Her sky-high shoes almost lifted her rear up off the mattress, leaving her feeling extra exposed. Exceedingly vulnerable.

She'd never been naked in front of a man before. Ever. And this didn't follow any guidebook she'd read for sex. Didn't evoke any of the random novels she'd thumbed through looking for the good stuff.

But what she wanted never had. But that hadn't stopped her from wanting it.

She had no idea what he would do next. No idea what to expect.

He slid his tie from his shoulders, the stretch of black silk held taut between both of his hands. "You aren't allowed to come until I say you can," he said. "And you can't touch me," he said, his voice lowering, "until I allow it."

"But..."

"Shhh," he said, leaning forward, touching the stretch of black silk to her lips, like he meant to gag her with it. "No talking." Then he moved the tie, laying it over her eyes. "I like that idea," he said. "But I need to be able to hear you if you need me to." He lifted the tie higher, to where her hands were resting above her head. The position had seemed natural to her. And now she understood why.

He slipped the expanse of silk behind her wrists and then wrapped it around one, then the other, before binding them together. She knew that if she told him no, he would stop. So she said nothing. Because she wanted it. Because she liked the element of feeling as though he'd done it without her permission.

He rose up above her. "So beautiful. And mine," he said. He put his hands on her legs and pushed them even farther apart, his gaze roaming over her. "All mine." He lowered his head and pressed a kiss to the tender skin on her inner thigh before moving on to more intimate territory.

He began to pleasure her with his mouth again, pushing one finger inside of her, then another, pushing her higher, closer to the edge before stopping, pulling back.

She wanted to tell him to stop. That it was too much. But then he would stop, like he'd promised, and she didn't want that, either.

She bit her lip, flexed her hips, tried to force herself closer to him.

"No," he said, sliding his tongue over her clit. "You aren't in charge here, sweetheart. I am. Stop trying to break the rules."

He withdrew his fingers from her body and slid them upward, white-hot pleasure spiking through her as he did. "Open," he said, and she did. "Suck on them for me."

This was a test. To see if she would obey. And she wouldn't fail his test. She opened for him and he slipped his fingers between her lips and she could taste her own pleasure on them. Could taste the evidence of what he'd done to her.

She ran her tongue along his fingers as he pushed them in her mouth and out again and she felt him shudder, the muscles in his body tensing.

He reached around behind her head, braced one hand on her neck, grabbed the end of his tie with the other and brought her into a sitting position, with her hands neatly in her lap. Still bound.

"On your knees," he said, drawing back and getting off of the bed, his hands working at the belt on his slacks.

He placed the belt on the edge of the mattress, his movements just as controlled and methodical now as they'd been when he undid his cuffs and tie.

He moved to unbutton his shirt, working silently as he released the buttons, exposing a wedge of tan skin. He shrugged the shirt from his broad shoulders, muscles shifting with the motion.

She couldn't take her eyes off of him. Off of each sharply defined line. How each movement sent off a ripple effect through his torso. He straightened and her eyes locked on to the dark hair that covered his chest and ran in a line down the center of his perfectly defined abs. Just enough to remind her that he was a man, not enough to conceal up all those gorgeous muscles.

She wanted to touch him. But she was still tied.

"I said on your knees," he repeated.

She repositioned herself, her hands in front of her, her heels beneath her butt, her knees denting the mattress.

He put his hand behind her head and started releasing her

hair from its pins. It fell around her in a dark, silken wave, moving over her shoulders, covering her breasts.

"I've been having fantasies about your hair," he said, his expression tense. Hard. Like a man carved from stone. Like a man trying, so very hard, to hold everything—his emotions, his desires—at bay.

She watched as his hands went to the closure on his slacks. Her throat went dry and she swallowed hard, finding breathing difficult.

She'd never seen a naked man in person before. And here she was, about to be confronted with her first, her hands tied.

You could tell him to stop....

No. She didn't want that.

He shrugged his underwear and pants down, exposing himself to her for the first time. She'd had a fair idea, judging from the bulge, that he was not a small man. But that was a bit of an understatement.

He wrapped his hand around his shaft and she watched, mesmerized, as he stroked himself once. Twice. Closing his eyes as he did, muttering something. A curse, a prayer. She wasn't sure.

He kept one hand on his erection, and cupped her cheek with the other, before moving it to her hair, sifting the strands through his fingers.

He pushed her hair back, gathering it in his fist and twisting it around his hand, his hold firm. He didn't pull; he simply held her. Captive. At his mercy.

Pleasure and excitement shivered along her spine as she waited to see what he would do next. What he would demand next.

She bit her lip, her eyes on his arousal.

"You want that?" he asked.

She nodded slowly, waiting for his order.

He moved closer to her and she tried to lean in but he held her fast, pain tingling around her scalp as he held her hair tight, keeping her in place.

"I didn't say you could do that yet," he said.

He tugged her hair again, forcing her head back. She looked up at him, their eyes locking. "Please," she said, breaking his rule.

She was hungry. For him. For every experience he could give. Everything she'd missed.

She parted her lips and waited for him to come to her. He moved closer and she touched the tip of his shaft with her tongue, her eyes on his face. She could see the tension there, could see how much he wanted it. That he was denying them both for some reason.

She opened wider and took more of him in. He held her tight, guiding her, setting the pace. She watched him, watched to see if he was getting the same pleasure from this that she'd gotten when he'd done it for her.

And it was her turn to deny him. To push him to the edge. To feel him shake, even while he held her in his iron grip.

He pushed his hips toward her and guided her head down and she took him in deep, her tongue moving along the hard ridge of him.

He swore and pulled her back. "Not yet. Not like that," he said.

He released his hold on her hair and stepped back, sweat making his chest and shoulders glisten. She just wanted to stare at him for a moment. At that hard flat stomach, the lines that framed the part of his body she was enjoying so much.

"I'm not waiting anymore," he said, opening the drawer by the bed and pulling out a condom. The amenities he'd requested in his phone call earlier, no doubt. "Turn around," he said. "Face the headboard."

She turned away from him reluctantly. She wanted to keep staring at him. She wanted to memorize this moment. This night. No, it wasn't sweet lovemaking. But it was what she needed.

And she had no idea when she would have the chance to do something like this ever again. Hell, it would *never* be like this again.

Because she'd never had a connection like this with anyone else. This raw, visceral understanding that went beneath their social veneers and touched on something real.

She hadn't made the choice to be honest with him. She'd had no other option. She suspected it was the same for him.

This man who was clearly from a life so obviously different from hers. A guest at the party, not the help. And yet he knew her. And she knew him.

She felt the mattress depress behind her, his hand on her hip, the other on her arm.

He swept her hair to the side and kissed her neck, the action surprisingly gentle. He slid his fingertips along her elbows, then gripped her wrists, lifting them slightly and looping them over the thick, black bedpost.

He let his hand drift from there, over her breasts, down to her stomach, between her legs. He repositioned her, bringing her ass up against him. He was hot and hard behind her, his fingers teasing her now, ramping up her arousal, keeping her nerves at bay.

She gasped as he pushed two fingers inside of her again, testing her slickness, testing her readiness.

She wasn't sure how much it would hurt. But tonight, there had already been some pain, and he'd made it okay. More than okay—he made it good. He would make this good, too.

He knew her body. Knew how to keep her walking that fine line between pleasure and pain. Knew when to pull back, when to push for more.

So she trusted him to do this, too.

He withdrew his fingers and repositioned them both. Then he was pressed against the entrance to her body, sliding in slowly, his grip tight on her hip.

She bit her lip, trying to keep from whimpering. It was the burning pain she hadn't expected. Pain, yes, but not quite this kind. It made her eyes water, made her shake.

"Stop?" he asked, his voice hard.

"No," she said, pulling down hard on her restraints, the bedpost biting into her wrists.

He tugged back on her hip and thrust hard, driving himself in to the hilt. He cursed again and started moving inside of her, the pain gradually decreasing, pleasure slowly blooming in her stomach and spreading outward.

All of the fire, the need, from every touch, every tease, every glance since she'd first seen him came roaring through her, the heat threatening to consume her completely.

He moved his hand between her legs, his fingers teasing her in time with his thrusts. "Come for me," he said. "Come for me now."

His words hit just as his fingertip brushed against her clit, just as he filled her with another hard thrust, and pushed her over the edge.

Her release was hard. Bursting inside of her, leaving shock waves of heat behind. Leaving her shaking, her shoulders aching.

He let out a harsh growl, both of his hands tight on her hips, fingertips digging into her skin, his hold so hard she thought it might leave a bruise. And in the wake of her orgasm, she prayed it did.

That there would be a physical brand of what he'd done to her. How he'd changed her.

There was no sound in the room beyond their splintered breathing. Until his voice broke the silence.

"Damn," he said, his forehead resting on her shoulder blade, his breath hot on her skin. "You should have said something."

"I wasn't allowed to talk," she said.

He swore again, reaching over and tugging her hand from around the bedpost. He moved away from her and started to untie her hands. "You should have told me."

"What exactly?"

"You have blood on your legs," he said, his tone grim.

"Oh. That."

"The fact that you were a virgin should have come up," he growled. "How the hell were you a virgin?"

"You're so sure I was?" she asked, feeling shaken. Unsure of what to do with herself.

"Yes," he said, though he didn't sound sure now.

"You an expert?"

"I'm not. That's the thing. Never done that before, but

then, that's why it seemed different." He turned away from her and discarded the condom in a wastebasket by the bed.

"Or maybe I just feel different. Maybe I'm just different," she said, only realizing after that the statement sounded just a little needy.

"Are you going to tell me you weren't a virgin?"

"I don't get why you're angry," she said.

"Because!" he shouted, turning back around, his chest pitching sharply. "You let that be your first time? What the hell is wrong with you? Didn't I warn you?"

She bit the inside of her cheek and rubbed her wrist, where the tie had left red marks on her skin. "You don't even know my name. Why would I tell you how many men I've been with?"

"Or haven't been with."

"Whatever." She rolled her eyes. "I got what I wanted."

He curled his lip. "How could that have given you anything you wanted?"

"It just did. Also not something I need to share with you. My reasons are mine. And I'm sure your reasons for getting off on telling a woman to get on her knees and suck your dick are yours. But you know what? It's none of my business."

"You should go," he said.

"Actually," she said, getting off the bed, her ankle rolling thanks to her damn four-inch heels, "I should. I... Thanks for the sex, or whatever it is you people of sophistication say in situations like this. I am just a poor, hapless virgin, so I'm at a loss."

"Get your clothes."

"I'm not taking orders from you right now," she spat, bend-

ing down to get her dress. "If you're in the mood to give orders, though, order me a car. How about that?"

"No problem." He bent down and picked his pants up,
tugging his phone out of his pocket. "Send the car up front.
You're just picking up my friend for now."

He hung up and she stood there, her dress crushed against
her breasts. He was still naked. Still beautiful beyond reason.

And still bleeding emotion. It was hemorrhaging between
them. Their needs mixing, mingling into one giant pool of
regret.

"I have a feeling we're both a bit too many levels of screwed
up to be able to deal with each other," she said, looking down
at the ground. At her feet, still clad in those patent-leather
black high heels.

"I imagine you're right."

She stepped into her dress and zipped it up. And they stood
there. Like two strangers. Like he hadn't been inside of her
only a few moments ago.

Like he hadn't left marks on her. Inside and out.

His phone buzzed. "That would be your car."

"Spiffy." She turned, and the moment she couldn't see
him anymore, her heart squeezed so tight she thought she
would suffocate. "Hey, before I go," she said, turning par-
tially, "did you want my name?"

He shook his head. "I don't need it."

More than that, he didn't want it. She could see it. That
he was almost afraid of it. Afraid to put a name to the virgin
he'd just violated, or whatever the hell issue he was having.

Afraid to have a name for the woman he was throwing out only minutes after having sex with her.

"Katy," she said, her hand on the doorknob. "My name is Katy Michaels. It was nice to have met you."

Chapter Three

My name is Katy Michaels.

Those words kept echoing in his ears. They had been for three days.

Because he knew that name.

Sarah had talked about Katy. Her younger sister. One of her inspirations for working so hard. One of the reasons, in the end, why she'd put up with Jason's abuse instead of leaving the firm.

Because there weren't a lot of ways out of the pit of poverty. Not easy ways. Many needed a hand-up, that was for sure. But there were very few people willing to give one without strings attached.

Which had been the situation Sarah had found herself bound up in, and he hadn't even realized it.

She'd been sending money to her younger sister. To her younger brother.

Katy had been in school; he knew that much.

He was a dick. There was no way this could be worse. None at all. He'd used her to feel in control of his own miserable life, a life that he was in the process of exploding so that he could make right what had been done to her sister.

He'd chosen to, for the first time ever, unleash his domination fantasies on a woman and it turned out to be Sarah's younger sister. The sister Sarah had protected with everything in her.

Sarah had died, in all likelihood, under a stress she never would have endured if she hadn't had Katy and their brother to take care of.

And he had debauched her. Holy hell, it was like he was destined to screw up everything. Like he was destined to be the villain no matter how hard he tried to avoid it.

One slipup with regards to his self-control and he'd done the worst thing imaginable.

"Stephanie," he said, approaching the reception desk in the front of his father's office, "is my father in?"

"Yes, he is, Mr. Treffen, but he's in a meeting." The woman looked down and Austin noticed that she seemed dull. Tired. It made his chest ache. "I can let him know you're here and see if he wants to interrupt?"

She lifted her hand to brush her hair behind her ear and he noticed finger-shaped bruises curving around her wrist.

And he saw a flash of his hands on Katy's hips. He wondered if he'd left bruises behind, too. If he were any different from his father, a man who used others to his own ends. For his own pleasure.

Even if it left them damaged beyond repair.

Then he saw red.

"I'll be interrupting the meeting, thank you, Stephanie. I find I'm not in the mood to wait." He strode past reception. If Stephanie were arguing, he couldn't hear her over the roar of the blood in his head.

He kept seeing flashes of his night with Katy.

And he wondered now if Sarah had gone through something similar. But he wondered if she'd ever been told she could say stop. Or if his father had unleashed all of that on her without ever giving her a choice.

It made him sick to think about it.

He walked down the long, bland corridor, the walls closing in on him as he went. Then he heard a familiar voice and stopped cold outside his father's door.

It was cracked slightly, and he couldn't see the speaker, but he could hear her.

My name is Katy Michaels….

What was she doing here?

"Thank you, Mr. Treffen, that will be all. I'll be handing over my case to another events coordinator. I'm sorry that the party of the other night wasn't to your specifications." Her tone was tight, stiff.

"Not at all, Ms. Michaels. I apologize that the complaint found you in trouble with your firm."

A sliver of ice wound down Austin's spine.

Jason wasn't sorry at all. He had that tone in his voice, when he spoke to a victim. A woman he intended to draw in. Austin recognized it now, and he had no idea how he hadn't seen it before.

"It's nothing, Mr. Treffen. I'll do other accounts."

"Of course it's not nothing," his father responded, his tone cajoling. "I know that Treffen, Smith and Howell is a big account. Losing it would be difficult for anyone. I imagine you receive a commission per event?"

"In addition to my regular salary, yes."

"So you'll be suffering financially."

"A bit," she said, her voice clipped. "But I'll soldier on."

"If there's anything I can do, let me know. I have other work."

Austin tightened his hand into a fist. What the hell was this? What was her game? What was his father's? Did he know who she was? It wouldn't be hard to place her. Michaels was a common enough last name, but Austin had figured out the connection easily.

And as for Katy...had she been using him to get to his father? Was that why she'd given him her virginity? So that she could maneuver her way into a better position?

Of course, their night together had gone to hell, so it hadn't worked that way, but he could see the logic in it.

"Thank you," she said. His father was seemingly unaware of the edge in her voice. Sharp and cutting, and, Austin had the feeling, prepared to verbally castrate him at a moment's notice. "Mr. Treffen, perhaps we'll see each other again soon?"

"I hope so, my dear."

Austin curled his hands into fists. To keep himself from pushing the door open. To keep himself from storming into his father's office and committing acts of violence he would regret later.

He moved back in the corridor before she opened the door and closed it tightly behind her.

Then she froze, her eyes round as she looked up at him. "What are you doing here?" she asked.

"I might ask you the same thing. But I realize that both of us never asked why exactly we were attending the Treffen, Smith and Howell Christmas party the other night. We forgot, I think, that we have someone in common between us."

He watched as her face changed. Horror lighting her eyes,

her top lip curving upward into something like a snarl. "We do, don't we?" she said. Her voice was monotone, not reflecting any of the war of emotion raging behind those blue eyes.

But she couldn't hide it from him.

"I suggest we take this elsewhere."

"Do you?"

"Yes," he said.

"I have to go back to work," she said.

"And do what? You've lost a major account." Which he suspected was by design. One of his father's sick, sadistic designs. "And we need to talk."

"I don't think we do."

He reached out and took her arm, held her there, and hated himself for doing it. But he had to hold on to her. She was Sarah's sister and she'd walked right into the lion's den. And he didn't even know if she knew it.

She was stupid enough to come back to his hotel room, either by design or by accident. She was stupid enough to come into his father's office today. Alone.

Or maybe *naive* was the better word.

He thought about how tight she'd been when they'd been together. The fact that she'd never been with another man...

Yes, perhaps *naive* was the word.

"You will speak to me now, or I will march you in there and we can have this conversation in front of Treffen. Which do you prefer?"

"What's your connection with him?" she asked, her voice breathless.

"It's genetic, I'm afraid. Now, let's go outside."

She didn't argue this time. She let him lead her. Past reception—and a wide-eyed Stephanie—and into the elevator.

The doors slid shut behind them and she rounded on him. "We seem to spend a lot of time in elevators," she said crisply.

"We've spent a vast amount more time in bed, but yes, some time in elevators. But what we haven't done is talk."

"We talked. About shrimp, and you told me to get on my knees."

"So we did," he said, his tone clipped. "But I think we skimmed over something very important. Katy Michaels."

"You remembered. I would have thought it would have sunk down into the annals of your memory by now. Just one of the many women you've deflowered in that ridiculous hotel room. It looked like a vampire brothel, by the way."

"One, I have never used that particular connection before. But a man would have to be an idiot not to keep said offer in his back pocket. Because he never knows when he might need a vampire brothel, as you called it. Two, I've never been with a virgin before, and I never do one-night stands."

"I have one nightstand but that's completely different."

"Entirely."

The doors opened to the lobby and he waited for her to go first. Like he had that night. Except he didn't own the right to do that now. He never had. To give her orders. To make her his.

He shook his head and continued behind her, out the front door and to where his driver was waiting. "Get in."

"This is like bad déjà vu."

"Would it be so bad?" he asked, and then he closed the door and took a deep breath of the cold air before rounding to the other side of the car and getting in.

When he closed the door and settled in, she looked at

him. "I think, after the way things ended between us, yes, it would be so bad now that you mention it."

"You like bad, though," he said, his eyes fixed firmly ahead, on the divider that kept his driver out of the conversation. "I remember." And so did he. A slug of desire hit him in the gut. Wrong time. Wrong place.

"Could we not?"

"Sure. Why don't you tell me exactly what it is you're doing? Because I don't think it's a coincidence that you're here in New York. And I don't think it's random you ended up doing event coordination for the firm."

"Oh, no, Mr. 'it's genetic,' it's your turn first. You tell me who you are, and what your connection to Treffen is. And then you hope I don't see your name anywhere in the invoices that I snagged."

"My name is all over it," he said. "On every single one. My last name, anyway."

He looked at her, at her waxen face, and felt a twinge of guilt over not just telling her who he was. Not just laying it out. But he felt guilty by association. By blood. And by deed.

No matter how much he might want to absolve himself of this entire situation, he couldn't. He'd failed to really listen to Sarah. He'd failed to keep her safe.

And now…and now here he was with Sarah's much beloved sister. Sweet Katy, whom he'd…

Well, yes, he remembered exactly what he'd done to her. In perfect, graphic detail.

He would never forget it.

But then…he wanted to see her response. To gauge whether or not she'd been using him the other night.

Like you weren't using her? To get your sense of control back through her submission? You sick bastard.

He had been. He'd used her. But he still needed to know what her game was. So he could try to…protect her. Yeah, that was what he wanted to do. Because he'd failed in protecting Sarah. He'd failed her in every way. The most basic of ways. She was dead, and who had taken care of Katy since then?

Yes, they'd gotten a payout. But what then? Money didn't replace a smile. It didn't replace the light in someone's eyes. Didn't answer the phone when you called.

It didn't breathe life back into a broken body.

He'd grieved for his friend. But Katy had been grieving a sister. A sister he'd failed. In so many ways. And now he had to try to make it right.

Otherwise…otherwise there really wasn't anything separating him from his father.

Katy closed her eyes. "Oh…no…please don't…"

"He's my father."

"Oh." She bent over at the waist, her face between her knees. "I'm going to be sick." She straightened. "Do you buy women, too? Do you whore them out? Are you a pimp just like your dad? You're a lawyer, too, aren't you?"

"Yes. To the lawyer part."

"And do you advocate for women?" she spat.

"Yes," he growled. "I do."

"You're just like him, aren't you? Should I be asking for payment for my services? All things considered, your little domination game, my virginity, I think I could have commanded a pretty high price."

Panic was building inside of him. Even though he hadn't

put every piece together yet, he could feel them locking tight, the picture starting to form. He could tell that what she was saying was true. "What the hell are you talking about?"

"You don't know? Do you expect me to believe you don't know?"

"I know that my father is a bastard. I know that he... sexually harassed a woman, to the point where she felt so distressed that she... I know he did that to a woman we both cared about. And I suspect there are others and he's been paying them off."

"Don't talk about Sarah," Katy said. "Don't talk about caring for her. You're his son."

"I am his son, but I didn't know what he was doing to her."

"Why not?" she asked. "Why didn't she tell you? Why didn't you *see?* If you cared for her, why didn't you see?"

Every question hit its target. Because they were questions he'd asked. Over and over again. And he had no answer.

"I don't know," he said. "No, I do know. Because I was a selfish, entitled asshole who never looked past himself or his own achievements. Because life was always good for me, so I didn't look for suffering because I'd never really seen it before." Because he hadn't wanted to see it. "But it's not an excuse. It's just the answer I give myself when I get in bed at night. So I can sleep."

"Well, I don't have a neat answer that helps me sleep. So that's nice for you. I just have to lie there and wonder what they did to her...what they did that was so bad she thought the only way out was to throw herself off a building."

"My name is Austin Treffen," he said.

"Great. Now we're all acquainted."

"It seems so." Silence fell between them in the car.

"I don't think we have anything we need to say to each other."

"No, we have a lot to say to each other. Starting with why you're here. Moving on to what it is you think is going on with my father, those women and the payouts."

"Do you honestly not know?"

"I don't know," he insisted.

"Have you had your head up your ass for the past, what? Thirty-five years?"

"Thirty-three."

"Sorry. Did I wound your ego?"

"I'm not going to run off and get BOTOX. So don't worry."

"Yeah, it would make that scowl you have going on a lot more difficult to accomplish."

"Stop deflecting. Katy, I need to know what you're here for. What you think you're going to get from my father."

"Why should I tell you?" she asked. "You're his son. Why should I trust you at all with anything?"

"You trusted me quite a lot that night we were together," he said. "You let me take you to a hotel and tie you up. The fact that you won't tell me anything now…"

"Stop. I didn't know who you were then."

"But I was the same man I am now."

"Well…I didn't know that then. So it's *not* the same." She shook her head and looked out the window. "It's not the same."

"No. Nothing is the same."

"You want me to believe that you aren't like your father?"

"Yes. Sarah was my friend, Katy, and it's an empty thing to say because my friendship didn't do anything for her. Not in the end. But I'm trying now. I need to know what you know, and until I do, I can't risk telling you too much."

"And you think I can?"

"I think you're one woman, Katy, going up against a man who has ruined hundreds of women. Women who were more well connected than you. Women who had more money than you. Women who were stronger than you."

"And you're going to bring him down with your big muscles? But I can't because I'm a woman?"

"I'm going to bring him down with a hell of a lot more weight behind me. With connections, with status and money and the inside track to his wife—who happens to have a large amount of influence in the community. And who, if she divorces him, will end up with half of what he has since he had less than she did when he came into the marriage. That's not the case now, obviously, but back then... Let's just say things change."

"And you want to bring him down?"

"Do you?"

"I want his head on a pike out in front of the city gates. Barring that? I'd like to see him rot in jail. For what he did to Sarah. For what I think he's done to a lot of women."

"What is it you're thinking?"

"This may be where I pull a Jack Nicholson and say you can't handle the truth," she said.

"Are you trying to protect me?" he asked, something warming inside of him.

"Protect you? Not really. But I'm really not sure you're going to be able to handle this."

"Because?"

"Because prostitutes, Austin. That's where all this has led

me. I've been working my way around the edges of his circles for months. As a server first, then as an event coordinator. I've talked to people. A lot of people. I contacted a pro bono law firm...."

"Dammit," he said, putting his head back on the seat. "That was *you?* Did you not do any research?"

"What?"

"I own that law firm. It's an arm of Treffen, though I keep them very separate."

"What?"

"I got your letter. It's the thing that mobilized me. And my friends."

"Wow..."

"You—" he said, raising his hand and pointing, shaking his finger like he was a concerned parent or something and he couldn't seem to stop "—you are a hazard to yourself and to others. What if that had managed to get into my father's hands?"

"I didn't sign it. I just wanted to...test the waters."

"To what end?"

"So that maybe there would be some investigating. So that when I found some concrete evidence I wouldn't be going in cold."

"Trying to make it look like more than one person was involved, maybe?" he asked.

"When the system isn't going to do you any favors, sometimes you have to game it," she said through clenched teeth.

"Granted," he said. "However, for all intents and purposes, I'm 'The Man,' so if you want to work the system from the inside, you might want to start by giving your information to me. You were going to anyway. Even if it was going to be unintentional."

"I've been speaking to some people. But Stephanie the receptionist was the biggest help. I found her crying one day when I was scoping things out for the party and asked her what was wrong. She'd just been propositioned by your father," she said, the words dripping with disdain. "He'd asked her if she needed extra money because he knew she had some big student loans and also major credit-card debt. He asked if she felt like he'd helped her, giving her the reception job, working it around classes... Of course, she felt like he had. Then he offered her a full payoff of her credit card if she would go on some...dates. With some of his associates. She agreed and...and it became clear very quickly that these were supposed to be something more than dates."

Austin felt dizzy, like he might vomit on the leather seats of his very expensive car. "What do you mean?" he asked, knowing full well what she meant.

"She was meant to sleep with them."

"And?"

"She said no the first time. But it was made very clear that she couldn't ever do that again. Not if she wanted to keep her job. Not if she ever wanted to get a job after college. At least in any sort of high-powered law firm. She knew too much, so it was either go along with it, keep her job and have her debts paid off...or lose everything."

"I don't really want to guess which she chose."

"She's working at the reception desk, so it's pretty clear."

"So, what? My father is running a full-on prostitution ring?"

"Escort service," she said. "No sex demanded up front. But

the expectation is there. There's a lot of money, a lot of gifts. And a lot of invoices. Your father is paying for these debts by wrapping them in expenses and charitable donations. He's shielding the money he's taking in from it, as well."

"How many women?"

"Right now? I'm counting about eight if the invoices are complete. And if it's current."

"How did you get ahold of the invoices?" he asked.

"Again, Stephanie. She doesn't want her name on any of this. That's the thing.... She's already told me she can't testify. Her loans are paid off. This is her last term. She's not bringing her name into this. She wants nothing to do with it. And I'm afraid that's...by and large what we're going to find."

"It seems like the women would want to help bring him down."

"You would think. But these are all ambitious, smart women. They have goals, and...let's face it, Austin, scandal like this? It would stick to them. They're women. And..."

"I know how it works," Austin said, his heart pounding, the sick feeling spreading through his veins. Like poison. Each pump of his heart making it move faster through him.

"You can see why it's going to be hard."

"Sarah?"

She bit her lip. "She sent me a letter before she died. But I didn't get it until after she was already gone. She said that things were bad at her job. She said that there were...things she was being asked to do that she didn't want to. That were never supposed to be part of it. It was sort of rambling. I didn't really...understand."

"I didn't, either." *But you could have. You could have asked questions. You could have picked up the phone. You just didn't want to. Because the truth scared you too much.*

He closed that voice down. He didn't have time for regret. He'd had ten years of it. It was time to take action.

"So yes, I came from a dung-heap mill town in Connecticut. There's nothing there…nothing but a great depression that never ended. There are jobs that will break your body. There's mud, and there's alcohol. And lots of drugs. I left my diner job behind, that life behind, so that I could finally put an end to this. So that I could try and fix this for Sarah, and I found out that it was just the tip of a very massive iceberg."

"Explain."

She shook her head. "Men in influential positions. Some of the country's wealthiest businessmen. Politicians, but then, that's not too surprising. There isn't a lot of hard evidence, but there is some."

He blew out a breath he hadn't known he'd been holding. "You know you're going to end up with a target on your back."

"What do you mean?"

"Do you hear what you just said? You're talking about sexual scandal that's going to touch people in the most powerful positions. Do you know how hard old white guys fight to keep their power, Katy? Do you know just what you're stepping into here?"

"It's worth it. It's for Sarah. It's for every woman they've taken into this, before and since. And all the women who won't be taken in in the future."

"And what happens if they get ahold of you?"

"I don't…"

"Do you think this is some kind of game? Do you think

you matter to them at all? They buy and sell women. They reduce them to nothing more than a commodity. They broke Sarah. What do you think your life means to them, Katy? Nothing. You're just a woman from Crapsville, Connecticut. You're just a thing. And if they have to break you to save their asses, they will do it, and don't think for one second they won't."

"You don't honestly think they'd hurt me...."

"Do you honestly think they won't? Listen to yourself. To what you just said to me. Jason Treffen is a charming man, and I bet he could charm someone even while he cut their throat."

"You think your own father would...kill me, and you mean that in the literal sense?"

"He'd pay someone to do it," Austin said, his blood so cold in his veins he thought it might stop flowing altogether. "After what you just told me, I have no reason to doubt it. He thinks nothing of killing someone's spirit. Why would he stop there?"

"I'm not going to do anything different, Austin. I have to stop him."

"That's what I'm trying to do, but I have a lot more backing me up. Work with me, and I can help. We can help."

"Who's 'we'?"

"Friends. Friends who knew Sarah. Alex Diaz, he's a journalist. And...Hunter Grant."

"Sarah's ex?"

He nodded slowly. "Yes."

"He broke her heart, you know?"

"I know. I think in the end we all did. And now...all we can do is try to fix it."

"It's too broken to fix."

"I know. So we'll do it for the women who are still here. For the victims he's left broken but not destroyed. That's what you want, isn't it?"

"Yes. Mainly, though, I want justice. I want to watch the man who drove my sister to suicide lose everything. I want to play the metaphorical fiddle while his empire burns. And if that's wrong, I don't really care."

Austin ran his hand over his face and leaned back in the seat. "Great. You can have your revenge, your justice. But you need to be where I can protect you."

While he was forming the plan, while the words were coming out of his mouth, he wasn't really sure what he was going to offer.

Until he said it. "You need to come and live with me."

Chapter Four

Katy stared at Austin, her mouth hanging open. "I what?"

"Come and live with me."

"No. No, no, no. Hell to the no."

"Excuse me, I have a call to make." He reached into his pocket and pulled out his phone. And she couldn't help but stare at his large, capable hands as he dialed the number.

She didn't know what was wrong with her. Why when she looked at his hands she could feel how it had been when they were on her skin. Gripping her hips. Holding her.

How it had been to feel those fingers in her mouth. And... elsewhere.

"Yes, this is Austin Treffen. Recently, you hosted an event for my father that was coordinated by Katy Michaels."

The hair on the back of her neck prickled and she shot him a deadly glare.

"She disappeared midway through the event, and we ran out of food and had no one to contact. I spoke to her the day after and asked her about it," he said, looking at her as he spoke into the phone, his dark eyes burning into hers. "She had no explanation. She just said she was tied up all evening."

Her face burned as wretched, embarrassed heat flowed

through her. Worse than the embarrassment was the quick, assaulting heat of arousal. How the hell could she still be turned on by this guy? And really, really, how could he turn her on even now?

"I found the whole thing quite unprofessional and if this is the way—" He paused. "Yes, I understand she was removed from the Treffen account, but honestly, I don't know that any of the people in attendance would be inclined to use your event-planning services when... Oh, she's no longer working for you? In that case, perhaps we can give you another chance. I'd hardly let one bad employee spoil your reputation. Especially as you've taken corrective measures. Have a nice day." He hung up and she exploded.

"What the hell? What the actual hell. I don't even..." She heard her phone ring in her purse on the floorboard of the car. "This rant will continue in a moment." She bent down and pulled her phone from the side pocket of her bag. "Katy Michaels, Life's a Party, how can I help—"

"Katy, this is Alexandra." Her boss. Oh, great.

"Hi," she said.

"I'm really sorry to have to do this, but we received another complaint regarding your performance at the Treffen event. With all the media attention Jason Treffen is getting right now, there's simply no way mistakes like this can be tolerated. I'm afraid we're going to have to terminate you. Effective immediately."

"What?"

"I am sorry, Katy. You're very nice to have around the office, but events like these are very demanding and they simply aren't for everyone. I'll have the contents of your desk waiting at reception. There is no need to come upstairs."

And with that, her boss hung up. Her ex-boss.

"You…" She twisted in her seat as best she could while belted in. "You utter bastard! You just cost me my job!"

"And now you're in dire financial straits. I guess you take my help or my father's."

"What's the difference between you and your father?" she spat.

"I won't whore you out to my friends. I think that's a pretty substantial difference."

"Look, the dominant-male thing was hot in bed, but it's jerky in real life, just so you know."

"This isn't about being dominant. This is about keeping you safe."

"In that case, can I use the safe word?"

"No," he snapped. "I didn't protect Sarah. I failed. I will not fail when it comes to protecting you. Do you understand? If I have to put you under lock and key until my father is behind bars, I will do it. Because I will not have your blood on my hands."

"If anything happens, my blood will be on me," she said. "I make my own choices."

He shook his head. "No. Sorry. You don't. Not right now. Because you might know what it's like to grieve your sister, but I don't think you have any idea what it's like to know you could have stopped it. I was here, Katy. I was here and I did nothing. I didn't see it. I see the danger now. I see it coming. I see what could happen to you. You're not going to end up staining the sidewalks of New York because of your pride. I can't let it happen."

She tried to take a breath, tried to breathe around the knot of grief in her chest. The anger she felt. At him for making her lose her job. At him for letting Sarah die. Just...mainly at him. "You don't get to control what I do," she said. "I know how to keep myself safe. If I find anything that you need to know, then I'll call you. Put it in my phone." She handed her phone to him and waited while he punched his number in and saved it. "But I'm not moving into your place. That's ridiculous."

"You are going to do this," he said, his voice low, rough.

She leaned in, her heart thundering hard. "Are you going to grab me by my hair and drag me back to your penthouse?"

"If I did, would you come?" he asked, letting the double entendre hang between them.

"You're disgusting."

"It wasn't disgusting to you the other night."

"Tell your driver to take me home. West 79th."

He punched the intercom button. "West 79th." He moved his hand away from the call button. "There, I did."

"Thanks. You're a gem," she said, every word dipped in a thick coating of sarcasm.

They spent the rest of the drive in silence, maneuvering through the nightmare traffic at a pace that made Katy sweat. She was used to taking the subway and not dealing with roads, which seemed to have all the driving laws of a demolition derby.

She looked out the window and saw a side mirror from a neighboring vehicle so close that she could have rolled down the window and touched it.

Worrying about a collision was a lot easier than worrying about Austin, her job loss and the possibility of Jason Treffen coming to sell her into sexual slavery.

When they pulled up to her apartment, she got out and

slammed the door behind her without saying anything to Austin.

She heard his door open and she turned, just as he stood up out of the car and looked at her over the top of it. The impact of his eyes meeting hers hadn't lessened since that first time. Not rage, not finding out he was a Treffen, not knowing what he looked like naked—nothing had stolen any of the heat that burned between them. "I'm serious, Katy. Call me if you need something. Call me if you hear from Jason."

She looked away. She had to. "I will. On that I'm going to work with you. I'm just not moving in with you. And now...I have no job, so if I end up on the street..."

"You'll come live with me. You could stop posturing and just come with me now."

"Here's a posture for you, Treffen," she said, throwing up her middle finger at him. Her younger brother would be so proud. Then she turned and walked down the steps that led to the lower level of the town house she shared with her roommate, Leah.

She slammed the door behind her and locked every lock before heading upstairs, trying to ignore the building panic. She had no cushion for this. No savings. She'd been so focused on landing the account for Treffen, Smith and Howell that she'd happily gone on a "trial period" pay grade, taking a cut from when she'd been working the lower-level accounts as an assistant.

As a result, at this very moment, she was two months behind on rent, and now unemployed.

Her roommate was not going to be happy. Not in the least.

"Leah!" she called.

"I'm in my room."

"Leah," Katy said, coming to the doorway of her room-mate's tiny bedroom. The whole town house was small. And old. And it stole about three quarters of their monthly in-come. But such was Manhattan. "You aren't going to believe what just happened."

Leah knew nothing about Sarah. Or Jason Treffen. Or her night with Austin. They weren't all that close. But they'd met during Katy's brief stint waitressing, and when she'd found out Leah had needed a roommate, Katy had jumped at the opportunity to get out of her studio apartment in a very seedy part of town.

"What?" Leah asked, sitting up, her blond hair falling over her shoulders in a frizzy halo.

"I got fired."

"What?" Leah's jaw dropped. "Do you get severance? How much severance will you get? What about rent?"

Well, that was the last question she wanted to be asked, because there was no easy answer for that, and she was al-ready treading on thin ice. And she knew it.

"I don't...know."

"You have to find out, Katy. I can't pay for any more rent on my own. I barely make what we owe in rent every month."

"I know. But I mean...I've been buying food."

"Ramen isn't equal to putting a roof over our heads!"

"I know, and I'm sorry. I'll find another job."

"When? And how long until you get paid?"

"I don't—"

"If we miss even once you know Mrs. Czarnecki is going to throw us out on our butts."

"I know," she said, thinking of their thin, pinch-faced

landlady. Yes, she would indeed evict them as quickly as possible. Eviction might be a complex process, but the older woman had honed it into a fine art.

"Affordable" Manhattan housing was hard to come by, and it was competitive. That meant the moment she booted someone for missing a payment, she had five new applicants beating down her door, just dying to give her first and last month's rent.

"I'm sorry but...Katy, you're going to have to go. Logically, there's no way you can get a job that pays well enough to cover your share, plus what you owe me, in the amount of time we'll need you to. I can't cover for you anymore. I just can't. This is... It's been a while coming."

Katy stood there, feeling like she'd been hit over the head, by an anvil she should have seen coming, honestly. "I thought we were friends."

"We are," Leah said, looking almost sympathetic for a moment, before shrugging. "But I've ditched friends for a lot less than a good apartment in Manhattan. And I know another girl who will come room here who has a great job. It's my name on the lease, and I'm the one that has to make sure it's covered."

"Leah..."

"I'm sorry. You're a great roommate, and you never take the food with my name on it, which I really do appreciate. I've never even caught you stealing a Kiss from my candy jar. But I have to cover myself here."

"I don't...I don't even know what to say."

"I'm sure you'll find something. I'll give you a week."

"Don't bother," she said, turning and storming out of her

ex-friend's room. "I hope whoever takes my place offers you thirty pieces of silver!" she shouted back.

"What?"

"Read the Bible!"

She stormed down the hall and into her room, slamming the door shut behind her.

Un-freaking-believable. She was being turned out onto the streets by the woman she'd lived with for the past eight months. Not that it should surprise her, since, in many ways, nice as Leah was, she was kind of a weirdo. Labeled food and all.

And fine, *fine,* Katy had missed rent for two months. Which was lame, and she knew it, but she was singularly focused on roasting Jason Treffen over an open fire like a chestnut. 'Twas the season and all of that.

If she and Leah were better friends, the betrayal would hurt her feelings. As it was, it just pissed her off. And this was New York for you.

Or rather, this was life for you. At least for her.

Her own parents would have sold her for a bag of dope if the offer had ever materialized. Lucky for her, it hadn't.

She didn't have time to job-search and apartment-search. She was so close to taking down Treffen. So close to getting her revenge. To getting justice. And now this. All of this!

Screw Austin Treffen. And not in a good way.

She pulled her phone out and looked up the number he'd entered, her fingers shaking. This was a win for him, and she hated that. But if it ended up being a loss for his father, then nothing else really mattered.

"Get your aristocratic butt back here, Treffen," she said

when he picked up. "Bring a car big enough to accommodate my things."

"I can do you one better. I'll send movers."

"I can't afford movers," she said. "I'm out of a job. I wonder why that is?"

"You might not be able to afford movers, but I can. And now you're under my protection. You might as well enjoy it."

"Oh, Austin, I'm sure I'll feel a lot of things while I'm 'under your protection,' but I doubt enjoyment will be one of them." She hit the end-call button on the phone and sat down on her bed, her hands shaking. All of her was starting to shake.

In the past few days, everything in her life had changed.

She'd finally slept with a man. And it had proved that all those shadowy, fleeting desires of hers were very much real. That there was another half to them. Someone who fit into her strangeness like a very weird puzzle piece.

She'd discovered that what she wanted couldn't be wrong, because there was a match to her needs.

Then she'd discovered that man was the son of her mortal enemy. And she'd lost her job. Lost her home.

She'd looked Jason Treffen dead in the eyes. The man who was responsible for her sister's death. She'd spoken to him. Been in his office.

So many things had changed in the past few days but that was the most important.

And that was what she had to remember. That no matter how much it felt like a loss to let Austin do this to her, it was a small part of a very big picture.

She would use this, use him, use the information he was getting and his muscle, to help get to Jason.

She'd had her night off. And it had been blissful, until she'd been smacked with the reality of it all.

Now it was time to get back to work. What she wanted didn't matter. It never had.

All that mattered was doing what was right. She wouldn't be distracted again. She wouldn't be giving in to her desire to let go again, either. Not until all of this was finished.

So if Austin thought she was just going to jump back into his bed again, he was going to be disappointed.

Me, too! Her body shouted at her and she ignored it.

It was one thing to sleep with a stranger. It was another to sleep with the man who had failed her sister in the way that he had done.

He might be her ally in this, but at the end of the day, he'd played a role in Sarah's downfall. She would work with him, but they would never be friends.

She would never forgive him for what he had done. And nothing would change that.

Austin felt a vague sort of triumph as he watched the movers bring the boxes into his penthouse.

Vague because it was battling with a sense of disquiet at the thought of sharing his space with this woman for an indefinite amount of time.

But he had to protect her. He had to. It was like some raging, primitive urge. Maybe Sarah's ghost possessing him. Or maybe it was just the guilt from the past, piling on with the regret he felt over having unleashed his darkest passions on the last woman on earth he should have ever touched.

The problem was, when he looked at her, he still wanted her. When he saw that brown hair, coiled into a bun at the base of her neck, he wanted to unravel it again. Pull it hard, until she cried out from the pleasure and pain. And that brought him back to what it was like to have her sweet red lips on his—

He cut off that line of thinking.

She was currently standing in his kitchen, in a pencil skirt and prim blouse, her arms folded beneath her breasts and her shoulders curved like she wanted to collapse in on herself.

Her expression, on the other hand, was much more confrontational than her posture.

"I imagine this is larger than your place on 79th?" he asked.

"It's larger than any place I've ever lived ever, but the only reason that matters is that I'll be less likely to run into you."

"You don't seem to like me very much."

"Shall I list your offenses? I don't see why I should need to. You're a smart man. College-educated. A lawyer. I barely graduated high school, so it doesn't seem like I should understand anything you don't. All things considered, you should be able to state why I don't like you with perfect clarity."

"In point of fact, I know my offenses in this life," he said, leaning back against the wall, his hands in his pockets. "I could put together a comprehensive case and see myself damned for all eternity."

"I might find that entertaining," she said.

"Don't worry, the devil is saving me a seat in hell already. I don't need to wait for my day in court."

"Then why act surprised about me not liking you?"

"It's just that you did like me once."

"No. I wanted you. I didn't know you."

"True enough. But I want you to know that in terms of… in terms of what passed between us that night…I don't expect anything like that to happen again. In fact, I don't want it to. You're staying here and you're under my protection. And the last thing I want is for you to think that I asked you to come here so that I could seduce you, or so that I could take advantage of you. Because while I'm not a spotless lamb, I truly have no desire to be my father. I pour a lot of money into advocating for women who have been harassed. Into really helping them."

"That's good to know," she said.

One of the movers walked in through the door, a small box in his hands. His foot caught the carpet and he pitched forward, dropping the box, the top bursting open and spilling the contents onto the marble. A highly polished wooden jewelry box hit the tile and went into three pieces that skidded across the floor.

"No!" The word burst out of Katy's mouth and she dropped to her knees in front of the mess, gathering up papers, earrings and necklaces that had come out of the box. "Oh…no," she said, as she froze and clutched a piece of the box in her hands.

"Sorry, miss," the mover said, looking genuinely upset.

"Give us a second," Austin said, gesturing to the door. The other man obeyed, likely just relieved Austin had decided not to tear him a new one.

If it had been valuables, who knew, he might have. But this was something more. Something deeper. And he didn't want anyone here to witness Katy's pain.

It was a part of protecting her. And he would protect her. In any way he could.

"What was it?" he asked, still standing across the room. She wouldn't want him to touch her. He knew that already.

"It was Sarah's jewelry box. It's probably silly to be this

upset about it but…" She took a sharp breath, concealing a sob. "It fell and broke into pieces. Just like she did."

"Shit," he breathed, and then he was on the floor next to her, holding one of the pieces. He wanted to do something more. Comfort her or something. But he didn't know how. He didn't know how to touch her the right way.

All he knew with her was sex and control. And that wasn't what she needed. So he just sat with her on the floor, while she stared straight ahead. There were no tears, just a blank sadness. A sort of hollow look that echoed inside of him, in all the empty places.

And there were so many.

"We can get it fixed," he said. "It's the lid and body and… this looks like it was a false bottom." He picked up the middle piece and looked at the way the bottom was dangling open.

"I didn't know it had that," she said, frowning.

"It has something in it, too," he said. "A picture."

She ran her arm over her face, over her dry eyes. "There's one here, too."

"You weren't keeping pictures in it?"

She shook her head. "No. But I didn't know about the bottom, either."

She leaned forward and touched the picture that was face-down on the floor, then picked it up slowly. She turned it over. "Oh." She put a hand up over her mouth.

"What?"

She just shook her head and handed him the picture. He looked at it and dropped it like he'd been burned.

He closed his eyes and tried to wash the image away. But he couldn't.

It was a woman. Blond hair spilling over pale shoulders, her head down, a man's hand braced on the back of her neck.

"It's Sarah."

"I know," he said.

He picked it up again and studied it more closely. Then he picked up the photos that were still in the false bottom. Some were more graphic. And there was no doubt as to the activity happening in them.

But it wasn't the blatant depiction of sex that shocked. It was the pain in Sarah's eyes. Not physical pain. This wasn't a game with whips and chains. It was the emotional pain. He could see how dead to it all she was. Resignation tore at his heart.

It was sex. Simple, vanilla sex. Especially in comparison to his encounter with Katy. She wasn't bound. She wasn't being dominated in any obvious sense, and yet, she was a woman owned.

With a man who took delight in exploiting his power over her.

His stomach pitched. It was all too familiar. A hideous, twisted rendition of his encounter with Katy. His stomach turned, his throat tight, sweat breaking out over his skin.

Something compelled him to turn it over and look at the back.

Jason 9/04

Three months before Sarah's death.

And with his father. Jason wasn't stupid enough to be in a picture, of course. All that could be seen was a man's hands. There was the label on the back, but that meant nothing in any real sense.

But he knew it was true.

"I didn't know," he said. "I didn't even suspect."

"I want to see," she said.

He pulled them back. "You don't."

"I need to see, Austin."

"Why, Katy?"

"Because I'm going to ruin this man. I'm going to de-stroy him and mount him on my wall, and I want to know exactly what manner of monster he was when I'm staring at the carcass."

"Incentive, then." He handed her the photos and watched her work her way through them, her complexion pale.

She curled her hands into fists, her teeth burrowed so far into her bottom lip he was afraid she would draw blood. "I hate this."

"I know."

"No, I hate that ten years after her death…this is the extra thing I get to find. That one last piece of her. Do you know how much you wish for one more picture? One more letter?"

His stomach churned.

One more voice mail. "No," he said, his voice rough.

"So much, Austin. And I have these. Pictures of this… affair, whatever the hell it was. I have photographic evi-dence of the thing that drove her to her suicide."

Katy swallowed back the bile that was rising in her throat and tried to stop the shaking. Dammit, she was shaking ev-erywhere. Inside, out.

It was horrible to see just what had driven her sister over the edge. To see what she'd been subjected to. And for how long? Had she wanted some of it, only to find it went too far?

What did it say about her that she wanted that man's son? That he was the one she'd picked out of a crowded room when she could have had any guy there? That he was the one she'd trusted to live out her most secret fantasies with?

Clearly she was sick.

She handed the pictures back to Austin and their fingers touched. The hot surge of electricity that shot through her only served to make her feel even more shame.

How could she feel something for him? Even now. During *this* moment. Her head was so screwed up. Something was broken inside of her and she had no idea how to fix it, or how to deal with it.

Just slap some duct tape on it and keep going. Because you have to. It's for her. You don't have time for you and your issues right now. Just shut it off.

She didn't have time to break apart now. And she didn't have time to deal with her attraction to Austin. An attraction that crossed the border into *so freaking wrong* territory.

"I guess I put this with the invoices," she said.

"I guess so," he said, standing up. She couldn't stand yet.

"Why did she keep them, do you think? Why did he take them?"

"Do you want my guess? Because a guess is all I have. I didn't know just how deep this went. How far things had gone. So all I'm going off of is the man I grew up with, the man I thought he was for the first twenty-three years of my life. Combined with ten years of suspecting he'd driven a friend to suicide by harassing her, mixed with what you told me today."

"Give me your theories."

"He gets off on power. On owning people. He likes that he can be so purely civil, I think, while hiding all of this. That he can advocate for women in the courtroom while manipulating them into sexual slavery in private. I'm sure having the pictures, and even putting them in Sarah's possession, was him taunting her. With the fact that evidence of what they'd done existed. And with the fact that her having that evidence would never mean anything. That she wouldn't be able to do anything with it."

"He was making her feel powerless."

"Yes. And I'm sure that was fuel for every disgusting fantasy he has."

"Who does things like this? I don't understand it. I...I grew up surrounded by addiction. By all the terrible things it can make you do, or not do. Our parents were so checked out. It was all about their next high. They used to leave us, lock us in a bedroom with food. It was their version of taking care of us. It was what they could do. What they understood. I hated it. And I'm not overly fond of them, but I get that there was an intention to care. But that the addiction was bigger than the love. This kind of stuff? This intention to hurt? I didn't know it existed like this. He killed everything inside of her. Until all that was left was for her to go ahead and kill her body, too. He left her to bleed out emotionally then...then she finished the job."

Austin's expression was blank, his eyes unfocused. "Well, I think for today you should just settle into your room. Do you want me to keep these?"

She shook her head. "I think I should. I'll put it with everything else."

"I understand."

She picked up the pieces of the box and held it together, the pictures on the top. "But I think I will go to the room."

"I'll get your things situated tomorrow."

"Okay."

She was too numb to be angry at him now. Not when she just felt sick and defeated. Why was everything so messed up? She couldn't even begin to figure out how her life, how Sarah's life, had ended up this way.

The thing was, not a lot of people would be too shocked that a woman with their background had gone to New York, gotten caught up in the excess and hadn't been able to handle it all. Officially, that was the story.

Sarah Michaels was just a girl from nowhere who'd transcended the boundaries she was born into. She'd taken a leap, and discovered she had no wings.

Another sob story in millions of sob stories, only notable because it was Jason Treffen's building she'd jumped off of.

It was her name that was mud. Not his.

And if she could do anything to change that, she would.

Assuming she could survive living with Austin. Not that the living situation itself was a hardship.

The penthouse really was beautiful. Open and new. And it seemed to have working amenities. Heat that didn't sound like a dying animal when it kicked on. Totally different from what she was used to.

The wall of windows in the living room offered up choice views of the city. Only the beautiful places. So that Austin Treffen never had to look at any of life's ugly things. Too bad there were a lot of ugly things on the inside of his world. They were just better hidden than the ugly things that were in the world she'd grown up in.

Though, that wasn't strictly true. She'd hidden her own ugly things admirably for a long time.

She walked out of the kitchen area and up the sleek, curved

staircase to the mezzanine floor. "Which bedroom is mine?" she called down to him. And she knew she sounded whiny and she didn't care.

She was so tired she thought she was going to fall over. Every last ounce of energy drained from her like blood running from an artery.

Today was horrible. She was spent. She was done. She'd lost her job, lost her home, seen pictures that she needed to view, but hated the existence of. And being near Austin was just a drain all on its own.

From the moment she'd first seen him, he'd captured a piece of her and he hadn't given it back yet.

Asshole.

"End of the hall."

She nodded and walked down that way, pushing the door open, then closing it firmly behind her. She locked it for good measure. Because she didn't trust any of the people in this house. It was only Austin and her, but that was sort of the point.

The room was huge. Clean and spacious with cream-colored walls, a sleek, black four-poster bed and furniture in purple velvet. That part of it reminded her of the vampire brothel. The rest of it was extremely respectable. And the velvet probably wouldn't make her think of anything untoward if she couldn't remember, vividly, what it had been like to feel that textured wallpaper beneath her bare skin while Austin was on his knees in front of her....

She closed her eyes. No. No, no.

She walked across the room and threw the covers back, climbing beneath the sheets and pulling her knees up to her chest.

From this position, on her side, she could see out the windows and down into Central Park, to the naked trees and the blanket of snow over the green grass. The windows themselves had pristinely clean windowsills around sparkling glass. It was notable to her. And for some reason, it made her think of the view from her bed, not in her most recent apartment, but in her childhood home.

On her side, from her mattress on the floor, she'd had a view of an old carpet. Frayed in spots, the rotting wood splintered beneath it. There was dirt on it. Pieces of cat food, kid food and other crap all over. Fake wood paneling on the walls.

If she'd turned over onto her back she could see an edge of light coming through the window, where the old ratty baby blanket that was tacked over it had come loose.

There was mold where the floor met the wall. She'd made a game of keeping an eye on it. Watching it climb the wall and spread farther. Little black spores that she knew, now, she should have been kind of worried about.

Anyway, this was a better view.

Maybe that was how Sarah had gotten sucked into all of this. It was easy to see how it might have happened. This life was so different from the one they'd grown up in. And Sarah had always told them that they could get out, if they did well in school. If they worked hard. If they stayed away from drugs.

She'd instilled things in them that their parents hadn't. Things their parents had been unable to do for themselves.

Today was horrible. And it didn't matter that it was only six in the evening—she just wanted to go to sleep and call it done.

For a few minutes she needed to just check out of the world

and forget everything. Forget Sarah. And Jason. Those pictures. Forget Austin Treffen, and all the things he made her feel. All the anger, all the desire. All the everything.

Forget that he'd made her lose her job. Forget that she was in a bedroom in his home. Forget that she lived here now, and for the foreseeable future.

She even almost wished she could go back to that dirty little house in Connecticut. Because at least there the dangers were simple. At least there she'd had her brother and sister.

And now she was alone.

She wanted to forget that. Everything that had happened in the past ten years.

Too bad when she closed her eyes she saw a room with black velvet wallpaper, and felt strong hands on her wrists. A commanding voice in her ear, hot breath on her neck.

Too bad she couldn't escape the fact that everything in her was changed.

Even in her dreams.

Chapter Five

"Damn, Austin, a conference call. We must really be in trouble," Hunter said.

"It was either that or you get your lazy ass over here right now, and I doubted you wanted to do that." Austin looked out the window of his home office and down at the city, lit up and busy despite the cold and the late hour.

"No desire at all," Alex said.

"Then deal with the conference call. This couldn't wait." He'd waited a few hours. Until he was sure that Katy was asleep. Until he was sure he could recount what she'd told him without throwing something through a window.

"About Jason, I presume?" Alex asked.

"Yes. It's bigger than we thought. I've had some suspicions the past couple of weeks but I...I met her sister."

"Sarah's?" The question came from Hunter. He would remember hearing about Katy. Sarah had talked about her brother and sister a lot, and if Austin remembered, as her ex-boyfriend Hunter surely would.

"Yes." He was not going into the details of how they'd met, that was for sure. "She's been doing some digging into Jason's life, too, it turns out."

"How did you find her? Or did she find you?" Alex asked.

"We sort of ran into each other." *Naked, repeatedly and on purpose.* "She was coordinating my father's annual Christmas party. And she told me...she told me that she has every reason to believe that my father is running an escort service."

"What?" That response came in unison.

"I didn't exactly want to believe it, but I don't think you can argue with the kind of evidence we have. Combined with..." He started to tell them about the photos of Sarah, then stopped. It wouldn't benefit anyone to know she'd been sleeping with Jason. Most especially not Hunter. He could use it for his purposes, but in terms of the legal case...it meant nothing.

Why drag every ugly thing out into the light?

"Combined with my own suspicions," he said.

"Wait," Hunter said. "Are you f— Austin, are you kidding me? Escorts? As in hookers?"

"Paid dates is more like it, from what I understand. But sex is definitely not off the table. And if the girls refuse... there are consequences."

"So hookers," Hunter said. "Your father is a pimp."

Austin gritted his teeth. "I suppose so...."

"Why sanitize it?" Hunter asked. "It's money for sex. That's what it boils down to."

"Are they all college students?" Alex asked. "Interns?"

"I don't know," Austin said. "But Katy told me some of what my father's secretary told her. Basically do it, and have student loans paid off and connections forged in the business world, or...be discredited, lose work and still have all the loans."

"Coercion," Alex said.

"Yeah, a bit," Austin said.

"So we're on the edge of a major scandal here," Alex said. "Because there are clients. And they're high-powered, I would guess."

"As if my father would touch anyone who wasn't."

"What proof do you have?"

"Besides cryptic invoices, a story from a woman who won't testify and the suspicions from a victim's very angry sister? Nothing. I have jack nothing that will stand up in court."

"So there's no way we can take this public right now? Plant seeds of doubt?" Hunter asked.

"No," Alex said. "There's no point giving Treffen any time to clean this up before the evidence is incontrovertible. In other words—don't shove him off the damn building with enough time to get a safety net installed. Make sure he hits the concrete."

"Thanks for putting it in terms I understand," Hunter said drily. "I've taken a lot of hits to the head over the past ten years."

"Just thought you'd appreciate the mental image."

"Oh," he said, "I do."

"Could we please bear in mind," Austin said, his neck starting to sweat beneath the collar of his dress shirt, "that I have a last name in common with my father." He looked down at his hands, and remembered again, the way he'd gripped Katy's hips when he'd had her. Her wrists bound... "I don't like the image of myself hitting the concrete, thank you."

"Sorry," Alex said. "I think of him when I say it like that. Not you. You're not like him at all."

The problem was, Austin wasn't sure that was true. He'd

spent his entire life trying to emulate his father. Had gone to law school and become a lawyer because he'd wanted to be like the man who'd raised him. The man he'd looked up to more than anyone.

He'd wanted to advocate for women. To make sure that those who were at risk of being taken advantage of would have a voice.

He liked his scotch neat. He watched baseball on TV like it was a compulsion. He rooted for the Yankees and despised the Sox. And it was all because of his father. They were things that had made him the man he was. Pieces of himself he couldn't change now, because they were an integral part of what held him together. Things that had come from his father.

Things he'd been proud of until he'd realized the manner of man Jason Treffen truly was.

And there's the fact that you took so much pleasure in having her on her knees. Sure it was a game, but isn't that what he likes? To control people.

That didn't even bear thinking about.

"Well, I appreciate that," Austin said, even while he couldn't stop running all the similarities through his head.

That sense of crushing inevitability that seemed to be his new best friend these days.

"So what is Katy doing now?" Hunter asked. "She's not... involved in any of this on a personal level, is she? I mean... she's safe from Jason?"

Austin thought of the woman sleeping down the hall. Of how he'd manipulated her into coming here. It was for her own good, though. It was to keep her safe. Even Hunter was concerned, because he was right in fearing that Jason might pose a threat to her.

"She's safe," Austin said.

From Jason, anyway. Even if she wasn't strictly safe with him. He would make sure he kept his hands off. He would.

"Good."

"Do either of you have any leads? Any contacts?"

"I'm working on an idea," Alex said. "I have a connection that I'm thinking could be made a bit tighter."

"Good. Let me know if you find anything. Hopefully we can reconvene and pool what we've found into something that resembles actual evidence," he said, drawing a hand over his face and wishing he had some alcohol to dull the ache that was spreading through him, starting at his chest and working down to his fingertips.

A little alcohol could replace that with numbness.

Of course, he'd want a scotch. Which brought him back to the source of the ache.

He got off the phone with Alex and Hunter and stalked out of his office and down to the living area, going to the bar and pulling out a bottle of whiskey that he could hardly muster any enthusiasm for.

He poured some into a glass and knocked it back, wincing. It burned now. And if he drank enough, it would pound on him tomorrow.

So he decided to go ahead and make that a goal. A little suffering. For his sins.

And for the sins of the father.

How poetic. The world's most damn poetic hangover.

It was better than thinking of those pictures. Better than

remembering how Sarah's eyes had sparkled before his father had come in and stolen them.

Better than wanting the woman upstairs.

Yeah, anything was better than reality. And tomorrow his head would hurt so bad the rest of him might not hurt at all.

"I'd imagined you'd be at work," Katy said, pausing in the doorway of the kitchen when she saw Austin, sitting at the small breakfast table by the window, his chin in his hand, his eyes red, a cup of dark coffee in front of him.

She couldn't take her eyes off him. He looked like she felt. Exhausted. Defeated. The brackets around his mouth carved deep, pulled down into a frown. Lines around his eyes showed how tired he was. His dark hair was rumpled, like he'd been running his fingers through it. Over and over. He was a mess. And he was beautiful.

"Not today," he said, his voice rough. "I don't have a case. Right now. I'm shoving off as much work as I possibly can because I have a timeline ticking on this thing with my father."

"You look like hell."

"I feel like hell, too."

"What did you do?"

"I drank a lot. And this morning I'm paying for it. As planned, I might add."

She frowned. "Okay, two questions. Why?"

"Because I was in the mood to punish myself. And if you have to ask why to *that,* you haven't been paying attention to the fact that I'm into some weird shit."

She felt her face get hot at the mention of the sorts of things he was into. She remembered them well. "Question number two—do you drink like this a lot? Because you were drunk the night we met. And you got smashed last night, which is only the second night I've spent near you. I have a low tolerance for addiction and self-destructive behavior and I don't particularly want to be around yours."

"I don't usually drink like this. I promise."

"Those pictures…"

He winced. "I drank a damn lot of alcohol to try and forget them. So I don't really want to discuss them at the moment."

"They were of my sister. They're hardly my favorite thing of all time."

"No. Of course not."

"You did care about her," she said, realizing the truth as she spoke the words.

"I did. She was my friend. One of my best friends."

"How did you meet her?" she asked, coming a little bit farther into the room but still keeping her distance.

"When I first got to Harvard, I was rooming with a bunch of guys I'd never met before. Hunter Grant—"

"Her Hunter," Katy said quietly, remembering the way Sarah had lit up when she'd spoken about him.

"Yes," Austin said. "Alex Diaz, who's a big-shot journalist now. And Zair. The spare to a sultanate somewhere in the Middle East. At least that's how he described it. As though the details didn't matter at all, because what's interesting about being Middle Eastern royalty?"

"That's…an eclectic mix."

"It was. Anyway, Sarah was in a dorm the block over from ours. She and Hunter connected quickly. And…then she was just a part of us."

"Did she like school?"

"Yeah, she seemed to. She excelled. She always had a lot of friends, more than just us. Even when she and Hunter were serious, she was friends with a lot of other women. She didn't talk much about her childhood, but after what you said yesterday…" He cleared his throat. "I didn't know how bad it was."

"It's why school mattered so much," she said. "Why the life she was building at Harvard mattered so much. People like us don't get those chances, but…she did."

"And she did well."

"She…she was happy?"

"For a while," he said, thinking of how sad that last year had been. She and Hunter splitting up. How distracted and dull she became.

The calls for help he missed. And the one he'd ignored.

"I'm glad to hear that because I just need to be able to think of her having some happiness. Our life was… Well, it sucked." She walked over to the table and stood behind the chair across from Austin's. She didn't quite want to just sit down with him. Not yet. "I always hoped she had some real happiness in those few years away from us."

"She did."

"She should have had more," Katy said, angry now. "She should have had a lifetime of it."

"Yes, she should have. And that's why we're stopping this. Because no one should ever be put in the position she was put in. Never again."

Their eyes locked, a short burst of electricity sparking between them. She didn't know how that happened. How they were able to talk about the most dire, horrible things and still feel the current between them.

Shame crawled over her skin. She didn't know what was wrong with her. How she could want him now. How she could want him the way she did.

It was twisted.

"So, what am I supposed to do here?" she asked, gripping the back of the chair. "Unemployed and living with a stranger."

"A stranger?"

"Yes. A stranger." She met his eyes and dared him to disagree. He didn't.

"Well, obviously you'll be working for me. If anyone asks what you're doing here. And by anyone, I mean Jason or one of his cohorts."

"Living with you and working for you?"

He lifted a shoulder. "You have a good point there. So why is it you think that you would live with me after meeting me at a party, sleeping with me, then losing your job?"

Her face heated. "No. You have to be joking."

"Hopefully we won't need the excuse. But there's every chance we'll be seen together. And there's every chance you'll be discovered living here. In which case, why make up an awkward, convoluted story?"

"But what a fricking coincidence! You're suddenly doing it with Sarah's sister?"

"Had my father connected the two of you yet?"

"Probably not. I didn't work for him. I worked for someone else. There's a very good reason I put myself in his general vicinity and not in direct contact. But finding out would be easy. As you said yourself. I mean, that's why you're so worried about my safety. That's why I find myself homeless and jobless."

"At least you're here and not alone," he said. "At least you're under some kind of protection. My building is secure. You'll be safe with me. The alternative is to have no protection at all."

"But in this scenario, you and I are somehow together just when you're looking to reconcile with your father? Wouldn't the entire thing scream 'setup' to him?"

"You're missing something very important in my father's character," he said. "In the character of every man who strikes up a deal with him. These are men who buy and sell the bodies of young women. Who have set up a modern-day whorehouse in a law office dedicated to protecting women from unwanted advances."

"So they're assholes. I get that."

"No. What you don't get is the arrogance. You're just a woman—one related to Sarah, in point of fact. How could you possibly be involved in bringing my father down? When he holds all the cards. When he has all the power. He is above the law, above suspicion. He can see men jailed for sexual crimes then go straight back to his office, rifle through a file and sell a girl he has 'on staff' to one of his buddies. He believes he is smarter than all of us. Better than all of us, but you most of all. Because you were poor. Because you're a woman. And he would never believe, even for a moment, that you could outsmart him."

She swallowed, her throat dry, her body feeling weak. Shaky. "He thinks all of that?"

"You know he does. Look at what he chooses to do in

order to get into the spotlight. All while abusing his power behind the scenes. He's a comic-book villain."

She laughed, a hollow, breathless sound. "Well, that's a good thing. Because I sort of consider myself to be Batman."

"Really?"

"Sometimes tragedy turns us into superheroes," she said. "Or, if not that, then maybe twisted vengeance monsters hell-bent on some form of justice. Even if it's the vigilante sort in the end."

"He'll underestimate you, Katy. He'll underestimate me. And that will be where we win."

"And if he doesn't?"

"If he starts to suspect…" Austin smiled, an empty, dark expression that seemed further removed from the traditional meaning of a smile than any frown ever could be. "Well, I'll just remind him that an apple rarely falls far from the tree. After all, he liked your sister. I like you. I bet he'd enjoy that."

A shiver went through her, a chill crackling over her skin like spreading frost. When he said it like that, she almost believed it was true. That his seduction of her had been calculated. That his desires were somehow connected to those of his father.

And in a moment, the darkness was gone, and he was back to looking pissed off and hungover.

"Anyway, I think it's covered. If his natural arrogance fails, it will be easy to come up with a story. I could say you were working for me, but then if you were discovered to be living with me, in the public eye, I really might tar myself with the same brush. Better to just have it called what it looks like."

"I'm not, though," she said. "Sleeping with you."

"No."

"And I won't," she said, as much for herself as for him.

"The horse sort of left the barn already."

"What are you, a cowboy lawyer?"

"Hardly."

"Yes. Okay. Granted, that horse left the barn. But it's restabled and it's locked back up. With an electrified fence. And it's not getting back out."

"Would it be so bad if it did?"

There was no cool disinterest in his eyes now. It was all heat. All desire. And she wanted to reach out and touch the flame.

She curled her hands into fists.

"So bad," she said, clenching her teeth together. "So wrong."

"See, I happen to know you like bad, so I'm not sure if this is an invitation or not."

"Are you still into it? After knowing that your father was having sex with my sister, using her, are you honestly still okay with…us?"

He drew back as though she'd slapped him, the fire burning to ash in his eyes. He shook his head slowly. "No."

"I didn't think so. Because you *do* seem like you might be a decent guy. And like you did fall far from the tree."

"Do I?" he asked, his voice raw.

"Yeah. You're not as charming as your father. He oozes it. But it's like oil you can't wash off after. After talking to him…I feel like I'm covered in a film I can't shake."

"But you know how he is."

"Yes. I do. But you aren't the same. Just…trust me. You aren't."

"You have a lot of confidence in a strange man you hardly know. Since we're going with the 'I'm a stranger' story."

"Sometimes when everyone around you that you know is a horror show, you have to take a chance on the stranger, right? And gut instinct."

"I hope yours is right."

She blinked. "Are you telling me you don't trust yourself?"

"I think, all things considered, trusting myself would be the most dangerous thing I could do."

A shiver went down her spine. She didn't doubt his words. But, for some reason, right or wrong, they felt like they were part of the same game they'd started the night they'd first met.

And she had to stop thinking that way.

"All right. Noted. No trusting you. I'll keep a shiv on my person at all times."

"And I'll keep my distance."

"So what am I supposed to do while I'm here in your penthouse, playing mistress of the manor?"

He arched a brow and looked her over, his gaze hot, assessing. "You could bake me a pie."

"Probably not."

"Vacuum in high heels and pearls?"

That should not turn her on. It should make her want to punch him in the throat. Instead, she pictured him coming up behind her and...

Well, never mind.

"This is the part where you get shanked, my friend."

"I'm just offering up helpful suggestions."

"Well, you can put a cap on that anytime."

"You asked."

She shifted her weight from one foot to the other. "Do I have house rules...or...?"

"Whatever you like," he said, standing and wincing as a shaft of light crossed his face. "I do have to go to work. If only for a few hours."

"Great. Well...I'll hold down the fort. But I won't vacuum your fort. Or bake pies in it. So you can just let go of that fantasy right now."

"Katy, for the time being, this is your home, too. I don't expect you to adhere to any rules."

She narrowed her eyes. "Where did controlling Austin go?"

He took his suit jacket off of the back of the chair and slipped it on. "He only comes out at night."

The rough edge to his voice, and the promise laced in those words, sent a little spike of longing through her that came to rest at her core. Which was so stupid because she was supposed to be shaking off the attraction. He was supposed to be helping her shake off the attraction because he was supposed to shake it off, too.

"Well, then I will limit my interaction with you to daylight hours."

"Probably for the best." He looked her over, quickly, but she felt it burn over every part of her. "Yes. Probably for the best."

Chapter Six

It had been a miserable day at work. Because every case he'd reviewed, every potential client he'd spoken to, had made him think of Sarah.

Had made him think of Jason.

Every woman with a bruise and sad eyes. Every woman with stubborn pride who sat there, rigid, hating to admit the things that had been done to her, as though they were her failings in some way.

Even the print screamed at him. Documents that detailed abusive relationships, sleazy bosses. Hell, the standard divorce cases were calling up dark emotions. But he was in a pretty dark place, really.

Austin took his tie off and started up the stairs, the faint sound of a thumping bass the first indicator he had that something was weird.

He frowned and slipped his jacket off, draping it over his arm as he started to work on the buttons on his cuffs.

The music was coming from down the hall.

He passed by Katy's door, which was closed. The music wasn't coming from there. His frown deepened as he went

toward his own bedroom, and the music got louder, mingling with the sound of running water.

What the hell.

He pushed the door open and was greeted by a rush of
humid air and more discernible pop music. He was pretty
sure the lyrics were talking about taking a ride on a man's
disco stick, and all things considered, it was about the last
thing he wanted to hear.

There was no door on the bathroom, only an entry area,
then the sinks, and in the back and around the corner, the
toilet and the shower.

He walked through the room, which looked undisturbed,
his bed still made, everything in its place.

Yes, the song was definitely a thinly veiled euphemism.

He gritted his teeth and walked into the bathroom. There
was makeup all over the countertop. Makeup and some sort
of heat-related device for a woman's hair. He didn't know
what it was called because he'd never lived with a woman he
wasn't related to, and he'd never had the desire to ask what
sorts of things they did to get ready.

There was wax, too. A big pot of it with a Popsicle stick
sticking out of the top of it.

She might as well have taken a stamp that said *woman* and
put it all over the room.

He rounded the corner to the shower area and saw a pair
of pink panties hanging from the towel rack, along with a
polka-dot bra and, beyond that, the shower, which was still
running.

The shower, like the rest of the bathroom, was open, with
the main part of it concealed by tiled walls.

He was about to say something. Let her know he was

there, something. Then he saw her round the corner and her eyes went wide when she saw him. She jumped and slipped.

He reached out as quickly as he could and caught her by the waist, her body bowed backward, her stomach flush against his pelvis. She was wet from the shower, completely naked and breathing hard.

The only sounds in the room were the running water and the music now.

"You okay?" he asked.

"Fine," she said, wiggling a little bit now. "You can let go of me now."

He did, stepping back and searching for a towel. When he looked back at the shower, she was gone, disappeared around the corner again. "I have your towel," he said. "Putting it on the hook right here and I'm turning around."

"You could leave the room."

"Fine. I'll do that," he growled, walking back into the bedroom and trying not to think about the wet spots on his shirt, which represented the places her body had made contact with him.

Her naked body.

He fought the surge of heat that shot through him.

He had no right to be lusting after her like this. Not now. Not when he'd walked in on her like that without an announcement.

Of course, she'd been the one in his shower. His shower, when there was one right near her bedroom that she could have used. And all her girlie crap was spread out all over his counter. As though she had every right to come in and take over his space, her things landing everywhere like a cloud of frilly locusts.

That was her fault.

She appeared a moment later, looking freshly scrubbed and wary, wearing a pair of gray sweatpants and a long-sleeved pink top, her hair wet and hanging loose.

"Didn't anyone ever tell you knocking is polite?"

"You were in my shower, baby. I didn't expect to find you there."

"The music and running water weren't a clue?"

"They were a trail of bread crumbs I felt obliged to follow. I honestly didn't expect to find you naked and dripping wet in my shower when you have your own."

"Well, you told me to make myself at home."

"So you decided that meant going into my bedroom?"

He'd never had a woman in his personal space before. Ever. He'd had girlfriends, yes. But he spent the night at their places typically. Or he took them out and they spent the night in hotels. He wasn't a hugger. He didn't talk about his feelings. He didn't let women leave their trappings all over his room.

There was room for one toothbrush in his bathroom, and that was his.

"Well, yeah. You railroaded me into moving in with you. You're a Treffen, therefore my trust in you is…eh. And so I decided to snoop around in your stuff. Then I saw your shower."

"You went through my things."

"Yes. And I'm not going to apologize. Anyway, no whips, chains or invoices for sexual favors. On that score you check out."

"Disappointed?"

"About?"

He crossed his arms. "The lack of whips and chains. You like that sort of thing."

She arched a brow. "You got your rocks off that night, too, so don't go putting it on me."

"You were out of line going through my things."

"Are you really all up on my butt for being intrusive?"

"Excuse me?"

"Are you really getting on my case for being intrusive?" she repeated, her hands on her hips. "Because the last I checked, you got me fired from my job. You effectively got me evicted from my apartment. You forced me to move here by default and then you said make yourself at home. And so I have. And now you're mad at me? You've interfered in every corner of my life and you're pissed because I used your shower?"

"And left your girl crap all over everything."

"My girl crap? What are you, fourteen?"

"No, but I don't share my space."

"Yeah, well, news flash, Austin. I haven't done anything but share space my entire life. I've had to make sure my schedule was conducive to taking care of my younger brother. I had to make sure my emotions never made a blip on the radar, because I had to keep things smooth and stable for Trey. Then I moved to New York and moved in with a roommate who had her name on the lease and who I had to tread softly with so that I wouldn't find myself out on my ass. Then guess what? Because of you I *did* find myself out on my ass. And now? Now I'm sick of treading lightly. You said make myself at home, I'm going to make myself at home. I'm not here because I want to be, buddy. I'm here because you stuck your all-powerful Treffen hand in my life and screwed with things."

"So that means my punishment is…leg wax on my bathroom counter and music that… Was it talking about…?"

"Yes," she said, her cheeks turning pink. "Yes, it was. I like that song. Sorry if it bothered you. Or maybe I'm not sorry if it bothered you. Grow up."

"Did you just tell me to grow up?"

"Yeah. I did. Like you can't handle song lyrics about sex. Again I ask—are you fourteen?"

"It didn't bother me."

"Well, then why are you complaining?"

"You have a bathroom. You could use that one."

She arched a brow. "It doesn't have three showerheads in the shower."

"So? You don't need three showerheads," he said.

"Says the man who has three showerheads," she said, putting her hands on her hips. "Personally, I value the ability to cleanse myself with the 'rainforest mist' setting on. It makes this whole ordeal feel less traumatic."

"I think you're milking it," he said, crossing his arms over his chest and leaning back against the wall.

"Do you?" she asked.

"Yes. I do."

"I don't know if you know my pain and suffering. I was fired and thrown out of my house on the same day."

"All right. If you want to use my bathroom, that's up to you, but I'm not knocking on my own bedroom door and I will use my bathroom when I feel like it. If you're so married to the showerheads, that's your business, but you may end up with a guest."

Her eyes widened. "I thought I told you I wasn't sleeping with you."

"And I thought I told you not to trust me." The air thickened between them, her lips parting, her eyes darkening. "And you definitely shouldn't look at me like that," he said.

"Like what?"

"Like you're considering letting the horse out of the barn again."

She blinked. "I'm not. I just wanted your shower, not your body. Calm the hell down."

"Have you eaten?" he asked, deciding it was best to change the subject. And to take the conversation into neutral territory. And to move *them* to neutral territory. Territory that didn't have a bed with a very useful-looking headboard…

"No," she said. "I was going to order something."

"Anything in particular?"

"I was sort of craving Thai."

"I'm very good at ordering takeout," he said. "Cooking, not so much."

"I can cook," she said, following his lead and leaving the bedroom, heading down the hall a couple of paces behind him. "Really gourmet stuff. Ramen noodles, with some vegetables for added nutrition. Mac and cheese. In the blue box. I don't screw around. Also, Beanie Weenies. A can of pork 'n' beans and some cut-up hot dogs. My skills cannot be beat."

"I don't think I've ever had any of that."

"Not even in college?"

He tossed a look over his shoulder. "No. I had a meal plan."

"Oh, yes, of course. How could I forget? You're all steeped in privilege. Which I guess I should remember since I just used your shower. Three showerheads." She held up a matching number of fingers. "Three."

He shrugged. "Yes. Yes, I'm privileged. Lucky, lucky me. My dad is a pimp." He headed down the stairs and he could hear her behind him.

"There are different kinds of privilege. I mean, sure, that's a sucky reality you have to face. But I grew up in terrible circumstances and I didn't get to eat good food. So you know..."

"Yes. Life was easy for me then. I won't lie to you and pretend I had any great struggle. But looking back and realizing just how little I saw outside of my bubble? That's hard. I'm not stupid. More than that, in my line of work, I'm trained to read people. I have to know how to read between the lines, how to reinterpret what they're saying. I have to know how to manipulate. But even with that, my world was so insulated, so damned perfect, that I just couldn't imagine the kind of thing my father was doing. I couldn't have imagined Sarah's pain. I've seen more since then. I know more about human nature. About how truly horrible life can be. I look back... I hate that idiot that couldn't see past the glitter all around him. Who thought bad things happened to other people. To other *classes* of people."

"And since then you've learned...?"

"Life is shit for everyone. It's just that for some people it's shit with three showerheads. Pad Thai sound good to you?"

"Pad See Ew."

"I'll get both. Chicken or tofu?"

"How about one of each. I'm living it up today and you, I assume, are buying."

"Sure. Why not. You can be on the Austin Treffen meal plan while you're here," he said, his tone dry.

Katy watched Austin make his way over to the kitchen

area. He pulled a menu out of the top drawer and picked up his cell phone.

She still felt shaky from their encounter upstairs. The way his arms had locked tight around her. The way it had felt to be up against him like that. He was all strength and heat. Strength and muscles and heat. And muscles. Oh...the muscles.

"Oh, my gosh," she said, her tone overdramatic. "Now I feel steeped in privilege."

"You are," he said. "Look around you. Hello?"

He started to give the order and she just watched him. Watched the way his hand held the phone, watched the way he stood, one hand in his pocket, his watch visible. There was something about the way a watch looked on him.

There was something about *him*.

Maybe it was just because he was her first lover. Her only lover.

Except that wasn't it because she'd felt that way about him before they'd slept together. The fascination, the strange connection, had been there from the moment she'd first seen him. It was strange she felt that way toward him.

This man who hadn't been able to even imagine the kind of poverty she'd grown up in. Yet they did connect. Somewhere, down deep. Probably in their pain.

And there was a physical connection. No point in denying that. She could feel it now, with him way over there. Just looking at him made her hot inside. Made her feel like parts of her were too close to a fire.

It was a distraction she really didn't need. She had to remember that she was here to bring down Treffen, to get justice for Sarah. That was why she'd gone through his things earlier—thoroughly. If there was anything he was holding back, she wanted to know.

"Ordered," he said, hanging up. "Now we wait."

He shoved both hands in his pockets and stood there, looking like he'd come straight from a designer catalog. There to model sexy watches and perfectly fitted pants.

He made her feel like a scrub. In her sweatpants, with her hair hanging limp...

Of course, he'd just seen her naked, so it was an improvement on that.

She tried to swallow and moisten her suddenly dry throat.

"I do have something to ask you," he said, his voice taking on that hard edge that said he wasn't going to be doing any asking.

He was about to command her to do something.

And that scared her. Because her entire body tightened in anticipation of it. With the desire to do as she was told.

Only for him. Never for anyone else. In the rest of her life, she was in charge. She kept things moving. She kept things together. She made the rules.

But not with him. And it was as natural as breathing.

He spoke with that hint of authority and everything in her went to jelly. Only sometimes, though. Only when she had sex on the brain.

Other times, his orders ticked her off just as much as anyone's.

It was weird. But then, the whole thing was weird. Getting off on any of it was weird.

"What?" she asked, trying to sound defiant, and not melty.

"How many parties did my father have coming up?"

"Oh, well, he's got the more exclusive Christmas Eve party, and then he's got the New Year's party...."

"And I need to attend both. Considering we're reconciling and all."

"And?"

"And I've been thinking. Since you're going to look like my lover anyway, we might as well go ahead and play it up. It was benefiting you to be there as an event coordinator. Think how much more we can find out if you're there as my mistress."

"Your mistress? What is this, some bad black-and-white film?"

"Girlfriend. Lover. Whatever you prefer."

"Love slave?"

"All things considered, anything that speaks of sexual slavery might not be the best label to put on it."

She blinked, her eyes stinging as she thought of Sarah, of those other women, subjected to the orders of men. Her cheeks burned as she thought of what it had meant to obey his orders.

She didn't know her own body right now. Not at all. There were too many conflicting emotions in it. Too many contrary desires.

She wanted to step out of it. Leave all that stupid lust, the regret, the pain, the desire behind. She wanted to step out of her skin before all of those feelings sank down beneath the surface and wrapped around her bones.

Being Katy was too hard. Had been for a long time. But right now the years had rolled together, collected into a heavy weight that rested on her, that made it difficult to breathe. Right now she felt desperate to escape.

And she knew only one way to do that.

In Austin's arms, she'd felt free. Taking orders from him, she'd somehow felt liberated.

No. You can't go there. Not again. How can you even be tempted? How could you possibly want that?

"You want me to play the part of dream date?" she asked, her tone tart.

"Sure. I'll even by you a corsage if you like."

"I do like. I didn't get to go to prom, you know?"

"No?"

She shook her head. "Nope. I was doing double shifts at the diner. What about you?" If she could keep talking, mask the tension, mask the weight of what they were dealing with, maybe she could survive.

"Gave a corsage. Lost my virginity. Prom was memorable."

"Senior prom?" she asked, her brows arching upward.

"Yep."

"Bit of a late bloomer."

"Says the woman who lost her virginity less than a week ago."

Heat stung her cheeks. "We're not talking about me. Who was your girlfriend?"

"She was more experienced than I was. We got a hotel room. You know, normal for that sort of thing. It's what most people do, isn't it?"

"I think missing prom may be why I was still a virgin," she said. "I missed that normal, crucial step."

"There you go. That explains it."

"This is painfully awkward," she said.

"What is?"

"Trying to talk to you like we're normal people who just

met. Rather than people who just met, got naked and then found out they shared a common tragedy."

"It's not the easiest thing I've ever done," he said. "I'll grant you that."

"Why bother? Maybe we should just eat our noodles in silence."

"We could do that. But then what will we do when we have our dates? We do have to look comfortable with each other."

"I suppose so."

"There's no 'suppose' about it."

"I thought Jason's magical arrogance would put an invisibility cloak over my true motives?"

"In many ways, it will. But it would be nice if we looked somewhat authentic, don't you think?"

"I don't know. So many couples have nothing in common and don't know what to say to each other anymore."

"Not new couples," he said.

"No? Enlighten me. Obviously I've never been the other half of a couple."

"Never?"

"I was a virgin, dumb-ass."

"That doesn't mean you never dated."

She let out a long sigh. "I dated. But no guy ever lasted longer than two dates. And I didn't date often. I think the reasons why are fairly obvious."

"When did you move out?"

"I was eighteen. I took Trey with me. My brother, Trey."

"I remember Sarah talking about you both."

"Anyway," she said, skimming over the mention of her sister, "I didn't date because it was too much work. There was already too much to handle. I didn't need another...thing to contend with. In my experience, men were just another hassle and I didn't have the energy for it."

"Can I ask what made you change your mind that night?" he asked.

"Okay, I'll be honest. Being busy wasn't the only thing it was.... I knew what I wanted, Austin. I knew I wanted a guy to hold me down and tell me what to do, to take my control away, take my decisions away, and...that's a scary thing to want. A scary thing to admit you want. Then I met you and for some reason I trusted you wouldn't abuse that power. And I could also see that you wanted it. On top of that, I didn't see you as a hassle because I saw you as sex. And it turns out, I could not have been more wrong."

"Funny how things work out."

"Mmm."

"Except you're right about something," he said.

"About what you wanted?" she asked, heat settling low in her stomach now.

He looked down. "Yes."

"There's a little bit of magic to how all of that lines up, isn't there?"

"I suppose there is. Though...black magic."

She nodded, feeling compelled to lean into him. To touch him. But she didn't.

"Anyway," he continued, "we will have to be more than a distant, brittle old couple because we are, theoretically, in the beginning stages of an affair. You're the first woman who has ever spent the night in my house, much less lived in it."

"Am I really?"

"I told you, I don't share space. But you know that must mean there's something very special about you."

"Maybe I'm double-jointed in interesting ways."

"Or maybe we just play up the chemistry we have between us?" He leveled his gaze with hers and her darn unreliable throat went dry again.

"Well, yeah, we could do that, too," she said. "Or...I mean...the flexibility."

He walked toward her, his eyes locked with hers, and she literally felt her knees get weak. She couldn't look away from him. Couldn't do anything but watch as he closed the distance between them.

He reached his hand out and cupped her cheek, sliding his thumb along her skin. "I don't think we'll have very much trouble convincing people there's something pretty explosive between us."

"You don't?"

"No. I have a harder time convincing myself that what happened between us last week...how good it was...wasn't real. That I'm making it bigger in my mind." He put his other hand on her cheek and she couldn't breathe at all. "I'm trying to make myself believe it. Because if I don't—"

An alarm buzzed and she cursed and blessed the timing.

"That would be the food," he said.

"Yes." She let out the breath she'd been holding and stepped away from him. Saved by the takeout. Any longer and she was sure she would have kissed him. And from there he would have gripped her hair in that iron fist of his and...well, she would have followed any command that had come after.

She watched him go to the door. Watched him take the delivery. She was powerless to do anything but watch him when he was around. She was missing some brain cells when it came to the man, and she couldn't quite figure out why.

"Want to sit...?"

"Anywhere," she said.

He lifted a shoulder and carried the bag into the kitchen area, to the small table he'd been having his coffee at that morning.

Had it only been a few hours ago? It felt like days.

It felt like weeks since they'd slept together. And like only a moment ago, too. Because she was pretty sure she could still feel the impression of his touch lingering on her skin, burning, as though he'd only just touched her.

"I guess we'll be spending the holidays together," she said, wandering over to the table and sitting. "Do you have soda?"

"Soda?"

"Yes."

"I have beer."

"I don't really like to drink. I mean...I will. But I don't often."

"I see. Too responsible?" he asked, opening the fridge and pulling out a can of soda.

"No. It's just that some kids think it's cool, I guess. Because it's forbidden. Because they're drawn to the idea of losing their inhibitions. That part of it, I don't find appealing." She shrugged. "I saw my parents drunk and high.... It's one of my first memories. That and the first time I got high."

His shoulders tensed, his entire body going rigid. "Don't look so surprised," she said. "Do you really think kids can be in a house like that, with garbage like that, and never try it? In my case, I got into it sort of innocently. It was E, I'm pretty sure. Which wasn't their usual drug of choice but... they weren't that picky."

She held her hand out, waiting for the soda, looking for a distraction. He handed it to her, the can cold, the tips of his fingers warm. She wanted to hold his hand while she told the story. To take in his warmth. Instead, she clutched the can and let the ice seep through her skin.

If she told it like it wasn't her, it was easy. And she had told it like that. A few times. For Trey. For some community-outreach programs. Because it was one of those stories that helped people.

Even if it cost her a little bit of herself every time she told it. Because of the hypocrisy. Because of the parts she didn't tell. But it was a good story, a valuable one. And if she broke herself apart from it, telling it felt like the right thing.

She's not you. She's a little girl. A different little girl.

And the girl she'd become? She wouldn't think about her at all.

"Anyway," she said, popping the top on the can, "I got ahold of some Ecstasy that was sitting on the bedside table in my parents' room. I took one pill. Which, being a kid—I was, like, twelve—I was sort of light, and that meant I was, as they say, rolling pretty hard."

She took a drink and watched Austin's expression closely. He was blank. Damned lawyer face.

"I saw a lot of weird things. And it kind of freaked me out, but it made me really euphoric, too. My parents lost their minds when they saw me, and that scared me. I couldn't stop shaking. I was out of control, completely. I probably needed a doctor but that meant taking me to the emergency room, which would have been detrimental to them. They would

have lost us. They would have been arrested. So instead...
they put me in my room to wait out the high." She closed
her eyes then, reciting some of the stats she used when she
spoke to classes. "One pill can last six hours. But comedowns
can last even longer. It can take days to feel normal again.
For me, it took about three days. And they were the worst
days of my life." She broke from what she told people then.
Broke from the script, from anything she'd ever said out loud
before. "I was sadder after coming down from that high than
I've ever been. Sadder than I was when Sarah killed herself.
Because...even though it wasn't the whole time, there were
moments during that high when I was happier than I've ever
been. It's not a natural feeling. At least it wasn't for me. I'd
never been really happy before. And I achieved it, in drug
form. I understood then why they did it. What they were
running to when they took all that stuff."

"But you never took them again?" he asked, his words
slow, cautious.

She took a breath, deflected the question. "E was not a
good experience for me. You know, as nice as the euphoric
feeling was, the comedown was...hideous. And it lasted longer. Plus, I hated understanding them. I hated having an in-
kling of why they let their children fend for themselves for
days at a time. Why they loved a substance more than they
loved us. And I hated being out of control. I've had so little
control in my life that what I could have, I've taken with
both hands and held on to it as tightly as I could."

She opened the box of food and starting dishing out noodles, not paying attention to what it was she put on her plate.
No, false euphoria wasn't her thing. Though, if not for the
hellish comedown...it might have been.

She liked sleep. She liked to be numb.

She wasn't going to talk about that.

"Not always," he said, his eyes meeting hers, heat arching between them.

"Everyone needs a break, I guess." She looked down at her food and broke the chopsticks in two, taking a scoop of noodles. "Anyway, now you know why I'm not big into altering my mood." Not anymore at least. There were limits to her honesty. She didn't owe him her every sordid detail. She didn't owe it to anyone.

"That's...awful, Katy. I don't even really know what to say about it. Sarah...never told us any of this. She never... I never got the impression she'd been into drugs, or around them."

"I don't know what her experiences were with drugs. I don't think she ever took any. She warned us away from them, but...she was in college by the time that happened to me. Trey never tried anything because I threatened him within an inch of his life and told him I saw a white light and angels the only time I took that garbage."

"You lied to him."

"Yes. And I don't regret it. I did what I had to do. Because I was a kid raising a kid. Basically, a mother bear with a cub in a den full of bear traps."

"So why did Sarah leave? You never did."

She took a bite of the food and chewed methodically to avoid answering for a moment. "She believed in education. She thought it would make a long-term change. Something lasting. Yes, she could have stayed. And she could have protected us, but she could never have changed things drastically. Plus, Sarah had the mind to change things. To change the whole world."

"And you don't?"

"I'm a waitress, essentially. Well, I was an event coordinator for a few months, but even so, there was a lot of busing tables involved. But that's what I do. I work. I worked to keep Trey in food and clothes. I worked to keep him safe. I worked my way up to Jason Treffen's inner circle so that I could be a part of taking the bastard down. Sarah was a thinker. I'm a doer. It was better that I stayed to get things done while she went forward."

"But she didn't come back," he said.

"No. In the end, though, it wasn't her job. It was their job."

"Your mom and dad?"

"Yes. And they didn't do it." She took a deep breath and stared ahead, not really looking at anything. "They love us. It's so strange to think about, all things considered, but they do. My mom said to me one time that...that we were the very best of them. The pieces that weren't ruined." She swallowed hard. "But he ruined Sarah. And then they wanted to spend the money he gave them on more... I wouldn't spend it. The money your father gave to my family. I gave them some. I lied and told them that was all and I put the rest in an account and never touched it. I didn't want money in trade for my sister's body. Sorry. I make a very poor dinner companion."

"No. I should know. I feel like I should understand. Because all of this stuff...it explains Sarah. Where she was coming from. Why she didn't feel like she could leave the job."

For some reason, his words sent a shot of pain straight to her heart. Just a small twinge. But it was very real.

Because what she'd told him mattered, but only in context to what it meant for Sarah.

What? You expected something else? He was her friend. He's nothing to you. He had sex with you once, and to a guy like him that means nothing.

Everything in her life was about what she could do to fix it for other people. To find ways to manage her own pain so it never got in the way of what she had to do. It always had been. It wasn't a sob story and an invitation to a pity party. It was how things were. There was no point in bitching about it.

She had her life. She'd never been abused the way that Sarah had been. And because of her role in Trey's life, she'd very likely spared him from going down the same path as her parents.

So yes, her life had often been about other people. Fixing things for them. Avenging them if it came to it.

But she couldn't complain about it. Not really.

Not when it was so utterly necessary.

"Yeah, well. I understand," she said, even though sometimes she didn't. Sometimes she didn't understand why jumping off a building was better than coming home. As soon as she'd thought it, she felt guilty for it. Because there were the pictures. The obvious evidence of what she'd been subjected to. Sex with her much older boss, probably under duress. Probably whether she really wanted him or not.

Maybe she'd felt too far gone to come home. Maybe she'd felt too changed. Too broken.

But she hadn't been. She never would have been as far as Katy was concerned. No matter what she'd done, no matter what had been done to her. No matter how much she'd done willingly, and how much had been forced on her…none of it would have mattered.

Not if she could have had her back.

"You both felt a lot of responsibility," he said.

"Yes."

"For your brother."

"Of course. He was so much younger."

"And for your parents."

"What?" she asked, freezing.

"You do. You feel responsible for them, and she must have, too. Because neither of you reported them."

"Well...what's the point, right? Of letting them go to jail. Getting us put into the foster-care system. We were made afraid of 'the system' very early on. The scare tactics were effective. Plus, there was strength in being together. Even when Sarah was gone, Trey and I had each other."

"Sarah still has you," he said.

"Yes," she said, thinking about all the things in her life that had led her to this point. About what had motivated her. "Yes, she does."

"Think you're ready for another party this weekend?" he asked, changing the subject.

"The party planner attending as the son of the high-powered host's lover? I'm not sure. What exactly will we tell them?"

"The truth," he said. "That we met at the first party. That we went to a hotel together. And beyond that we can get a little creative."

"Uh...meaning what?"

"Meaning we don't have to tell anyone that we didn't see each other for a few days after. Or that I made you lose your job."

"And made sure I was homeless so I had to come live

with you? Yeah, that sounds more like the story of *How I Filed for My First Restraining Order.* Not so much *How I Met Your Mother.*"

"So we'll change it. We made love," he said, his voice a caress, lingering over the words, making an illicit shiver wind through her body. They'd never made love. Of that she was certain. What they'd done had been great, but it had not been making love. Making love was something that grew between lovers, wrapped itself around them both. It was something that was for two people.

What they'd done hadn't been that way. She'd wanted what she'd wanted. He'd taken what he'd needed. It just so happened those desires were compatible.

"We made love," she said, trying not to blush.

"Yes, and then after that we were inseparable. We came back to my place. We ate takeout on the floor. We didn't leave the house for days. We just stayed here, wrapped up in each other. And then, well, then I asked you to stay because I couldn't bear to let you go."

His words painted a warm picture in her mind. One she could see clearly. One she could feel without ever having experienced it. He made her feel like it might be real. Made her feel like she wanted it to be.

What might that have been like? To have been possessed by him, claimed by him utterly, and then…kept by him?

You don't have time for that.

No. She didn't. And she didn't have time to sit here and weave fantasies about it, either.

"Nice case you're building, Mr. Lawyer-man," she said, as much for her benefit as his. To remind herself that words were his business. That spinning the truth from lies was what had bought him this house they were currently sitting in.

His skill had paid for her Thai food. Suddenly, it tasted a little bitter.

"Well, we may not have to say anything at all. But if we do, we both know the story."

Yes, they did. And like the brief, false high she'd gotten from the drugs so long ago, she felt a warm glow in her chest connected to vapor. To something insubstantial and false. Something that would never be. Because it didn't exist. Not outside of a pill, or a well-constructed story designed to make other people believe in a lie.

"Well, hopefully they won't need it. But if they do, we can be all legit." She continued to eat, even though the food didn't really have a flavor anymore. Not to her.

"That's the idea."

"What would he do?" she asked. "I mean…if he finds out we're out to get him, to take him down."

"I don't know. Because I didn't know he would go as far as he did. He'd probably make up some great stories about my childhood. Me? He'd cut me off at the knees in my professional life. He'd make sure I couldn't get cases. That I was discredited. You? I don't think you'd be that lucky. Which is one reason I need to keep you safe."

She couldn't remember anyone ever trying to protect her before. And even if it was for Sarah, it was real. He was taking care of her. That was such a strange feeling. And it was a little bit magical.

Suddenly, dinner tasted good again.

"So the next party is this weekend," he said.

"Yes, I remember. I planned it."

"So you did. What's on the menu?"

"It's going to be good. There's this little appetizer with a bit of tortilla, some quail egg and an heirloom-tomato rel-ish...."

"They were stupid to fire you."

"Or they felt intimidated by the big bad son of the man signing checks. Well, and the man himself. I think your fa-ther is hoping I'll come to him on my knees and beg for work. As it were."

"Oh, it's going to make him angry that you didn't," Austin said, smiling. "That you got on your knees for me instead."

She blinked rapidly and tried to ignore the pricks of heat in her face. She had indeed done that for him.

"So what are we doing at this thing? Besides poking dear old dad with a stick?"

"Again, I'm playing at reconciliation so that I can get closer and hopefully get a small bit of...something. And I need to get enough evidence to bring to my mother."

"You're really going to do that? To your mother?"

"I don't want to," he said, sounding weary. "I don't want to do it at all. But the fact is, she shouldn't be with him. She should get free. Cut ties. I need to make sure that Addison doesn't even get near these sorts of men."

"Addison?"

"My sister," he said, his voice rough. "My younger sister."

"I didn't realize you had a sister."

"I know what it feels like to care about someone like that," he said. "Wanting to protect them from...everything. Un-fortunately, I think the best thing I can do to protect them both is make sure they know the truth."

"The truth sucks." It did. She could remember, very well,

being the one to tell eight-year-old Trey that Sarah was gone. Telling her parents. She could remember the desperate sadness that had surrounded her. The feeling that she couldn't give in to her own grief, because if she did, if she stopped holding tight to everyone, they would all just splinter apart.

"But it has to be told. And in order to do that...I need something convincing. It doesn't have to hold up in a court of law. Just the court of Lenore Treffen."

"I think that's possible. Although, I will need something fabulous to wear."

"Will you?"

"You're designer-suit man. I can't go off the rack," she said, her tone dry.

He leveled his gaze with hers, sending a spark down to her toes. "Don't worry. I'll take care of you."

Yes, of course he would. Because he was Austin Treffen, and hadn't he taken care of everything already? Her job. Her apartment. Her virginity.

Yeah, he was good at taking care of things.

But she wouldn't leave everything up to him.

He could manage the wardrobe for the event, but she would be the one making sure that they didn't lose sight of their goal.

Jason's blood might be in him, but Sarah's was in her. And that meant she would be the one, in the end, who would make sure it was avenged.

Chapter Seven

"It's a bit much, don't you think?"

He damn well did. He hadn't anticipated her looking quite that good in the gown. But he'd seen it in the window on his way to work and he'd known that she had to have it.

Katy had, after all, demanded something fabulous. Something to match his custom suits. And just any dress wouldn't do.

Austin had passed a little bit of time, more than he wanted to admit, looking at dresses online. The current trend of frothy and sparkling for the holiday season just wasn't suited to a woman like Katy.

A woman who could twist the most tragic moment into a snarky comment. A woman who had a backbone of steel and a razor-sharp tongue.

He thought if he put her in a frothy skirt it might wither and die on her body.

And that was when he'd seen the black dress in the window. Fitted to the mannequin. With bands of satin and sheer mesh in strategic places over the bodice, all dark so that the hints of skin would be subtle.

At least, that had been his thought.

On her, though, the subtlety was lost. Or maybe it was only lost for him.

He could see, very clearly, where heavy satin gave way to chiffon and showed the pale loveliness of her skin. Then there was the shape of it.

The mannequin had possessed the simple, androgynous shape so well loved by the fashion industry. But God had not embraced that shape when He'd made Katy.

She was an homage to the female form from the days when a lush shape had been a thing to celebrate. All rounded curves, from her breasts to a slow indent of the waist, and another sharp curve for her hips. Hips that he knew were perfectly shaped to fit his hands...

The dress followed the line of her shape, tapering in at her knees before flaring out and falling in soft folds to the ground. As she walked toward him, it made a soft, whispering sound that reminded him of quiet breaths in a dark hotel room.

Her hair was loose, in dark, glossy waves around her shoulders, her eyes outlined in black with hints of gold in the corners, making the blue in them stand out even more.

And her lips were red. Like candy. Just begging to have the sweet sucked off of them.

"It's perfect," he said, extending his arm and ignoring the burn when the heat from her body connected with his as he slipped his arm around her waist and drew her close.

"I feel like I'm on display," she said, kicking the skirt to one side as she walked with him out of his penthouse and into the hall.

"Well, you are," he said, letting his eyes drift down to

her breasts, which were on spectacular display, speaking of displays.

"I feel as though I should have a tiara."

"We can swing by the tiara store on our way there."

"Oh, well, I don't want to hold things up. It seems a little bit precious."

He pushed the button for the elevator and waited, his arm around her waist, the feel of her under his palm a slow burn. A good burn.

"A little bit, maybe. But then, perhaps being precious isn't a bad thing. You are playing mistress to a billionaire."

"Shut the front door," she said, leaning against the back of the elevator and pulling out of his grasp. "You are not a billionaire."

"I am, I'm afraid."

"How? I mean, don't get me wrong, I'm sure you're a kick-ass lawyer, but seriously, where did the money come from?"

"Investments," he said, flashing her a smile he didn't feel. "Kick-started by my father, naturally, because…"

"Well, because he has money. It seems fair that you should get a head start with it. I mean, maybe *fair* is the wrong word, but unsurprising. I inherited my parents' poverty. Seems about right that you'd inherit your parents' wealth."

"I multiplied it," he said.

"That's the problem," she said drily. "Damn multiplication. You know what happens when you multiply by zero, I assume? Yeah. Math has always been out to get me."

"You don't have nothing," he said, his stomach tightening. "You seem to have done well for yourself."

"I've done okay."

"Your brother is in school?"

"On a football scholarship. He worries me a little bit. I mean, because he's so lucky to have it and if he screws it up... It gives me heartburn."

"I can imagine."

"There are no safety nets when you're in our position. Which I think is a really terrible metaphor, all things considered. But that's the fact. There is nothing to catch you if you fall. Not when you're alone like we are. Not when there are no stacks of dollars waiting to catch you."

"Let's hope that wads of cash don't cushion my dad's fall, huh?"

A small smile curved the edge of her lips. "Yeah. I really do hope so."

The party was perfect. And it should have been since Katy planned it. She had loved the job. She knew a lot of people would find something like that frivolous. But Katy loved it. The attention to detail it required. The organization.

There were binders dedicated to food. One for decor. Another with contacts for various bands and orchestras that were available to play for different events.

There was control and order available for every area of a party. And all Katy had to do was make sure it was planned, so that it went off without a hitch. She was good at that. Because the budget was all set, and she had the tools she needed to pull it off. It was nothing like trying to play the bills game she was used to playing.

Pay the bill you had to pay, put the other one off until they were threatening to shut off your power. Then pay that. Don't pay the car payment until they're threatening to take it. Rinse, repeat.

No, planning high-profile events was nothing like that. It gave her a neat and orderlygasm. And she missed it.

Especially standing there on Austin's arm like a piece of bling. There was no control in that at all. No way to control the fact that everyone was looking at her, making judgments and speculations. Whispering behind their hands about who the woman with Austin Treffen was.

No, she didn't like that feeling at all.

Though, it wasn't half as bad as the way having his arm around her waist made her feel. Because that was a whole new level of out of control. It made her shake. Not just a little tremble in her fingers, but a bone-deep tremor that started inside of her and radiated out.

Like an earthquake was moving in her. She knew exactly where the fault line was, too.

Her wretched, unruly lady parts. Oh, she was not happy with them at all.

If not for them, she could keep her head in the game. If not for them, Austin's nearness wouldn't send her into a spiral of lust and need. Of hot memories and hotter desires.

But she had them. And they had woken from their slumber. And now they would not settle down.

He leaned in, his lips brushing her neck, just beneath her ear. "Look, my father is charming the masses," he said.

She looked up and saw Jason, laughing, with a large group of people around him. Austin's mother was on his arm, a pristinely put-together blonde with a slender figure and expertly applied makeup that verged on the line between full coverage and a full-on mask.

"He's good at that. But I suppose if the devil looked like the devil..."

"No one would listen to him."

"Exactly," she said. "Do we have to go talk to him?"

"No," he said, shaking his head. "We don't have to."

"But should you? I mean, reconciliation yada yada."

He let out a slow breath. "I suppose. We used to talk all the time. But then, he used to be my role model, so things change."

"I guess they do."

"But I won't ask you to do something you find too difficult."

"I'm not afraid of him," she said. "In my head he became a monster. But then I met him, and I realized he's just a man. It's the power given to him by other men that makes him dangerous. And it can be taken. So whatever we have to do to see that happen? We'll do."

"Very true," he said.

"This little happy family chat won't take long, will it?" she asked.

"It's best that it doesn't. Since I don't know if there's enough booze at the bar to make it bearable. Why?"

She looked across the room, at the double doors that led to the corridor. That led to Jason's office. "I have a plan."

He quirked a brow. "Should I be afraid?"

She lifted her own brow in response. "No. Yes. Maybe. Let's find out."

"Fair enough." He started to guide her toward the knot of people that were surrounding Jason Treffen. Her heart began to pound, hard and loud in her ears, her shoulders knotting with tension.

Being near him…it was like being in the presence of evil. He was a chameleon. A man who could make himself as good or as bad as he wanted to appear to be. But she was far too aware of the artifice of the good to fall for any of it.

Some people only saw the shiny red apple. She knew there were maggots inside. And that meant no matter how enticing it looked, she would never be tempted to take a bite.

"Great party," Austin said, the crowd parting in a wave for him, as though he gave off some sort of magical power beam that warned everyone of his importance.

"Thank you," Jason said, a half smile curving his lips. "Very kind of you to grace us with your presence. The second Treffen event in a row. Unusual."

"As I said, I'm interested in bringing the family closer together again."

"Good of you to say, Austin." This came from Lenore, and she could feel Austin tensing up beside her at his mother's words. Because, of course, he was planning on proving those words a lie very, very soon.

"It's been too long," Austin said. Katy could hear the layering to those words, and it resonated in her. Yes. It had been too long. Too damn long that Jason Treffen had been allowed to go on with his life.

"You're the event planner," Jason said, his eyes, far too sharp, far too interested, landing on her, looking her over. It felt like a slug crawling over her skin, leaving a visible trail behind.

"I was, rather," she said.

"No hard feelings, I hope," he said.

"None at all," she said.

"How could she have any?" Austin asked, shifting his stance, his fingertips drifting across her arm. "If she were still working on these events, she couldn't be here as my date. And that's important to both of us," he said, his eyes on her. Intense. Sensual. Far too believable for her liking.

"You're...together?" his father asked, one eyebrow raised. He was still looking too intently at her.

"Yes. And can you blame me? I'm afraid I was responsible for her absence at the last event. She didn't feel at liberty to say. But she's left the company now, so it's not a problem."

He'd skimmed through all that easily.

"Interesting," Jason said, taking a sip of champagne.

"Wonderful," Austin said, tightening his hold on her. "I've never met a woman like her." He turned his focus back to Lenore. "Mother? Are you and Addison free for lunch sometime this week?"

"Yes, dear, I'm certain we are. You haven't been out to the house in ages. Perhaps...?"

"Of course."

"And bring your friend..."

"Katy," Katy said, offering her hand to the older woman. "My name is Katy."

"Nice to meet you," she said, smiling, the expression curving her lips but not making a dent in her makeup.

"Very much."

Katy felt a twinge of guilt lying to the woman whose life they were about to upend.

But she didn't have a moment for guilt. She had to have guts now. Guts and glory and all of that crap.

She looked Jason Treffen right in his snake eyes. "I'm going to have to steal your son away now. I have plans for him. It's our first Christmas Eve together and I intend for it to be... special."

She'd never had a special Christmas Eve in her life, but if

she did…well, there was no doubt it would include Austin wrapped up with a bow.

Unfortunately for her hormones, that was not on the docket for the evening. But Jason didn't need to know that.

Jason's answering smirk made her skin crawl.

Gah.

She wouldn't let him see how it unnerved her. Wouldn't let him see her sweat. He'd broken her sister. He would never, ever break her. Austin took his cue from her, and acted like any man might do when promised a naughty Christmas Eve. He tightened his hold on her and nodded at his parents, steering her away from them.

"What are we doing?" he asked.

She sucked a breath in through her nose, eyes on those double doors. "I'm about to take you home and screw you senseless, baby," she said.

"What?" he asked.

Her face burned, but she kept her eyes on the prize, on the doors, held on to him tight and dragged him along with her like she was about to do just that—throw him down and have her way with him.

"You heard me," she said, weaving through the crowd.

"I heard you," he said. "But I don't believe it."

"I have ulterior motives," she said. "Surprise, surprise."

He shifted their stance and wrapped his arm around her waist, his fingers resting just above her ass. She tensed. She couldn't help it. Because his touch was like fire, burning her, turning her insides into molten liquid.

It made her dress feel too heavy, too itchy, too thick. Made her want to strip it off and press herself against him…

"Don't react like that to me," he said quietly. "Not in public. You'll spoil the show."

He thought he made her nervous, but that wasn't it at all. Still, he was right. This was all about the show.

She wasn't taking him home to do it with him. This was all for the people, and that meant allowing herself to melt into him, not fighting it.

Her heart started thundering hard, and part of her wished that sex was all they were leaving for. Not because she wanted him, but because more breaking and entering chez Treffen was nerve-racking in a serious way.

She really didn't want Austin.

No, she didn't.

She had more self-preservation than that.

"What are we actually doing?" he asked as they exited the ballroom.

"We're digging for evidence, of course," she said, craning her neck to get a look down the hall.

"More?"

"Yes, more. If there's an iceberg tip, the rest of that bitch has to be around somewhere. And your father is a fan of pictures."

"Yes, that's true," he said, his tone grim.

"I also know he has a safe in his office. I put in a call to Stephanie earlier, so I have keys. Or rather, they're waiting for us, under her weird daisy-ladybug-clock thing. Her preferred location for covert exchanges. Weirdly."

"Yes, I know about that safe."

"Well, I think we need to get into it, don't you?"

"It's not a bad idea. Though, you seem to have a fondness for breaking and entering, it has to be said."

"Better than a fondness for whoring out women, I say."

"Touché." He approached the reception desk and skimmed his hand for a moment before lifting the little clock shaped like a flowerpot, with electronic daisies in the top that ticked from side to side, ladybugs nestled in the stems. "Funny," he whispered, pulling the key from beneath it. "How this is in here, on her desk. Like this is some friendly fun place to work." He set it back down and straightened. "What a load of crap."

Katy had to take short fast steps thanks to her dress and heels, and thanks to Austin's long legs, which ate up ground at a much quicker pace than hers could.

They paused at the door and she took a deep breath. "I think this is where it will all be," she said. "All the evidence."

"I doubt it," he said. "We're more likely to get shot with poison darts."

He opened the door and they slipped inside, closing the door behind them. "This is all so cloak-and-dagger," he said.

"Yeah, I feel a little like I'm trapped inside a *Murder, She Wrote* episode."

"Let's hope we avoid murder," he said, crossing the room and going to the bookshelf. "Ready to feel even more like you're on TV?" he asked.

"Oh, sure. Okay, how do we do this thing? Do you know? Don't tell me—you crank the arm on a statue and a false wall falls away."

"Not so dramatic." He went to the middle of a bookshelf and started counting shelves, then put his hand on an upper one, in the center, and pulled out six books, which weren't books at all. "Just fake literature."

The books were hollow, and fitted around a safe, set back into the wall.

"Well, I'll be damned. Your father really is a comic-book villain."

"That's why the potential for poison darts seems a legitimate concern."

"How do you know about all this?"

"From back when I was heir to this evil empire," he said.

"So...the combination," she said. "A birth date. His birth date? I know it. A...social security number? That I don't know. Random? Maybe we can tell by which numbers are most worn?"

"You're prepared," he said drily.

"I'm acting. I'm getting it done, and I'll do it however I can."

"Fair enough."

He stepped up to the safe and assessed it, then touched the keypad, frowning slightly before putting in the numbers. Then he tested the handle and nothing happened. "Not his birthday," he said.

"Your mother's?"

He tried that, too. "No. And I'm afraid if we're wrong too many times we'll alert someone." His frown deepened. "I wonder..." He typed in a series of numbers quickly, and this time, when he tested the handle, it gave.

"How did you guess that?" she asked.

"It is a date," he said, the words leaden. "On that you were right. I hoped I was crazy but...I was right. I'm not sure you want to know it."

Silence fell between them and he started to pull contents out of the safe and put them on the desk.

"It's the day she died, isn't it?" she asked.

"Yes," he said, his voice hoarse. "It is."

"How did you know?"

"I guessed. I don't like that I was right."

"It's pretty twisted," she said.

"Like a serial killer keeping a memento of a victim. A piece of her. Of what he did to her. And I'm sure there's more in here. That arrogance we talked about. That's why I was able to guess the number. That's why I think there will be evidence of some kind in here."

He started to rifle through the documents that were in there and paused at a small white envelope. He opened it and took out a stack of pictures. He started to sort through them, and she could see a tremor in his fingers.

"Are they the same?" she asked.

"Yes," he said, his voice rough. "Oh...there are more of them."

"More?"

"More girls. With different men. The men's identities are protected.... The women..." He shook his head. "This is sick. He's holding this over them, holding evidence because he knows in the end they'll be the ones hurt by it and not him. Because he is that arrogant."

He flipped through the pictures and paused, his hands trembling.

"Sarah?"

He nodded slowly. And then he held the photo out to her. It showed the profile of a man's face, leaning down to whisper in the ear of a naked woman, whose head was facing the camera, her expression distressed.

Jason and Sarah.

It was from the same series of pictures. They were obviously engaged in intercourse. And while the man in the picture had only part of his face showing, he was recognizable as Jason Treffen.

Again, not enough evidence to get him locked up but…

"I think this is all my mother will need," he said. "And in that sense, it serves my purposes."

"Not mine," she said, feeling pale, defeated and on the verge of passing out.

"It will in the end, Katy. Trust me."

"I want him in jail, Austin. More than that, I want him destroyed. This won't do it…this…"

"This is another stick of dynamite." He turned and looked at the desk. "You need a lot of dynamite to bring down a fortress. We need as much as we can get." He put the photo on a newspaper that was sitting on the otherwise pristine surface and snapped a picture with his phone. "For the date. To show when I found it. And…" He snapped another shot with his father's nameplate in the background. Then he took photos of each and every picture.

"Put these back," he said, handing them to her, while he continued to go through the papers he'd pulled out of the safe. "Nothing I can decode here. And it could all be nothing. His favorite fishing spots upstate, for all I know." He put them all back in order and stuck them in the safe, locking it and putting everything as it was.

"We should go," he said. "Quickly."

"Agreed," she said, releasing a breath she hadn't realized she'd been holding.

He took her hand and squeezed it, leading her from the

room and closing the door behind them, making sure he locked it.

They made their way through the halls of the office, deposited the key back where they'd gotten it and then headed toward the elevators. And they nearly bumped into Lenore Treffen.

"I thought you'd left," she said, a smile brightening her face.

Katy looked at Austin, saw the color drain from his face. "Sorry. You know how it is," he said, his voice tight. Stilted. "We were delayed."

She arched a well-groomed brow. "I see. Well, you will come up for lunch next week?"

"Yes," he said.

"To the house, not a café in Manhattan. I'm glad to have you back at the estate. It's really been too long, Austin. Whatever happened between you and your father, I'm glad you're setting it aside. So that we can be a family again. We're so much stronger together. Maybe you can unite the law firms? Treffen and Treffen. That would be something. I would be so happy to see our name in the media with that attached to it. With both of you getting the credit you deserve for all the good work you do."

She could feel the tension move through Austin's body, could feel everything in him locking up.

"I look forward to it," Katy said. "Lunch, I mean. It was very nice to meet you. Really. And I'm sorry to rush, only I'm not feeling well—" which made no sense since they were still lingering instead of already being gone, but who cared "—so we really do need to go. Come on, darling." She tugged at Austin's hand. It felt like ice.

She pushed the button on the elevator and shot his mother an awkward smile. She smiled back, seemingly unaware of just how strange it had gotten. Then waved as she headed toward the restrooms.

The elevator doors opened and she all but dragged Austin inside.

"I'm sorry," she said.

He leaned back against the elevator wall, his breathing ragged, his body shaking.

"That was really unfortunate timing, all things considered. But she didn't know and…and I know it makes things really uncomfortable but—"

"Stop talking," he said, his words rough.

It might have hurt her feelings if she hadn't been able to see, very clearly, that he was having some sort of a breakdown. So, all things considered, she wasn't going to take a little bit of grumpiness personally.

She stayed silent in the elevator, and all the way to the car. Then from the car, all the way back to the penthouse.

She could feel his tension growing, could feel it building in him like a raging beast. His hopelessness, his grief. His anger.

And when they got inside his penthouse, something broke inside of him, and it all poured out.

Chapter Eight

Austin hadn't been able to breathe since they'd left his father's office. Seeing his mother, hearing her talk about happy times, about a togetherness that would never, ever be, had left him feeling like he was breaking apart from the inside out.

Which, when he really thought about it, was about right.

When he'd found out about Sarah, about his father harassing her to the point of death and hopelessness, it had felt like a spanner had been inserted into his ribs. And since then, it had been spreading. Pulling him into pieces, and he had no control over it.

Everything was being torn, ripped to shreds. His family, his name, his very being.

In a few days, he was going to take his mother's life, his sister's life, and break them into shards so small nothing would ever be able to put them back together.

And there was no other course to take. The ball was rolling, the truth giving it weight, momentum. There was no stopping it now.

It was bigger than he was. He had no control over it; he had no say in its movements.

And when it came down to it, nothing in his life, nothing familiar, nothing his, would remain the same.

He was a Treffen. The destruction that would be left behind after the bomb was dropped would be his inheritance.

It would be his life.

A hovel where a palace had once stood.

He looked across the room, at Katy, standing there in that beautiful gown, the heavy satin strips wrapped around her body like stark, black binding.

I'm about to take you home and screw you senseless, baby.

Her words echoed in his body, in his blood.

She was so perfect, so lovely. She was like a Christmas present. She could be his Christmas present.

His.

Something to hold on to. Something to control.

Something to have that would be his. All his. He didn't share Katy with his father. He didn't share her with the world. He didn't share her with any other man.

She was his.

All his.

At least she had been, for a while one night a week ago.

But she could be his again. And why not? Everything in his life was coming undone. He could find something with which to anchor himself.

So maybe he could grab on to Katy's hips and ride it out. Ride her hard. Pour it all out on her. Make her hold him to the earth.

"Come here," he said, his voice demanding and raw, even to his own ears.

She obeyed, walking toward him, her blue eyes wide, her red lips parted slightly.

And for one moment, the man he wanted to be saw the man that he was, and despised him.

But just as quickly, he lost his perspective, lost it in her eyes.

"Yes?" she asked, her voice so sweet. So docile. So unlike Katy was during the day.

"I need you," he said.

"What...?" She swallowed hard, looking down. "What is it you need?"

He reached out and took her chin between his thumb and forefinger, forcing her to look up, to meet his eyes. "You. I need you, all of you. I need you to do exactly as I say. I need you to be mine tonight. To do with as I please."

"And what is it you want?"

He started to loosen his tie, to undo the buttons on his shirt. He shrugged the shirt and jacket to the floor, then started on his pants. She didn't say anything. She just watched, until he was naked in front of her.

"I want you on your knees in that pretty dress. I want you to suck my cock like a good girl."

For a moment, she held his gaze, and a spark flared in her eyes. He wondered if she would obey. It was like being in a free fall. Weightless, terrifying. If she said no, there was no amount of force that would ever satisfy. No coercion that would give him what he needed.

He had to have her willing submission, her complete and utter desire to give him what he needed, or it meant nothing. Less than nothing. If the submission wasn't her choice, then it would never be true submission.

And his control would be nothing more than force. Nothing more than farce.

Then, with the lights of the city behind her, the windows open providing a view of the Christmas Eve snow that was falling, she obeyed.

She sank down to the hard floor, her dress flaring out around her like a dark cloud, her hair sliding forward, a glossy brown curtain that shielded her actions from him.

That wasn't acceptable.

He reached back, wrapped her hair around his hand, as he'd done their first time together. He tugged it, pulled her head back. "Are you going to give me what I want?"

"Yes."

"Good."

He gave her a bit more range of motion, didn't hold her so tightly, and watched as she leaned forward, the tip of her tongue sliding over the length of him before she took him into her mouth.

He swore and fought the urge to close his eyes, fought the urge to let his head fall back. He wanted to watch her. Wanted to enjoy the sight of her, giving to him as he'd instructed.

He hadn't kissed her. He should feel guilty about that. About ordering her down on her knees and demanding she suck him off when he hadn't even given her the smallest kiss on her mouth.

But he didn't. Because this was his. She was his.

She would like it, because he'd told her to.

He flexed his hips in time with her movements, holding tighter to his as pleasure pooled in his gut, white-hot, threatening to boil over.

He pulled her away from him. "Not yet."

She sat on the floor, still on her knees, her hands in her lap. He was breathing hard, his whole body tense.

He needed more than release. He needed control.

He moved back to her, bending down and forking his fingers through her hair, guiding her in to kiss her lips. He could taste salt on her tongue from his skin, evidence of what she'd just done for him. It sent a hot rush of need through him, one that left him trembling.

Put him closer to the edge than he'd already been.

"Now I'm going to take this dress off of you," he said.

She rose slowly to her feet, and he allowed it, his fingers still woven through her hair.

He reached around with his other hand and gripped the zipper tab on the back of the dress, drawing it down slowly, letting it fall away from her curves. Revealing her slowly for him.

She didn't have a bra on. Her breasts, plump and perfect, sank slightly, as the structure of the bodice gave.

Then the dress slipped down past her hips and she stepped away from it, a butterfly emerging from a cocoon. Wearing nothing but a black thong.

"Go upstairs," he said.

She nodded slowly, and he watched her walk. As he'd done in the lobby of his father's building a week ago. Watched the way her hips swayed. Watched her perfect ass as she walked up the stairs, her eyes straight ahead.

"That's right," he said. "Keep looking ahead." He started to follow her. "Don't look at me."

His eyes drifted upward, the line of her spine, to her hair, dark against her pale back.

She turned her face to the side, lifted her gaze, her eyes

locking with his just for a moment before she turned away again.

Something tightened in his gut. Not anger. Excitement. Because she was daring him. Challenging him. Asking what would happen if she didn't obey.

"I forgot," he said. "You like the idea of being a bad girl."

He could see her slight nod as she looked ahead, walking down the hall and into his bedroom.

"Stop," he said.

She did and he walked past her, going to sit on the edge of the bed. "Now come here."

She did, keeping her eyes on his the whole time.

"What should I do now?" she asked.

"Sit with me."

She sat next to him, her lashes fluttering as she looked down and bit her lower lip. Her teeth stark white against the red.

He cupped her face with one hand, holding her, and kissed her. Hard. Delving deep, sliding his tongue against hers. He was starving for her. Making up for the lack of kiss earlier.

"Now I want you to bend over this way." He guided her so that she was over his lap, her knees on her side, her head on the other. "Lay down."

She did, her hair spilling over the blankets, over the edge of the bed. She wasn't nervous. She was like a cat, her body heavy and warm over his, at complete ease. As though she were waiting for him to pet her.

But that wasn't quite what he had in mind.

He put his palm flat on her ass, smoothing it over her rounded flesh, before lifting it and bringing it down hard on her, the sound loud in the silent room.

A small sound escaped her lips. Pleasure and pain in one. "You shouldn't disobey."

He brought his hand down on her again, eliciting another sound that echoed in him, fueling him, amping up his arousal.

She was his. She had submitted to him entirely, was enjoying everything he gave to her. Allowing him to open up a part of himself and beg for control.

In that moment, he fully realized how much control she held. On her knees or over his, she was the master of the game. Because it was her allowance that gave him power, her pleasure that let him release this part of himself.

Her willingness that let him feel that, even for a moment, she belonged to him.

But he needed more. He needed to be in her. Suddenly he needed it more than he needed air. To be surrounded by her. To be able to watch her face when she came. To feel it around his shaft.

He bent down and kissed her back, between her shoulder blades, grabbing hold of her hair, pulling her head back and kissing her neck.

"I want you," he said. "I need you. Do you know how much? Do you know what you do to me?"

"Yes," she said.

He released his hold on her hair and moved his hands over her curves, bending again to kiss the red mark he'd left behind on her skin.

He shifted his hand, felt the wetness between her thighs, pushed one finger deep inside of her. "You need me, too," he said. "Say it."

"I need you, too."

"Say my name."

"Austin. I need you, Austin Treffen."

She'd known, somehow, that he'd needed to hear all of it. In that moment, on her lips, his name felt like his own. Because she felt like his own.

He slipped away from her. "Lie on your back and put your head on the pillows. Spread your legs for me and wait. No touching yourself."

He went into the bathroom and got a box of condoms, took a strip out and tore a packet open, rolling the protection onto himself quickly. When he walked back into the bedroom, she was there, ready for him.

He joined her on the bed, gripping her thigh and tugging it up over his hip as he sank into her. He watched her face as she took him in, sliding in slowly, making sure she felt every inch. Making sure he felt it, too.

"Austin," she said, his name on her lips better than any alcohol.

He could have drunk it all away. But losing himself in her was so much better.

He thrust in deep, taking her hard, swallowing the little gasp of shock she made. He kissed her as he drove into her, the thrust of his tongue matching his movements inside of her.

She was perfect. So tight and hot. It was better than anything he could have imagined. She was more than he'd imagined. Her scent was around him, her body around him. And he felt driven by a deep, primitive need to make her his. To brand her. So that she would never forget that she belonged to him and no one else.

He slid his hands down and cupped her butt, pulled her

up to meet his every thrust. She wrapped her legs around his waist, opening her to him, letting him deepen his thrusts.

He was close, so close. And he could see that she was, too. In the flush of her skin, her short, quick breaths. She put her hands on his shoulder, her fingernails digging into his skin, a sharp spike of pleasure butting up against the pain, nearly sending him over the edge.

Her hands hadn't been free last time. And he hadn't been able to watch her face. The way her brow creased, the way her lips formed an O, a silent scream working her throat.

She arched into him, her breasts against his chest.

"You have to come for me, baby," he growled, "because I can't last much longer."

He pushed into her again, pulling her up so that his body would make contact with her clit. And that was when she went over the edge, her internal muscles contracting around him, her fingernails digging in so deep, he was sure she drew blood.

And he liked it.

Mine. The word throbbed through his brain with every beat of his heart, with every thrust into her beautiful body.

She was his. And he would make sure she didn't forget it.

He felt his orgasm rushing up on him and he pulled out of her, tugging the condom off and stroking his hand over himself as he came on her stomach, the strong need to brand her the only thing in his mind as he did it.

His muscles turned to jelly then and he leaned forward, breathing hard, bracing himself on either side of her as he slowly came back to himself.

As he started to see himself clearly again.

A monster of some kind. Who used a woman in a vulnerable position. A man who unleashed his demons on someone who had enough of her own.

He looked down at her, fully expecting to see disgust. Fully expecting to see her anger, her hatred.

Instead, she was looking at him with a sleepy, satisfied expression. Not quite a smile, but then, they hadn't had much to smile about lately.

"I…I'll be right back."

He went into the bathroom and found a towel, then came back. He stopped and looked at her for a moment, sprawled on the bed, looking completely relaxed and satisfied.

He bent over and ran the towel over her stomach, cleaning her skin.

"I'm sorry," he said.

"For what?"

"For…that. For hurting you. For doing a bunch of crazy shit without even talking to you about it first."

"I appreciate it. But it's not necessary."

"No?"

"I like it when you're in charge. I figured the same rules from the first night applied. That if I told you to stop, you would. Am I wrong?"

He hoped not. "No," he said.

"Okay, then." She sighed deeply and rolled onto her side. "It's midnight."

"So it is." He wasn't sure if he should get in bed with her or not. He wasn't sure what the rules were, or what they should be.

She scooted to one side and got beneath the covers, patting the spot next to her twice.

He took a deep breath and made the decision. He got in beside her, covered them both, his arm draped over her waist.

"Merry Christmas, Austin," she said.

He lay there, awake, listening to her breathe, watching the snow fall outside, his heart still beating like a bloody, raging beast in his chest.

After an hour, he gave up sleeping and got up again.

He could go burn off the tension in the gym. Hell, his muscles already felt like jelly. His heart was already on the verge of cardiac arrest. Why the hell not punish himself for a while?

Like he'd punished her.

The memory made his neck prickle with shame.

He went to his dresser and tugged on a pair of shorts, heading down the hall to the room that had all of his workout equipment.

Yes, working himself to the point of exhaustion was definitely better than getting back in bed with her. Than putting his hand on her bare skin, cupping her breasts. Covering her mouth with his other hand while he thrust into her from behind.

He scrubbed his face with his hand and went toward the weight bench.

This was what he had to do. Not that. He wouldn't touch her again. At least not until he could get himself under control.

He lifted weights until the bench was slick with sweat, until he was shaking. Then he ran on the treadmill until his legs were ready to give out.

He wiped his chest and back down with a towel and went

toward his home office, sat in the chair and leaned back, closing his eyes and hoping he might get a couple hours of sleep.

"Merry effing Christmas," he said.

Katy shifted and stretched, rolled onto her back. It was Christmas morning. That had never mattered to her very much. Christmases growing up had been inconsistent. When Sarah had gotten older she'd made sure they had trees and gifts. She'd come back home for the holidays often, bringing good food and her warm smile.

Until that last Christmas. She hadn't come home that year at all.

For some reason, this Christmas morning felt different from most. She felt a sense of change. Of possibility. As if when she got out of bed, things would be different. Like there was even something to look forward to.

It was a wonderful feeling. A perfect, newly formed hope that hadn't met up against reality yet.

She couldn't recall ever feeling anything like this before.

She burrowed down deeper into the blankets, desperate to hang on to the feeling. To put off reality for as long as possible. The bedding was so soft, so heavy and warm. She could feel the quality against her skin. Her bare skin.

She didn't usually sleep naked.

Except… Oh, yeah.

Flashes of last night popped through her mind. Austin and his intensity. The desperation with which he'd taken her, from the moment he'd first turned to her and said he wanted her, to that last moment when he'd come on her skin.

He'd given her every feeling. Pain, pleasure, aching, deep need and satisfaction. For a woman who had spent years aspiring to numbness, seeking out this sort of thing, reveling in it, was foreign. And intense. He gave her so much more than she'd imagined sex could be.

Oh, wow. She put her arm over her face and took a breath then rolled over onto her side.

The mattress was big. And it was empty of anything but blankets and her.

And her little happy glow waned a bit. Because Christmas morning would have been a lot sweeter if she would have woken up in his arms.

But no, he wasn't there. And she had a feeling there were reasons for that she wasn't going to like.

She slipped out of the covers and went into the bathroom, looking at her naked reflection in the mirror.

She turned and let out a sharp breath when she caught the reflection of her butt. It was still a little red, but she found she liked the lingering evidence of his passion.

Though, she had a feeling he didn't see it as passion. Not the way that she did.

He got all weird and self-loathing after they had sex.

All two times.

So strange. She felt like it had been more. Like there had never been a time when she hadn't been intimate with him. Maybe it was because they'd known each other only about an hour before they'd gotten it on the first time.

Or maybe because being with him was such a soul-baring experience. So it made her feel like they must know each other.

Because she'd shared her body with him. And pieces of her childhood trauma, over noodles and diet soda. It was a level of intimacy she'd never had with anyone else.

Still, Austin felt like a mystery to her. Even knowing what he was going through. Even understanding why he acted the way he did.

There was something deeper. Something that she didn't have a hope of reaching without a pickax. To dig through all the rock he had walled around his heart.

Not that she wanted to reach his heart. Nope. She didn't have the inclination for that. They had to see this through. To see through the destruction of Jason Treffen, and after that, she could start making a life for herself.

But it wouldn't be with Austin. It wouldn't be wrapped up in Sarah's death. This entire situation was too close to parts of her life she despised, and when it was over, she was leaving New York and never coming back.

She was leaving all this to burn to the ground behind her.

For now, though, she did have access to Austin's triple showerheads. And she was going to take that.

Chapter Nine

"I suppose I should have realized by your lack of decked halls that you weren't super into the season."

Austin turned in his chair and saw Katy, standing in the doorway. She was wearing sweats and had that just-showered look that made his cock jump a little bit. The only explanation being that thoughts of her being freshly showered put his thoughts onto her being slick, wet and naked. Which was in no way neutral territory.

"No tree flocking or menorah lighting in the month of December for me, I'm afraid. I continue on in my dull, undecked, semi-heathenous existence."

"Since when?"

"Since Sarah," he said. "It's left a bad taste in my mouth for Christmas."

"Oh." She sort of shrunk back after that. "You did care about her, didn't you?"

"I told you, she was my friend. I was an asshole who failed her. But I did care. A lot."

"You didn't love her, did you?"

"Not like that. She was dating Hunter. I never looked at

her as anything more than my friend. Sometimes I liked her better than I liked him."

"She had a pretty strong effect on people. A good one."

"Yes," he said, his chest getting tight, "she did."

"So, to change the subject awkwardly and inappropriately, why weren't you in bed this morning? And why do I get the feeling you weren't there for most of the night?"

"Because I wasn't. I slept in here."

"Right...and why?"

He looked straight ahead, his posture rigid. "Because what happened last night wasn't okay."

"Why?"

He felt like he'd been punched in the chest. "What the hell do you mean *why?* Does it not seem like some seriously sick stuff to you that your sister was in some sort of weird manipulative relationship with my dad and the minute I meet you...I want you. And now that I have you I suddenly want to turn you over my knee and spank you? Usually, I'm a huge fan of my penis, but lately, not so much."

"Interesting. I recently became a fan of it."

"Stop," he said, his throat so tight he couldn't breathe. "It's not happening again."

"Because you know what I should want?"

"Because I know what *I* should want, and it's not this. I don't like the fact that I'm using you. And that's what I'm doing, Katy, make no mistake. I'm not going to fall in love with you and live dominantly ever after with you. I'm using you because I'm going through something hard. Because I want to control something, and right now, the only thing I can control is you. That is a special kind of screwed up."

"And you're protecting me from it because...I'm just so

normal and well-adjusted you're afraid you'll screw me up? I mean, seriously, Austin, I almost begged you to spank me harder. Because I liked it that much. Shall we psychoanalyze just why I enjoyed you punishing me so very much?"

"No. Because I have issues of my own. I'm not taking yours on board, too."

"Fair enough, not asking you to. But just be aware that I was using you, too. Because I'm so damn sick of carrying everything. And letting you have the control? It lets me drop it for a while. So I can honestly say, your issues suit me."

"They don't suit *me*," he said, meeting her gaze. "This isn't who I want to be. This isn't what I want to do. I do not want to do anything that even remotely resembles... I am not my father. I don't want to be, not even anything close. If I have to give something up to distance myself from him, it's going to be this...*relationship,* or whatever you want to call it. The alternative is giving up baseball, and I damn well won't do that."

She blinked rapidly. "Oh. Okay. So I rate somewhere beneath baseball?"

"No, but my enjoyment of baseball doesn't terrify me to my very soul. How about that?"

"I terrify you?"

"The things I want to do to you? The things I have done? That terrifies me."

"You know," she said, "inexperienced though I am, I do know there are plenty of normal people who have relationships where they do this sort of thing. And there's nothing wrong with them. Not if it's mutual and consensual, and you can't doubt for a second that what we did was just that."

He let out a sharp breath. "Yes, that's true. But this has

nothing to do with them. It has nothing to do with anyone but the two of us, and as far as we're concerned? There's nothing normal or healthy about it. You're Sarah's sister. I've never done things like this with a woman. What my father enjoyed doing to your sister didn't need handcuffs for there to be a power differential, and I'm afraid... Sure, there are plenty of people who do this and it's not screwed up, but between you and me? It is."

"I guess right now isn't the best time to be exploring something like this," she said, her eyes on the ground.

"Everything is horrible right now," he said, hating to admit it. Hating to admit just how deeply all of this affected him. Just how utterly hopeless and out of his hands it all was. "I can't change that. I can't stop it. I have to go and ruin my mother's life sometime next week because...because it's for the greater good. You know...it's not personal for them."

"For who?" she asked, her long, delicate fingers curling around the doorframe.

"For Alex and Hunter. I mean, they loved Sarah, too. The revenge, though... It doesn't hurt them. It heals something for them, atones for things. And nothing else. Jason Treffen being brought low doesn't change a thing for them. It just gives them the ability to look at their hands and hopefully...not see her blood there anymore. For me? For me it's different."

He didn't know why he was telling her this. Why he was pouring all this onto her. But he supposed if he could spill himself on her stomach, he could try to explain what was going on inside of him.

"I can't destroy him without hurting myself. I can't let him go on without hurting other people. But this... When I was a kid my father seemed perfect. My family was perfect. My life was perfect, and nothing went wrong because…because things went wrong for other people, not for me. It's like I'm paying for that now. Like there's only a certain amount of good you can have before it all goes bad."

She laughed, the sound hollow and bitter. "Does that work in reverse?"

"It should."

"Then stick with me. I'm about to win the mother-effing lottery. I'm sure of it. I may also find out I'm the long-lost princess of some little-known island nation. Probably I'm also an heiress to a shipping magnate, too."

"Been that bad, has it?" he asked. He felt like an ass going on about all of his stuff when she'd never had a good day in her life. At least, it didn't sound like she had.

And how fair was that?

Katy was a hard worker. Someone with a strong backbone, a sense of loyalty. And what was he? Just a lucky guy who'd been born into money. Without it, what would he be? Nothing. Without his family name? What was he?

Maybe nothing. But at least he'd still have his money. So there was that. He wasn't sure what else there was, to be honest.

"If I covered it up…" he began, his voice ragged as he tried to voice his deepest, dirtiest desires. And why not? She'd seen his dirtiest physical desires. Parts of himself he'd never wanted to expose anyone to. Because that wasn't respectful. It wasn't right. And he'd grown up believing in that. Dominating a woman went against so much of what had been instilled in him, so he'd done his best to ignore the fantasies. Even though he hadn't always managed.

But this was more shameful than a desire for spankings and bondage. Much more so.

"If I covered it up," he began again, "things could be like they were. My mother wouldn't lose her husband. My sister wouldn't suffer any repercussions. She's in college, you know. Tearing her way through Columbia, continuing on the tradition. She's part of the legacy that I'm about to destroy. And what will happen to her when I do? But if I don't...she can go on like she always has. And I...I can, too. When people hear my name, when they hear *Austin Treffen,* they'll think of a legacy of good works. Of achievements and advancements made for women. That's what they'll think of."

He looked at his hands, not really able to believe he was saying this out loud. Not able to believe how well-formed it all was. That it had been building in him like this.

"But if I go ahead with it...my mother loses her marriage. My sister potentially becomes a target at school. And every time someone hears the name *Treffen* they'll think of prostitutes and abuse."

He heard Katy swallow, saw her throat working. "I do understand how hard that would be, Austin. And I get that it's costing you. More than it is them, more than it is me. But as it is, my life is so damned expensive. It costs me all the time. Because I can't rest until this is fixed for her. I am truly sorry that people will think bad things when they hear your name, but what do people think when they hear Sarah's? They barely hear it. They barely think of it. And if they do, they think of some stupid drunk slut who jumped off a building. Not the woman who gave me sanity. Who taught me how to love people. Who instilled in me the value of hard work. She was my example." She swallowed hard. "When I lost her, I lost my way. I lost everything. She was the person who showed me that you could make it out of a situation like ours and go on to bigger things. And I know I haven't done that. I know I haven't done a lot of bigger and better things. But I believed I could. Just believing that brought me through more than you can possibly imagine. But no one knows that. They only know that she was a nobody from nowhere who just couldn't handle any measure of success, 'cause you know those dirty poors just can't."

That assessment shamed him. And he deserved it. All things considered, he sort of liked it. Since it helped him focus on something else.

"She deserves better than that," he said. "But you know that if they judged her before, they'll all judge her more now. She's the woman at the center of the scandal. He might have dealt in whores, but by default, whether she was paid or not, she was one. She will be one as far as the public is concerned. That's how these things work, trust me. I deal in sexual crimes against women all the time. It's what I do for a living. Until there is no way to blame a woman for all the sex, she will be blamed for it. It can come down to the fact that the rapist says she didn't say no loud enough. Or that she didn't fight hard enough. It's ugly, and it's something I hate, something I battle constantly in court and out, but it's the way things work. And when all of this hits? Every woman involved is getting dragged straight through the mud with him."

"But her name is mud already, Austin," Katy said, her eyes glistening. "And it will never be anything else unless this is finished. Not only that, he'll make more of her. How many other Sarahs do there have to be?"

Her question hung in the air, an accusation. Stark in the silence. Austin let out a slow breath.

"No more," he said.

"Because if you really need control that badly, I'd much rather have you tie me down and spank my ass than back out and leave these other women to be abused by your father."

"I'm not doing either thing. I'm not backing down and I'm not... We don't have time to mess around with whatever is happening between us."

She lifted a shoulder. "Right. I agree. So nothing is happening between us. And what did is..."

"Not important."

"Nope."

"By the way," he said, leaning back in his chair, "would you mind coming with me on Wednesday to ruin my mother's life? She really did want you to come."

"Probably not for what's actually happening," she said.

"No. But I think it would be good for you to be there."

"And can we trust her with my safety? You know, all the safety that had you forcing me out of paycheck and home?"

"If not, we're screwed, because I'm going to be very clearly letting her know that I'm actively attempting to stop Jason from ever doing what he did to Sarah again. So she'll have the chance to stop both of us, I suppose. If she sides with him, she'll tell him."

"She won't, though," Katy said. "I can tell just from that brief meeting with her."

"If she believes us, there's no way she would side with him."

"And your sister?"

"Addison is a spoiled brat. It's almost cute. But she's not

stupid, and she isn't cruel. I think once she sees the evidence…"

"The pictures. You'll even show Addison?"

"Life is so ugly, and she'll find it out sooner or later. I'd rather have her learn it this way than through being used by someone. This way, she can know that it happens. That people lie. That they manipulate. She can learn it without experiencing it."

"She is, though," Katy said. "It's her dad. I know you've been disillusioned about him for a while, but has she?"

"Probably not. I survived it, though, and so will she. We'll all survive it. Even if we come out of it without a reputation…we'll survive it."

"I know what it's like to survive things," she said. "It's not as glamorous as it sounds."

"In what way?"

"Survival is only the beginning. It's the living after that's the problem."

"Has it been your problem?"

She narrowed her eyes. "When you met me I was a twenty-six-year-old virgin with a vengeance complex. Now I'm a twenty-six-year-old with a vengeance complex. You tell me how well you think I'm living."

"You're surviving," he said.

"Exactly. Which is more of a half life. So I hope you do better than that. Though," she said, her lips twisting into something that sort of looked like a smile, "I think some of us are maybe better off. Focus on other things. Idle hands and all that."

"When you put it like that, I might be better off, too. But I hope that my mother and my sister do better than that.

Addison is too young for anything else. My mother... She's never hurt anyone. She's never been anything but supportive and loving. And she doesn't deserve this, not any of it."

"And you do?"

He shook his head. "I don't know." His chest felt heavy. With something. He wasn't sure what. He didn't understand what his feelings were doing. All this complex crap. He was used to happy, angry, hungry or horny, not necessarily in that order or frequency, and this...all of this...was not conforming to that.

This was something else entirely. All-consuming emotion. It filled him completely, making every word, every movement, a challenge. All he really wanted was to stand up and turn everything in the room upside down. The desk. The chair. To break glass and spread out the papers until everything was as big of a mess outside as it was inside of him.

But he couldn't do that. He had to get a grip on himself and keep it.

No outward signs of rage. No attempts at gaining control by using Katy's body.

"Sometimes I think maybe this is all keeping me from heading the same direction as my father."

"Do you really think you might have?" she asked.

"I don't know. Because I don't know how he got there."

"I said it before, and it's true—you're not as charming as he is," she said. "You're much more honest. I think there's something to that."

"I hope you're right," he said. "Anyway, I'm about to use some of that honesty to ruin my family. So here's hoping that it serves a higher purpose. Otherwise, I'm setting my entire world on fire for nothing."

★ ★ ★

The Treffen estate was impressive. Sprawling grounds, blanketed in crystalline snow, and a massive home with turrets rising from it, like an imposing old guard.

Which is what it was a representation of, in so many ways. The old guard. The system as it had been for so many years.

And, as Austin had so eloquently put it during their conversation on Christmas morning, they were about to set it on fire.

He put the car in Park and got out, and she followed. The snow muffled the sound of the doors closing. The silence seemed to press in on them.

It was so different from the city. Even different from her neighborhood in Connecticut. It had been a small town, but the houses had been crammed together. And there were always dogs and fights, eighties metal music and revving truck engines.

This was an isolation and silence that cost, and she could see why people paid for it.

"It's incredible," she said, the fog created by her words lingering in the air. "I mean...what a place to grow up."

He nodded slowly, slipping his hands into the pockets of his long, dark wool jacket. "It was. Do you see why I thought my life was enchanted?"

"Very much."

"You can't go back. You just start to wonder what's hidden in the corners. What kinds of skeletons are buried in the yard." He looked up and squinted against the sun. "But, hell, time to raise the dead."

"Séance time," she said.

She locked her arm through his as he pressed the doorbell.

Because they were supposed to be playing a couple. And because she knew that this was the hardest thing he'd ever done.

Things had been awkward with him for the past few days. They'd avoided each other. No more shared takeout. No more sex. Barely even a conversation.

But none of that mattered right this second. Really, none of it mattered at all. They had one thing they were united on. And that was bringing Jason down, seeking out justice for Sarah. That was why they were here. It was why she was still in his house. Because nothing else—not their relationship, not her feelings about him—really mattered.

All of this was for Sarah.

An older man in an honest-to-goodness butler getup answered the door.

"Good afternoon, Mr. Treffen," the butler said, sadly lacking in British accent.

"David, good to see you. This is my…girlfriend, Katy." He stumbled over the word, but then, what suited for his father—lover or mistress—did not suit for lunch with his mother and Katy well knew it.

She couldn't imagine being Austin's girlfriend. She wouldn't want to be anyway. Between the two of them they had so much baggage they'd require assistance carrying it all.

When she did find someone, it would be someone normal. And it would be when she felt normal. When she finally got her head on straight and learned how to live life without this endless need to fix everything.

For some reason, for just a second, that thought made her feel like she was in a free fall, with no idea of where she might land. It was terrifying. Nothing to hold on to, no idea of when she might hit bottom.

And then, just as quickly as the feeling hit, it was gone.

They were ushered through the expansive entryway, which was more like a grand antechamber to some palatial throne room, then through the living area and into a large, bright room with floor-to-ceiling windows that overlooked the snow-covered field outside, the white reflecting the sun and washing everything so that it looked overexposed.

There were bookshelves, a cluster of furniture around a fireplace and, by the windows, a small, round table. Lenore was already sitting there, a smile on her face. Next to her was a beautiful blonde that Katy assumed was Addison. She looked like her mother probably had many decades—and many face-lifts—ago.

She didn't have the same artifice to her beauty. Her hair was back in a low bun, her lips the same shade of pink as her cheeks and the dress she was wearing. She looked like a fresh rosebud. All new and pretty, and unexposed. Still closed up tightly, untouched completely by the elements.

Katy felt a pang of guilt that ran so deep it almost made her double over. Because today was the day that Addison Treffen would be shown what Katy already knew. That life was an utter bitch.

She took a deep breath and walked in with Austin. She was dimly aware that he was doing the polite thing. Making introductions, greeting everyone and holding her chair out for her. She sat, nodding at what she hoped were appropriate times.

Then the luncheon was served. And it was adorable. Pink lemonade, martinis and little sandwiches.

They ate while talking about nothing. The weather and

who wore what to where. And as lunch started to wind down, something in Katy started to wind up.

And she wondered if she should excuse herself before the big moment. Fake a bathroom emergency. Something to do with an eyelash in her eye or…

She caught Austin's gaze, just as everyone's plates were being cleared, and she knew that escape wasn't an option.

"There is a reason I wanted to have lunch with you today," he said, looking at his mother with a steadiness that Katy could only admire. Because she could hardly look up at him, and yet he was meeting his mother's eyes, giving her every respect, in spite of the fact that it was killing him to impart the news. "It's about Dad."

"What about him?" Addison asked, perfect lips turned into a frown. "He's not sick, is he?"

"Not the way you mean," Austin said, his tone dry. "I may be making the wrong choice telling you both at once, but it does affect you, Addison. And I don't particularly want to tell the story twice. I have evidence that Dad had an affair. Ten years ago with my friend Sarah. The one who killed herself during the party."

Lenore's face didn't move. Addison's did. Her brow crumpled, her expression turning fierce. "You aren't serious, Austin. She was so young and…"

"I am serious. And there's more. And the reason that I'm here telling you this is that it's all about to go public and I don't want either of you standing with him." He reached out and took his mother's hand from across the table. "I don't want you standing there behind him with that stoic supportive look on your face like some lobotomized politician's wife," he said, his tone intense. "Because he doesn't deserve it. He deserves for you to take his money and make his life hell."

Lenore blinked rapidly, her eyes glassy with tears. "You have evidence, you said, Austin?"

"Yes."

She shook her head. "I don't need to see it. I've suspected as much. That he was unfaithful. But...you know, in my position, in the world I'm from, we're taught not to care."

"You're taught not to care?" Addison said. "You never taught me not to care. I don't see how you can sit there so calmly and say that."

"I taught you to expect more, Addison," Lenore said, her tone turning to steel, "because I damn well wished I had expected more for myself. Because I didn't know how to ask for more, or go out and get more, because I thought you just had to sit back and endure it when you suspected your husband was having affairs. I must say, Austin, it's much harder to do when someone confirms it. Until now, I only had the suspicions."

"The affair is the least of your worries. He's been involved in illegal activity. Some of which...Katy has evidence of, as well."

Katy nodded slowly. That was her cue to take part in the play. "I'm Sarah Michaels's sister. I'm sure you know that name. Austin and I met...quite by accident. But after we... spent some time together, we found out why it was we were both at that party. Both of us were looking for answers. For Sarah. And we'd both found things. Putting them together..."

"We have a rough idea of what was happening. None of

it is very pleasant, Mother, and I hate to trouble you with the details. But my advice…"

"Is this legal advice, Austin?" she asked with a trace of dry humor.

"Yes. And advice as your son. Walk away. Make the break now, take him for everything he's worth. Make the public question the man they always thought they knew. You'll come out of it stronger. Better. Rather than ruined, because make no mistake, Jason Treffen is going to lose it all and you don't want to be part of that. You want to be someone who took something, not someone who stayed in Rome while it burned."

Lenore's shoulders lowered a bit. "Avoiding scandal has always been so important to your father."

"He created this one," Austin said. "It's his own mess and he's going to have to clean it up. You don't. I know it will be hard, but I'll be there for you. I brought it to you now be-cause soon it's going to be in the media, and I wanted you to have time to distance yourself from him before then. I hate telling you this," he said, looking tired now. Older. "Both of you. I hate knowing it. I hate that it's our life right now. But no matter how much I hate it, it doesn't change anything."

Lenore looked at Katy. "You aren't his girlfriend?"

The older woman looked so shattered. And she knew the devastating news wasn't really the question of Katy and Austin's relationship. But even so, she couldn't bring herself to disappoint her. She didn't see the point of making things worse. It was only Jason's blood she wanted.

"Oh, no, I am. We met almost by accident. I mean, at the party like we told you. But…but then it turned out…"

"Very convenient," Addison said, her arms crossed under

her breasts, her eyes now on Katy, and gone very sharp, digging into her. "And you have all this supposed evidence about my father?"

"I have my own, Addison," Austin growled. "And before you go accusing Katy of anything, remember that in doing so you're accusing me of being a gullible idiot. And I know you wouldn't do that."

"Will you excuse me, please?" Lenore asked. "I'm not feeling well. Thankfully, because of the weather Jason is staying in Manhattan all week. It will give me some time to process it all. I'll call you in a couple of days, darling." Lenore stood and bent, cupping Austin's chin and kissing him lightly on the cheek before she walked out of the room.

Katy felt nothing but sadness for her. For the position they'd put them in. Austin was right about the cost of all this. It wasn't light. Vengeance hurt more people than she'd ever wanted to hurt. But it was the truth, so that had to make it right.

Addison stood, too, her eyes on Austin. "Mom might not need your evidence, but I do. We'll get in touch later. For now...for now, I have to deal with Mom."

"I understand. Tell Mom I love her." Austin stood and Katy followed suit.

"I will." Addison gave Katy a hard look. "You'd better be right. If you're going to go saying things like this...you'd better be right."

"I'd rather be wrong," Katy said. "But I'm not."

Addison nodded once, then walked out of the room.

Katy felt like she'd misjudged Addison. She wasn't as soft as she'd seemed at first, but that shouldn't surprise Katy, really.

She was a Treffen, and she seemed to have that same spine of steel her mother had. That Austin had.

"It's time to head back," he said, "now that we've done our damage."

"Right. And you were right," she said, when they were outside and getting back into the car. "It wasn't fun. At all. Because I can appreciate ruining Jason's life. I can appreciate taking them from him. But I didn't really enjoy taking him from them, if you know what I mean."

He started the engine. "Yeah, I do. Damn, it's cold."

"Yeah." She turned on the heat before leaning back in the seat.

"I'm hoping that we're not driving on a sheet of ice the whole way back."

"Do you have studs?" she asked.

"No. I don't drive often enough to put special tires on."

"Chains?"

"No."

"You weren't a Boy Scout, were you?"

"Because I'm not prepared? Don't I always have a condom when we need one?"

She snorted. "Unless you can put condoms on tires to help give you more traction, I'm not really impressed with that right now."

"We'll be fine." He pulled out of the driveway and onto the two-lane road that headed back toward town and the interstate.

Not long into the drive it became pretty clear that the roads weren't fine. It was cold enough that the roads were frozen, and with snow falling, the cars that had come before them had flattened it into a hard, white sheet.

"How far is it to the freeway?" Katy asked, holding on to the door handle, like it might keep her safe if they slid off the road.

"A ways. But we're fine."

Except they weren't fine because the road up ahead was closed.

"There's another route," he said, his jaw set, that stubborn man-look firmly etched into his face. That look that meant he would drive them over a freaking frozen pond if it meant proving that he could handle it.

No. Thank. You.

"Another route that's less snowy? Does this other route happen to take us through Bermuda? Because if not, please just release the death grip on your pride. Because I don't want to die in an icy Aston Martin—shaped tomb."

"This isn't about my pride," he said, teeth gritted.

"Bull, Austin. I've seen your penis. I know it's big. So can you just find us a place to stay for the night so we don't end up dead in a ditch?"

He put the brakes on and the car slid for a few feet before stopping completely.

"That!" she said, hand on her chest, her heart pounding. "That is why the stopping somewhere for the night."

"I know how to drive in ice."

"I don't know how to be a passenger in it!"

"Fine." He turned the car around, the snow crunching beneath the tires. "We'll see what we can find."

Chapter Ten

What they could find turned out to be a nearly-booked-solid B and B in the center of town. An old Shaker-style house with an ornate entryway and a wreath on the door. It was like a Christmas card. And Austin hated that shit.

Now he was staying in one room with the woman who was driving him crazy, slowly but surely.

Today had beaten the hell out of him.

He hated his father; he hated himself. Mostly he hated how much all of this was out of his control. It was a beast that was bigger than he was. Part of him had imagined he'd be able to control it. To turn it all so that only those who deserved it were hurt in all of this.

But after seeing his mother receiving every hit quietly, after witnessing the hurt in Addison's eyes, he knew he was lying to himself.

He knew that this was a monster that would consume indiscriminately, and while part of him had come to that conclusion before today, it was only today that he'd truly seen it in action.

And this place, so full of Americana and the woman he

wanted like another hit of a drug, was getting under his skin. He would have rather chanced the blizzard.

The room the owner had shown them to was as quaint and precious as the rest of the house. Solid oak floors with oriental rugs, a four-poster bed with ornate carvings in the wood. Stamped, cranberry-colored wallpaper and a matching blanket for the bed.

"If the first room we stayed in together was a vampire brothel, what's this?" he asked, sitting on the edge of the bed and watching Katy explore the room.

"A respectable vampire family home."

"Is it all vampires with you?"

"It is when it has an edge of Gothic to it. And life in general seems to have that Gothic edge of late."

He planted his hands on the mattress and leaned back. "What's my penthouse, then?"

"Oh, you're that slick urbane vampire who tried to pass himself off as a mortal. You lure women back to your penthouse and turn them into blood slaves."

He snorted. "Blood slaves?"

"Sure. You make them crave things they've never wanted with anyone else. Things that are so very bad for them."

Her voice had gotten a little husky, her words reaching down deep into his gut and squeezing him tight. "If I were a vampire, I would, that is."

"Yeah. Sure." She jumped, then reached into her pocket and tugged out her buzzing cell phone. "Hang on. Hello? Trey! What's up?" She paused, her expression changing, her eyebrows locking together. "What do you mean your scholarship is being reviewed? What do you mean—" She started pacing. "I thought you said your grades were good." She paused. "You lied to me? You little worm! You need to tell me these things so we can try to work them out! Yes, I know I'm not your mother, but news flash, your mother doesn't care what you do! Or what *I* do! I *do* care, though. I care," she repeated. "And you didn't work this hard to— Fine, it's just a review. Whatever. You handle it, then, since you seem to know everything." He could hear her brother's voice on the other end, the terse angry tone of a teenage boy who knew when it was his fault, but who wouldn't admit it. "Did you know about this last time we talked? And you were B.S.ing me about it all being fine?" His response obviously didn't thrill her. She let out a long breath. "Don't pull this crap with me again. If you need me for anything, call me, you idiot." She hung up the phone and pitched it onto the bed, letting out a feral growl.

"Trouble in paradise?"

"My brother is an idiot. He didn't work this hard… *I* didn't work this hard for him to lose it all now. I did. I worked so hard, Austin," she said, her breath coming out on a sob. "I always worked. I had no personal life. No boyfriends, no friends. Nothing but work, and Trey, cooking him dinner, making sure I knew where he was, and then…getting high in my room at night to keep all the pain from crowding in on me when I needed to sleep."

"You what?"

"I'm so stupid. I didn't want to tell you. I've never told anyone."

"You told me you took drugs once on accident."

"I took Ecstasy once. And I never wanted to take it again. But I had a bad couple of years. When I moved out and took Trey with me. I was stressed all the time and depressed. Sarah was dead, and the payoff money was mocking me. A full savings account I would never touch because it was money I got in exchange for her blood. So I worked, and I did what I could to deflect all the stress and pain, and I used drugs to do it." She sat on the edge of the bed next to him. "I felt like an idiot. And a hypocrite. But I justified it because I was just doing really mild stuff, like painkillers. They work for the pain inside you, too, and they're pretty easy to get. My drug use was different than my parents', so I told myself. Because they were legal drugs. I was just using them illegally, but hell, what did doctors know about my pain? And anyway, it's not like I could afford a doctor."

He put his hand on her thigh, not caring if it violated their new no-touching, no-sex policy. "When did you stop?"

"When I woke up passed out on the floor, totally disoriented and late to pick Trey up from school because I'd broken my own rule and taken some during the day. Because it was a hard day. Because it was the third anniversary of Sarah's death and I wasn't able to cope with it. Christmastime, right?" She turned and looked at him. "I almost killed myself, and not on purpose. Just with my own denial. I didn't think I had a problem. I didn't think I was taking too much. Just enough to relax, to sleep. To keep the pain away. I didn't examine myself."

"And you never took them again?" he asked.

"Mostly," she said, the admission costing her, he could tell. "I threw them away. I kept a couple emergency pills. I used them, because sometimes...I could feel the numbness splitting open and without it there was just pain. I spent the year working my way off of them, but nothing was ever as bad as it was that day.... I just felt bad when I took them after that. Like a failure. Restarting the clock on your sobriety is tough. You get so many days, so many months…a year. And then you go back to zero because you were too weak to stop yourself."

"But you didn't share it with anyone?"

She shook her head. "I don't have anyone to share things like that with. I take care of my brother. I don't need him to know how tragically human I am. I don't want him to know I did that stuff because I don't want him to think that people in our position have to. Because we don't. But I'm part of the very large percentage of kids with our background who did get sucked in. But I got out. I've shared part of my story, not all of it. Because…I'm not really sure how to explain to people the way I dealt with my issues. It's certainly not healthy."

"All right, how did you deal with it? How did you quit?"

"Life hurts. It's so hard and…I was using pills to dull that. But then…then I got angry. I figured out how to cover it all up with that. Every other emotion was like white noise because the anger was just so strong. And I decided that I was going to do everything in my power to make Jason Treffen pay for what he did to Sarah. To make sure the entire world knew he was the man responsible for her death. I had her letter, and even though it was hard to make sense of, I felt like I had an idea of what she'd been dealing with."

"So instead of wallowing in pain you went out for revenge."

"Without something to drive me I just sort of marinate in the bad stuff. Not that revenge is good. But my only regret now is that I wasted any time in going after him. Though, I couldn't leave Connecticut until Trey was in school. Still, I started strategizing even then."

"You're frightening. And kind of incredible," he said.

"Just angry. Anger is more productive than grief."

"Yours is, anyway."

"So," she said, lying back on the bed and picking her phone up, before dangling her arm over the mattress and dropping it onto the floor, "the odds of us not having sex tonight are extremely low, so what do you say we don't even pretend it's not going to happen and just get down to it?"

He almost choked. "What?"

"Come on, Austin. We're in this room. I just opened up to you. I'm feeling very vulnerable. There's only one bed...."

"All the more reason for us not to have sex. It's practically forced."

"Good. Please just push me down and screw me senseless. That's what I want."

"What?"

"I need you to take control. I need...I need to not hurt. I just...hurt so bad. I'm afraid. Of what's going to happen to Trey. What's going to happen to your mom and your sister. And to me. When you touch me, when you take command, you make it all feel manageable. You make me feel like pain is a good thing. When you...spanked me...for a second it was like I could breathe again. It hurt, but only my body hurt, not my...not my emotions."

"That's not normal."

"Who cares? It works for me. It's about the only thing that's worked for me other than drugs and being numb. I like what you make me feel a whole lot better than I like being high. I like it even better than being numb. Who cares if it's normal? My whole life isn't normal, so why should I care if the sex I want is normal? There's no one else here.

Just you and me, and I know what you want isn't normal. You know it, too."

"No, it's not. I want to own you. I want you to obey me. To be here for me. To do exactly as I say, no matter what. And what does that make me? My father? A monster of another sort entirely?"

"What does it matter, if it works for both of us? Because tonight, I'd rather be yours than just plain me." She rose up onto her knees and cupped his face with her hands. "I'm so tired. Make me forget it. Make me forget how much it all hurts. Make me forget I'm me. Take it all away until everything I am belongs to you."

Something inside of him broke free. A beast on a leash that wouldn't be kept back any longer. She wanted it. She wanted to be his.

And he wanted to make her his. There was no room for civility, or concern about how something might look. No thought given to what was politically correct or strictly acceptable in polite society.

This wasn't polite society.

This was his domain, because she'd told him it was. She'd handed him the power and he would damn well use it.

"Don't hold back," she said. "I'll know if you do. I don't want your restraint. I don't want that white-collar bullshit. I don't want you to be all starched and together. Take what you want. Not what you're supposed to/want or allowed to want. Make me yours. Make me beg."

Her eyes were level with his, no shame on her face, no hesitation. And he wanted to give her everything. He wanted to obey her in his domination of her, and if that didn't sum up their twisted little relationship, nothing did.

She was demanding his domination, and in return, she would offer perfect submission. But he had to rise to that challenge. Give her what she wanted. If he didn't, he failed, because he was the one in control.

He had failed too much lately. He would not fail again.

"You want it all, Katy?" he asked. "Every dark thing in me?"

"Every one."

"New rules tonight, baby," he said, starting at the buttons on his shirt. "'Stop' won't be good enough." Adrenaline fired through his veins, his body on fire, burning with need for her. It had never stopped. Every day since the last night they'd been together he'd wanted her. But he hadn't allowed himself to cross that line.

Now he couldn't remember why. Why the idea that he might somehow beat this need for her had ever been a serious consideration. Why? When he could indulge it. When he could use her as he saw fit. Tie her up and pleasure her until neither of them could think, much less hurt.

But first, he had to get to the rules.

"If you need me to stop, I want you to say 'Help,' not 'Stop.' If you say 'Stop,' I'm not going to. That's part of the game. It's a test of our trust. But if you need help? If you need help I'll always give it. Say 'Help,' and I will. Do you understand?"

She nodded slowly, her full lips parted slightly, her beautiful eyes round. He hoped he wasn't pushing it too hard. Hoped that he hadn't abused his power.

That was the thing with being in charge. He had to make the moves, but she had to allow him. His control was nothing more than a vague facade around them.

If she said no then he was the one left standing there with a hard dick, looking like an idiot.

"I understand," she said.

Her acquiescence was a weight lifted off of him. A gift he needed, so very desperately.

Katy felt a shot of adrenaline spike through her, a desperation that made her shake. This was what she wanted. For him to take her like this. To make her feel something that took over her body, so that she didn't ache quite so much inside.

So she didn't feel so much like the Katy Michaels she'd always been.

So that she could choose to give up her control and have it feel good, instead of having control wrenched from her and getting nothing back but devastating consequences.

Life stole her control and gave her nothing but heartbreak and loss. Austin took her control and gave her pleasure that shattered her world.

She didn't wait to be asked to remove her clothes this time. She knew what he liked. Knew he liked to watch as she took off each piece of clothing.

When she took off her bra, his eyes dipped to her breasts and his tongue slid over his top lip. But he didn't touch her. He only looked, his power leashed, his control held tightly in check.

She unsnapped her black dress pants and pushed them down her legs, taking her panties with them. She wasn't embarrassed to be naked in front of him. Not when the glint in his eyes made it very clear that he not only liked what he saw, but he was also starving for it.

"Now…give me your hands," he said.

Katy stretched her hands out in front of her. They were trembling, not from fear, but from excitement.

He stripped off his tie and, like he'd done their first time together, started binding her hands together. This time he looped the heavy silk around her thumbs, then around both wrists, up her forearms before tying it off.

"All mine," he said, the roughness in his voice, the feral light in his eyes, sending a sensual shiver through her body.

He leaned in, his rough cheek scraping against hers, the day's growth of beard thick and nearly painful against her skin. He followed up with a light bite on her jaw, then one on her chin.

He wrapped his hand around her arms and pulled her so that she was up straight, before guiding her onto her back on the mattress, her arms stretched high over her head, her breasts offered up to him like a sensual sacrifice.

"Stay just like that," he said.

She loved him like this. His jaw set, his sexy mouth set into a grim line. Every part of him was devoted to it. To her. To being the master of her body. There was no hint of teasing, no hint of the man he could be, so sophisticated and polished.

No. There was no room for that man here.

He bit his lip, as if he were concentrating on making a very important decision. And the second it was made he acted. He planted his hands on her knees, driving her legs apart, exposing her to him. Utterly. Completely.

He leaned forward, his eyes never leaving hers as he bent to touch his tongue to her clit, circling the impossibly sensitive bundle of nerves.

Her hips shot up from the bed and he grabbed on to her thighs and pulled her back down to the mattress, pulled her hard against his mouth as he continued to pleasure her. Deep, long strokes of his tongue sending sharp, white-hot sparks of pleasure through her.

He pushed two fingers into her, working them in time with his tongue, pushing her higher, harder, then drawing back, stilling his movements entirely. Just enough to let her blood cool a little bit, before he started again, pushing her even higher, even closer to the edge before pulling her back.

She was so close, and he was arousing her even more intensely than she'd imagined possible. The pleasure was so acute it was almost pain. And when he added a third finger, it *was* pain. Not because it was too much to handle, but because the well of need it opened in her felt too deep to satisfy.

Because she was close to satisfaction, and yet so far, she thought she might die.

"Austin…" she said, the word a sob she didn't want to get out all the way.

He kept on going, his fingers working in and out of her, his tongue keeping time.

A rush of arousal hit, sensations that ran down deep beneath her skin. In her blood. It was too much. She didn't think she could handle it.

She knew what to say to make it end. But she didn't want it to end.

"Oh, please…" she said. "It's too much."

He didn't stop. He didn't have to. And she couldn't force him. And that turned her on even more, pushed her over the edge, her orgasm crashing over her like a wave. Her internal muscles contracted around his fingers. She tried to grab on to the blankets, to something, to hold her to earth. But she couldn't because her hands were bound.

Because he'd seen to that. That he could control everything.

"Oh, Austin…" He continued to pleasure her, pushing her further, harder. She was too sensitive. She wasn't ready. "Please, st—" She cut the word off. He'd promised he wouldn't stop, but she had to be sure he wouldn't. She needed him to keep going.

But she wanted to see what he could do. What he would do.

He growled and hitched her legs over his shoulder, withdrawing his fingers from her and holding her to his mouth, focusing on using his lips and tongue.

She couldn't even protest now, nothing more than sobs escaping her lips as he pushed her over into another climax, her breath stopping in her throat, everything going dark for a moment as it hit.

He moved away from her then, reaching for his wallet and a condom, and shucking his clothes. She couldn't do anything but lie there, her hands bound, sweat beading over her skin, her hair sticking to her neck.

"You're mine," he said, rolling the condom onto his length, his hand moving slowly, methodically, over the hard length.

Her mouth went dry watching. Her desire rising already. Impossibly.

She shouldn't be able to come for a week after what he'd just done to her, and yet she found she wanted more. Wanted it all.

"Yes," she said. "I'm yours."

"Did I make you forget yet?" he asked, leaning in, his lips close to her, his arms on either side of her.

"I can't even remember my own name," she said. Except she could. She could still feel the darkness creeping in around the edges.

She pushed it away and focused on him, only him.

"Katy." On his lips, it didn't sound the same. It sounded new. Unfamiliar and filled with possibility. This Katy could be something else entirely. Whatever she wanted, because from him, the name seemed new.

When he pushed inside of her, there was no room for darkness. Because Austin filled her.

"Katy," he said again. And she faltered.

She remembered who she was.

He kissed her neck, his teeth scraping her skin.

"More," she begged, fighting against reality. Against the pain that was pushing again.

"More?" he asked, dragging his teeth along her neck again.

"Harder," she said.

He bit down, a shot of pain going from that point down, sending a dart of pleasure to her core. "Yes," she breathed, as sensation that came from Austin took over, getting rid of all the rest.

Then he was moving in her. Hard, fast, one hand beneath her ass, and one covering her breast, teasing her nipples, squeezing them.

"Austin, please."

"Not yet," he said, his teeth gritted. "Not yet, baby. It has to last."

His movements slowed, and she could feel each inch of him as he slid out, then back deep inside of her. Exquisite torture. Perfect and cruel.

He kept her from coming again, kept her poised on the brink. Their pleasure in his control, and he knew it.

She arched her back, tried to urge things along, but he stopped her, holding her hips steady with his hand as he kept his thrusts measured, until sweat broke out on his forehead, the cords in his neck standing out, his muscles shaking.

"I can't hold back," he said. "Oh, Katy."

"Then don't." She was desperate for release, desperate for him to lose his control now.

He growled, lowering his head, his movements turning hard and erratic, pushing her over the edge.

She let out a hoarse cry, her orgasm tearing through her like an animal. No sweet crashing waves, no ebbing and slowing pleasure. This was a living, breathing beast intent on taking over her entire body.

On consuming everything in her and leaving nothing behind.

When it passed, she quieted, satiated for now. She lay there, trembling, Austin's arms around her. He held her close, his hands moving over her body.

"And tonight," she said, "don't leave."

"I don't have anywhere else to be, my Katy," he said, kissing her temple, untying her hands and throwing the tie down onto the ground. "After I take care of this." He kissed her again and walked into the bathroom, returning a moment later with the condom taken care of.

Then he lay down behind her, his arms around her. His chin resting on her shoulder.

From him, that was romance. She wasn't sure she wanted romance, but it made her feel all warm inside. Made her feel kind of fuzzy. And that was as unfamiliar as the screaming physical pleasure.

Being in Austin's arms made her feel safe and cared for. She wanted to be Katy. If she could be his Katy.

And for tonight she wanted that. Needed it even. And that brought a new guilt, pushing at the edges of her euphoria. She shouldn't want this. Not with him. She shouldn't want this with anyone, not when there was still work to be done. For Sarah. For every woman Jason Treffen had hurt. Later there could be rest, but she shouldn't be allowed this now.

Still, she was stuck in a blizzard. And they couldn't do anything tonight. She couldn't fix it tonight. Not for Trey, not for Sarah.

So maybe…maybe it was okay to rest in this tonight. To be his tonight.

He slid his fingertips along her arm. A soothing touch that had more to do with connection than sex. It was such a strange and powerful thing. To be in someone's arms. To be touched by them. Really touched. With purpose. With desire. Even unconsciously, nothing more than the drifting of his hands over her skin.

It was connection on a level she'd never experienced before. But it was always like that with Austin. From the moment she'd met him, before there had ever been physical contact, there had been a bond.

She couldn't explain it. Couldn't even begin to try. And she wouldn't want to, because she'd sound like a nut-bag. But then, she already did. She was sure of that.

And she would let herself have it. If only for now. This world of feeling, this desperate, raw, painful sensation that she sought out, was the direct opposite to the numbing bluntness she'd sought out from the pills.

"At least our crazy lines up and hits all the right places," she said. "And creates orgasms."

He tightened his hold on her, a laugh rumbling in his chest, vibrating against her back. "That's one way of looking at it."

"You're so good," she said. "Just so you know. Best I've ever had."

"I'm the only you've ever had."

"Weren't you listening? I've had a *lot* of things. None of them made me feel this good. Sexually? Yeah, okay, you're the only I've ever hard."

"Because? I'm asking now because now I know you weren't just hanging out being a paragon."

"It's easier to sneak pills past your sleeping brother than it is to sneak a man past him?"

"That's all you've got?"

"It makes more sense than the truth."

"Try me," he said, shifting so that his thigh was between her legs and he was all tangled up in her.

"That I felt like I knew you when I saw you. Like maybe you could know me. Because you were so composed and smooth. So sexy. But you were sad. And you were angry. You were so familiar even though I'd never seen you before. And I wanted to touch you. I've never…needed to touch someone like I needed to touch you."

He cupped her cheek and turned her face, kissing her. Deep and slow. There was no desperation, just a steady hunger that he fed, that somehow grew the more that he satisfied it.

"Now you've touched me," he said, kissing her again, "quite a bit."

"Yes. And do you want to know something else?"

"Of course."

"I wanted this. I had fantasies of it. A man who would hold me down. Tell me what to do."

"Is that so?"

"Does it shock you? That I've always known I had a submissive streak?"

"A little, because I can't say I was that articulate to myself about my own fantasies."

"I knew them," she said. "The moment I saw you, I knew. I knew you were the one I could share this with." The honesty came with a cost, but in truth, she was always honest in her actions with him. Laying herself bare every time she expressed a desire to submit to him.

"And do you regret it? Sharing this with me?"

"Never. Though you have a habit of tying my hands."

"And you like it."

"Yes," she said, happier now that she'd just gone ahead and admitted it. And she wouldn't think of anything else, of anyone else. Because she wouldn't allow any ghosts in bed with Austin and her. She wanted to have him all to herself. She wanted to give him all of herself without caring about Jason and Sarah.

Just for a little while.

"That's what I like to hear."

"You're such a control freak," she said, wiggling in his arms and turning to face him.

"And?" he asked, a teasing glint in his eye she couldn't remember seeing before.

"And nothing. Carry on."

He slipped his hands down to cup her butt, pulled her tight against him. "Don't worry about that."

"Again?" she asked.

"I need more time to recover than that."

"You're hard already."

"Still, I think the top of my head blew off sometime during my orgasm."

"And you're waiting to regrow it?"

"Something like that."

"Too bad." She slid down, wrapped her hand around his erection and leaned in, flicking her tongue over the head of his cock. "Because I think you really want this."

He grabbed her hair, jerked her head back. "Hey, that's not the game."

"This is a new game," she said, running her tongue along his length. "Where I get to play with you as much as I want. I've never seen a man like you." She moved her hand up, over his chest and stomach, feeling the rough hair that was sprinkled over his hard, hot muscles. "I've never wanted a man the way I want you. You own me," she said, sucking him deep into her mouth.

He grunted, his fingers still buried in her hair, pulling hard as she sucked on him. "Yeah, baby," he said. "Yes, Katy." He flexed his hips, pushing himself deeper into her mouth.

She held him steady, moved her hand in time with her tongue.

He swore, holding her tight while he gave up, his muscles shaking while he found his release. While he lost his control.

He lay on his back after, breathing hard, and she moved to him, lying over his chest, tracing shapes over his muscles with her fingertips. She took pride in the fact that his skin was slick with sweat. In the fact that, for a moment, he'd been the one at her mercy.

"You didn't have to…"

"Mmm," she said, licking her lips. "Shut up."

"Maybe we should stay here," he said. "Being snowed in isn't as bad as I thought it would be."

"Damned with faint praise."

He bit her ear and she jumped. "Best I've ever had," he whispered, his voice rough and sexy.

"And from you I guess that's something," she said, feeling breathless and sexy. Feeling like things were okay, even if it was just for a moment.

"There have been some women. But no one like you. Nothing like this."

"So you've really never done this stuff with a woman before?"

"You couldn't tell?"

She laughed. "A little bit I could tell. But only because you freaked out after. So what? You just discovered your inner dom?"

"No, not really. I would never have called it that. I'm still not sure I would. I don't know anything about clubs or… that kind of thing. But I knew what I liked," he said. "I've just never…acted on it before."

"Oh, really?" She situated herself so that she was partly on top of him, her breasts crushed against his chest. "This intrigues me, Austin. I want to know all about your sordid fantasy life. You're an overachiever. A go-getter. You're so confident and established in your life. You've had lovers. So it fascinates me that you knew what you wanted, but never did anything about it."

"Hey, I know what I jack off to. I was hardly unaware, naturally."

"I know what I used to get off to, as well. Fantasies of handcuffs and men in uniform—don't judge me. I have a thing for authority figures, which is ironic since in my real life I hate being told what to do. I guess that's sort of a window into my psyche. But this is your story. Do tell. Make it my very dirty bedtime story."

"There isn't anything to tell. I knew that I liked the idea of being in control in bed. That I got turned on by the thought of tying a woman up. But I thought…you know, that stuff wasn't for me. I mean, hell, all I needed was for an ex to tell the media that I, a lawyer who, like my father, takes a special interest in cases concerning women being harassed, was into domination games. Can you imagine the field day they'd have?"

"Image-conscious even in bed?"

"You have to be in my position. That's why my mother couldn't even cry in front of Addison and I when she found out my dad was having an affair, that he was in legal trouble. Because appearance is everything, and nothing else really matters." He cleared his throat. "So yeah, even in bed you have to make sure there's nothing that would damn you if it got out."

"Is that the only reason?"

"No. Because it takes a hell of a lot of…trust? Something. I don't know. And I never felt like I could with anyone else. Yeah, it is trust. To let this part of myself show. To let it have free rein."

"How could you trust me? You knew me for twenty minutes before you had me tied up in a hotel room."

He smiled at her. "I could ask you the same question. You said I was the first man you trusted to do this stuff to you."

"Well, I make unhealthy life decisions. I think we've established that."

"You've made a lot of healthy ones, too, Katy. Don't forget about all those just because you made bad ones, too. You got off drugs, you took care of your brother, you got work and you're doing all of this to try and get justice for your sister. To free these other women. The ones who were involved in the past, and now, and who would have been taken in in the future."

"You make me sound like a saint."

"No. Just a sinner who's done some pretty extraordinary things."

"Or maybe a sinner with good intentions? Though, you know what they say about good intentions and the road to hell...."

"I don't believe that," he said. "I think good intentions do matter."

"What the hell difference do they even make?"

"They make you who you are. If my father had a good intention inside of him then maybe things wouldn't have gone the way they did for Sarah. For any of the women involved in this."

"But it takes more than good intentions to fix a mess like this."

"And you're doing it."

"So are you," she said, thinking of his mother and sister earlier. Of the pain he'd been through. That they'd been through. "I think we can rest easy for a night."

"Tomorrow we have to go back. And we have to go to

his New Year's Eve party. I do wonder when my mother will drop the bomb."

"When she does, what will you do?"

"Me? I'll stick close to my father," he said, though his tone was less decisive than it usually was when he was stating something he considered to be a certainty.

She was starting to recognize his tones. Whatever the hell that meant.

"But what about your reputation, Austin? Shouldn't you distance yourself like Addison and your mom are? Shouldn't you protect yourself?"

"I can't afford to do that," he said. "And I don't deserve to do it."

"Why?"

"Because I was so close to Sarah. To what happened. I should have listened then. I should have stopped it then. You couldn't have done anything. You were a kid. You were a hundred miles away. I was right here. I don't deserve distance now."

She examined his profile, hard as granite, masking so much hurt. So much hate. For himself. He was so beautiful, the most beautiful man she'd ever seen. All hard muscle, and straight, perfect lines. And yet he hated himself.

She wanted to take it from him, shoulder it. Make him realize that he was worth more. Make him see what she saw.

And what do you see?

She didn't want to examine it too closely.

"How long are you going to punish yourself?" she asked.

"I might ask you the same question."

She took a deep breath and tried to shift some of the weight off of her chest. "I'd rather have *you* punish me. Let's just stick with that."

"For how long?" he asked. "How long are we going to do this?"

"I don't know. Until the end? Until we go our separate ways and ride off into the distance? That's what I plan on doing. I'm going to leave the city behind. I'm going to leave all the ugly behind. Wipe my feet on the whole damn East Coast, maybe."

"Where will you go? Not the Bible Belt, I wouldn't think."

"Why not? Maybe I want to try out being a Southern girl. Sit on a porch somewhere and drink sweet tea. Soak up the sun. Sounds easier than this."

"What else?"

"I was thinking California. As far the hell away from here as possible without leaving the continent. Sun. Palm trees."

"Swimming pools. Movie stars."

"Hell yeah."

"It's a nice dream," he said.

"Sure. What about you? What will you do when it's over?"

"What everyone does after a hurricane hits. Rebuild."

"Do you think you can?"

He chuckled. "No. But I'll damn well try. Because the rubble that will be left behind? That's my legacy. I'll live or die in it. Eventually we'll find out which."

Chapter Eleven

It was midmorning when they got back to the penthouse the following day. Austin had held her all night, and when she'd woken up, for the first time in her life, she'd felt like the one being protected.

She'd woken up with Trey in her bed before. His little body cold because the heat was off. Trembling, and with no one else to turn to. And later, she'd locked herself in her room, feeling like she was breaking apart from the inside out, and found her solace in a pill bottle.

This was different. This was...

It was nice to have someone there who made her feel safe. Who made her feel like she was sharing a burden.

And they were. She and Austin shared the weight over Sarah's death more than anyone else. More than Trey, because Katy had shielded him from it, and because he'd hardly known the sister who'd moved out when he was three. More than her parents, who'd never been sober enough to really understand.

Austin was carrying it. And he was going to see it finished.

He was her own, personal Samwise, helping her carry the ring to Mount Doom. Or something like that.

Whatever, she'd found something with him. Sure, their bond was made of grief and rage, but in between was incredible sex and the beginning of what felt like a friendship.

So, it wasn't all bad.

"What would you have me do, master?" she said, turning to face him in the hall.

"Do not mess with me like that, Katy. I could get used to it," he said.

"I wouldn't complain."

"You might if I made you my good little slave girl."

"I already am, aren't I?"

"Only when you're naked. The rest of the time you seem to fight me for control."

"I have no interest in being submissive when there's no orgasm in it for me." But she couldn't deny that "good little slave girl" made something inside of her tingle.

"What exactly were you looking for instruction on?"

"Where do you want me to sleep?"

"Your toothbrush is already on my sink. I might as well reap the benefits. You should sleep in my bed. Naked, naturally."

"So I'll be a good slave?"

"You said it, not me."

"I'm so tired. And we didn't *do* anything."

"Except have sex all night."

"Except that," she said drily, heading through to his bedroom, feeling a strange sense of intimacy close in on them when she crossed the threshold.

This needed to stop. Or at least...she needed to stop letting Austin take up so much head space. None of this was supposed to be about him. It wasn't supposed to be about her.

"I think I need a shower," he said, tugging his shirt up over his head. "Wash the travel grit off."

Her throat dried at the sight of his body. Hard, carved lines of muscle, dark hair over his pecs, thinning out down his abs, down beneath his jeans. She wanted to touch him. She wanted to lick him. It suddenly seemed more important than revenge.

She cleared her throat. "You have travel grit after driving a couple of hours? Sex-ay."

"It's a clever ploy to con you into the shower."

"Hell, dude, you have three showerheads. All you have to do is ask."

Just another couple of hours. Just a little more. A chance to feel something more than anger. Something more than numb. Something only Austin could give.

Austin looked out the window and leaned back in his chair. Damn. He still had two cases to review before he could go home and be with Katy.

Katy, whose panties had been on his bathroom floor this morning. Whose toothbrush was in the holder with his on the sink.

Katy, who had taken over his life, his brain and his body.

And he couldn't even be sorry. She made him smile, which was ludicrous in so many ways. With his world crashing down around him, she made him feel both in control and blessedly out of it. She made him feel bliss.

She even made him laugh.

It was New Year's Eve and they were supposed to go to his dad's party tonight, a part of making the reconciliation look like A Thing That Was Happening, but he couldn't muster up any desire to go.

Not when the alternative involved staying home all night with Katy. As soon as he walked in the door from work he fully intended to push her down on the nearest surface and have his way with her until neither of them could think.

He was in the mood to tie her to the bed tonight. To pleasure her until she was begging for him to stop. But he wouldn't.

No, he would pleasure her until he was done.

He looked at the files on his desk and growled.

He wondered how she was doing. If she were still stressed about her brother and his scholarship. There was really nothing she could do to fix it. If the kid was intent on slacking off, then that was what he was going to do. But he knew that she felt like it was her job to fix it.

Just like he would if it were Addison.

Just like he did now, because it was Katy's problem. And Katy's problem felt like his, God knew why. It did, though. He felt it like a weight on him, just as he felt it release, for both of them, when they were in bed.

And sometimes just when they were together.

That woman had gotten underneath his skin, straight into his blood. And he couldn't work out how to get her back out.

When it's all said and done, she'll be gone. And you won't have to worry about it anymore.

True enough, but for now, he *was* worried about it. And worried about her.

He let out a slow breath and picked up his phone. "Can you connect me with the athletics department at U Conn?"

★ ★ ★

Katy had never enjoyed takeout more.

Austin had just freed her hands, and now she was ready to eat. Completely naked, her wrists a little bit red from the way they'd done things tonight. It had been rough; it had been raw.

But she was happy. So happy.

"I liked your technique with the scarves," she said.

"Really?" He picked up a carton of noodles and stuck his chopsticks inside.

"Yes. I'm thinking, though…maybe we should get some handcuffs."

"You'd like that?" he asked, taking a bite.

"What did I tell you about my authority-figure fantasies? Arrest me and make me talk my way out of it," she said, leaning over and taking a bite of food from his carton.

"I'm not sure about that."

"Because?"

"It's a total miscarriage of justice. If a police officer ever really did anything like that, I'd prosecute his ass so hard he wouldn't be able to sit for weeks."

"That's so hot. I think I'm having lawyer fantasies instead of cop fantasies now. Would you prosecute me?" she asked, wiggling her eyebrows. "Would you prosecute me hard?"

"I think you know I would."

She smiled and stole more of his food. "So what has you in such a good mood?" she asked.

"Am I in a good mood?"

"You aren't as growly as usual. And also you seem to be smiling. An actual Austin Treffen smile. Those are rare, like a unicorn, and I treasure each one."

"Actually, I have something to tell you," he said, smiling again. Her heart kicked.

"You solved global warming."

"Dammit, Katy, now whatever I say is going to sound stupid. I'll fail because I didn't solve global warming."

"Fine, work on that next."

He reached over and took a bite from her food. "Great. Since my specialty is law and not science, I'll get right on that."

"Sorry, baby," she said, leaning in and kissing his lips.

"'Baby'?"

"Sure. You call *me* that."

He cleared his throat. "Anyway..."

"Yes, what did you do?"

"I called U Conn's athletic department today and offered a very generous donation. But only if they would look upon Trey Michaels with leniency."

"You did...what?"

"I called about Trey. I don't really have to repeat it, do I?"

"I just can't believe you would do that.... I can't...I can't believe..." She could hardly breathe past all the emotions that were cycling through her. Could hardly think. And then anger came to the rescue. Because it was the only emotion she had much practice with. And it was readily available.

"How could you do that without talking to me first?" she asked.

"What?"

"I was handling it, Austin."

"Oh, forgive me. I thought you were sitting here naked eating takeout."

"Are you serious right now?" She slammed the carton

down onto the blankets and a noodle spilled over the edge. "How much did you pay them?"

He named a figure that made her curse.

"I can never pay that back," she said, "and you damn well know it. You took…everything from me. My power, and now you're making me indebted to you in ways—"

"I fucking took everything from you?" he asked, his voice rising now. "Funny, I thought I gave you a whole bunch of stuff to balance it out. A place to stay, access to my father and help with your revenge. Plus, I recall an orgasm or fifty."

"I don't think you understand, Austin. Because no matter how much you care, no matter how much you give to people like Sarah, people like me, the power is always yours to command. I have nothing next to you and this just emphasizes that. I can't pay you back," she said again.

"I don't want you to. It was a gift."

"I already owe the Treffens money. The last thing I want is to take out…a…a loan on your guilt."

"A loan on my guilt? Screw that. Screw guilt. This has nothing to do with guilt. This is because I wanted to do something for you. Because I didn't want you carrying it all. It has nothing to do with my dad, and nothing to do with Sarah. This was about you."

"I…I…"

"Do you think I'm in bed with you thinking of them? Of her? I damn well am not. I can't think of anything else, of anyone else, not when I'm with you."

"You were thinking of her plenty right at first. With all your shame over tying me up. Like a little bondage makes you a serial killer or something. So don't throw me some line about not thinking of them."

"I don't now," he said, his voice tight. "Because...because like you said, it does something for both of us. And this was both of us, too. I don't like seeing you stressed out. I don't want you to be hurt, and I wanted to do something for you. And now it's not a solution for global warming, and somehow you think I'm paying you blood money, so I can't win."

That took some of the anger out of her. Replaced it with confusion.

"That's not what I meant. I just didn't expect for you to do something like this for me. Because no one ever has. No one has ever...no one has ever done anything like this for me. No one has ever done anything for me. It's always been...me. I'm the strong one. I fix things. And the only time I'm allowed to have a meltdown is in my room, and even then...I would take drugs to feel numb instead because I didn't have time to have a meltdown. So I just don't know how to take something like this. I don't know how to be much of anything other than angry and distrustful.... Austin, I want to believe you did that for me. I want to believe it. That there's nothing attached to it."

"There isn't, Katy. I promise. And I know it's a dick thing to say, but the money doesn't matter to me, because it's something I have. It's something I can give you. And I know it feels like a lot, but to me it isn't. Having the ability to do something for you is what means a lot to me."

"I don't know how to respond to this. To any of this."

"Just say thank you, Katy. That's what you do when someone does something nice for you."

And all the anger was gone now, replaced by a need so deep it frightened her. By a desire that went so far beyond the physical it crossed into unknown territory. It had nothing to do with revenge. It had nothing to do with anything she could identify and it scared her.

She cleared her throat. "Well, this has never happened to me before, so I was stumped on the protocol."

He cupped her face and leaned in, and her heart thundered hard and loud in her ears. "'Thank you' is enough. I'll have my thank-you now."

She blinked back tears. Frustrated tears. At him, at herself. Happy tears because no one had ever wanted to fix something for her before. No one had even tried. Austin had tried. "Thank you."

"You're welcome. This was just about you. Because I didn't want to see you upset like that."

"Well, the little bastard really should handle his own stuff."

"But you couldn't let it go."

"Of course not!"

"Neither could I." He kissed her then, and she felt it, not just in her body, but in her heart. She wished she didn't feel it in her heart. She wished the need was only skin-deep.

He pulled away and she looked over at the clock. "Oh, no! It's after ten. How did it get so late? We were supposed to go to your father's thing and you were supposed to pretend to be reconciling and stuff!"

"I could just tell him you were tied up."

"OMG. Do not even go there again. It was bad enough when you used that line to get me fired."

"But it's the truth. You were. Tied up and at my mercy. You couldn't exactly go put your makeup on. Or, you know, keep me from taking your panties off and licking your..."

"*Seriously.* You can't tell him that."

"Seriously, I won't."

"Good. He's sick. I don't want him thinking about me like that."

"*I* like thinking of you like that," he said, his tone suddenly serious, his dark eyes searching. "What does that make me?"

"Hot. But then, I *want* to be with you, so I suppose that's the difference."

"Even though I was a high-handed asshole who took over your life and did something for you that may well have compromised your agency?"

"Even then," she said. "Life is hard, Austin. Thank you for helping it feel not quite so bad."

"Now I'm the one damned with faint praise."

"Tie me up again and your praise will not be faint."

He put his carton of food on the nightstand. "This is a much better way to spend the evening."

"Is it?" she asked, her heart thundering.

They shouldn't skip the party. They should go. She should try to get back into Jason's office. But she didn't want to.

Austin picked up one of the scarves and stretched it between his hands. "No question."

Soon she would have to change her focus again. Soon she would have to build her walls again. Protect herself from all the feelings. Find her numbness. Her anger. Her drive.

Soon.

But for now, Austin was in control. He was going to bear the burdens, if only in bed, if only tonight.

And she was going to happily obey his every command.

Chapter Twelve

"Where the hell were you last night, boy?"

Austin's ear nearly bled from the screed coming through his phone and into his ear.

"What?"

"The party. You were supposed to be there."

"I know," Austin said as he rolled out of bed, looking at the sleeping woman that was still burrowed beneath the blankets. He rubbed a hand over his face, trying to clear his head. He hadn't slept. He and Katy had rung in the New Year in the best way he could think of. Their own personal party that had lasted until the sky had started turning a light shade of gray.

"What happened?"

"Just a second." He bent over and picked up his pants and tugged them on, then walked out of the room so he wouldn't disturb Katy.

He closed the bedroom door behind him and started down the hall. "Something came up."

"A business matter or a female one?" his father asked.

"I don't see what difference it makes. You would have

skipped an event for either reason, so let's not be self-righteous in our indignation now."

The words were a bit more honest than he'd intended. A bit too sharp. But he found he didn't care. For some reason, between darkness and dawn, or maybe just between Katy's thighs, he'd started growing more and more averse to the idea of playing at a reconciliation between the two of them.

The idea of going to one more party, offering him one more smile, had started to seem unbearable.

"You've grown a spine in the past decade, Austin," his father said, a vague hint of approval in his voice.

"Ten years is a long time."

"So it is."

"So now why are you jumping down my throat over missing a party, when we both know in these past ten years when I was busy growing a spine, I didn't attend a single one of your events?"

"I was expecting you."

"And I wasn't there. Why does it matter?"

"Your mother asked for a divorce—no, she demanded one in front of everyone."

Jason's words stunned him. He hadn't realized his mother had had that in her. That was scandal, on every level, something Lenore Treffen had a total aversion to. And yet she'd done it anyway.

He had to wonder what else his mother knew.

"Did she say why?" he asked, feigning ignorance. Because he would as long as he could.

"She's accused me of infidelity."

"And?"

"She has no evidence of it. Come now, Austin. You're a

man. You know how things are. Do you honestly think you would be faithful to one woman for thirty-five years of your life?"

He thought of Katy, warm and soft in his bed. The way her needs fit into his so very well. How he could be utterly selfish with her, a slave to his own needs in every way, and yet fulfill hers, too.

He could imagine her being the only woman he wanted for the rest of his life.

He had no idea what to do with that realization. Because reality was a far cry from that desire.

"Shit happens. I get that," he said.

"Meet me at your office in an hour."

Austin paused for a moment, unsure how to respond. Unsure of what he would do if he went. Of what he would accomplish either way.

"Okay. One hour."

He hung up the phone and tapped the screen, then went into the browser and did a search for Jason Treffen's New Year's party.

And got a video. He tapped Play and got a full-color viewing of the drama. He and... Damn, one hundred thousand views in the past ten hours.

He turned up the volume.

"I'm done, Jason. I won't stand for this anymore." It was his mother, onstage next to the band like she was about to give a toast, the microphone in an unsteady hand. "I won't be a part of this empire you've built. On lies and the pain of other people. I won't let you hurt me or anyone else anymore. It's time the world knew that you're not who you pretend to be. That you're not the man I thought I married. I want a divorce."

The crowd of people at the party gasped and he could see Jason moving up to where his mother was. "Get down, Lenore. Now."

"I don't belong to you anymore. I'll do what I damn well please."

There was more mayhem, and the video shook, then stopped.

Austin stood still, his heart thundering hard. He had to go and deal with his father.

Because if Jason were going to start confessing to try to keep himself in the clear when everything started breaking, Austin needed to know. This was his chance.

But first, he had to put in a phone call to his mother.

Austin had murder on his mind by the time his father walked into his office.

Reconciliation, whether fake or not, was definitely off of the table.

He'd spent most of the hour on the phone with his mother. And he'd learned things that had made his blood burn.

Abuse he hadn't even imagined.

He liked to put his hands around my neck…. He didn't even need to be angry to hit me. To threaten me. It was almost as though he liked the shock of it. To take me from laughing to crying in the space of the moment.

It's his power. And he loves to use it for pain.

Austin's stomach hurt. His father's sins went so far past what he'd originally thought. More than whoring out women. More than coercing a young woman into a sexual relation-

ship. He liked to hurt others. He got off on the fear he instilled in them. On the evidence of his own power, reflected
by the terror in the eyes of the weaker person.

Now it was his turn to instill a little bit of terror. To make
sure that Jason Treffen tasted his own poison.

If Austin could wrap his hands around the older man's
throat and squeeze, he would do it. But barring that, he
would make sure that he walked away from this divorce
with nothing.

And in the end, he would make sure he rotted in a jail cell.

For his crimes against Sarah. For his crimes against his
mother. For selling women like commodities, abusing them
like they were objects.

"Come in," Austin said. "Have a seat."

He was establishing the power dynamic now. He was the
one in command. His father was right; he had grown a spine.
And now he was ready to do what he had to do. To not just
destroy his father's empire, but to revel in it. To not simply
have a part in removing Jason Treffen from the map, but to
drive the initiative.

This was no longer about duty. There was no longer a
hint of regret.

There was nothing but rage. White-hot and purposeful.

And a sick, burning satisfaction that sat low in his gut.
Driving him on.

"I don't think I'll sit," Jason said.

"I think you will," Austin said. "Have a seat. You'll need
one for what we're going to talk about here."

When his father sat in the chair opposite his desk, Austin
stood, a file in his hand.

"What is it you expect me to do for you? You and Mom

don't have a prenup. So tell me what it is you think I can help you with?"

"I think you taking my side in the divorce will have an impact on the decision. Especially as you're typically an advocate for women. As am I."

"Oh, yes," Austin said, his lip curling. "A famed advocate for women in their time of need. Which is why you'd like your wife to end up with nothing? And you'd like me to help you do it?"

"Let's cut the crap, Austin," his father said. "I think you have an idea of who I am. And of what you're dealing with. I don't, for one moment, think you buy into the *media's* idea of who I am. You're far too perceptive. There's a reason you hardly spoke to me for ten years. And there's a reason you're speaking to me again. And your current toy...Katy Michaels. It's not an accident that you're screwing Sarah's sister."

A trickle of ice worked its way through Austin's veins. "I'm surprised you remember her name." Except he wasn't. Because the combination on the lock was the date of her death. Because he still had the pictures.

"Of course I do."

"You're not going to try and tell me you loved her, are you?" Austin asked.

Jason sat back in his chair, his expression flat, emotionless. "I had a train when I was a child." He picked up a small glass figurine from Austin's desk, a model of the New York skyline. "A small, wooden one. It was very intricate, lots of moving parts." Jason turned it over in his hand, his thumb moving over the Empire State Building. "One day I was playing with it, and it broke." He snapped the top of the building off, leaving a bead of blood on the top of his thumb. He stared at it for a moment, not reacting. Not even making the smallest showing of pain. Then he set the damaged skyline back on Austin's desk. "I remember crying. And feeling the loss of it, even though it was nothing more than a toy. And if asked, I would have said I loved that train, because I certainly missed playing with it." He put his hands behind his head, ignoring the blood. "What child isn't sad when he breaks his favorite toy?"

"Sarah was not a toy," Austin said, his voice choked. "Katy isn't my toy."

His father laughed. "At least I know myself. You're my son, and you've always been so like me. Let me guess…you like that she's young. Poor. That you have all the power in the relationship. That she has to live in your house, use all of your things. That you get off on her being your inferior. You like to dominate her. You probably like her even more because of whose sister she is. And a pity for me that you got to her first. Because I would have so liked to use her. Though, sharing is always nice. I enjoyed sharing Sarah. Because you should always share your toys."

Austin reached out, and before he could temper himself, he had his fingers wrapped around his father's throat. The older man's eyes went wide, genuine fear in them, fear that fueled Austin's rage, that offered a kick of adrenaline and satisfaction unlike anything he'd ever experienced.

He wanted his fear. He wanted him to know just what it was like to be afraid for your life. For your sanity. Like his mother had been for years. Like Sarah had been.

Like every woman he'd ever abused had been.

"You're about to learn a couple of things about me, and that spine I grew," Austin said. "I don't share. And I don't forgive. And I'm not that scared of what might happen to me if I tighten my grasp right now."

"You don't want to spend the rest of your life in prison."

"I don't know. Seems like it might be worth it." He pressed his thumb a little harder into the soft spot at the base of his father's throat. "We're both full of surprises, aren't we?"

The fear in Jason's eyes intensified, fuel for his own anger, for the feeling of utter, invincible power that was coursing through his veins.

"You wouldn't."

He loosened his grip, stepped away. "No, you're right. I wouldn't. The short road to hell is too good for you. I'd like you to suffer a bit in this life first. You're right about something else, too—I'm not naive. I do know exactly what you are. And I will take great joy in bleeding all your assets from you. In watching you fall to earth, like she did. I will break you. And I will enjoy hearing your bones snap." He straightened his tie and met his father's cold, hard gaze. "I can't take your case, because I'll be taking Mom's case. I am an actual advocate for women, after all." He turned to face the windows, looked at the traffic moving below. Then he turned back to Jason. "I'm going to enjoy this. Watching you suffer. Watching you lose everything."

Jason stood, his expression ashen. "I knew you were like me," he said, his voice tight and hoarse, thanks in part to the grip Austin had had on it. "You think you aren't, because you're fighting against me, but the fact that you like it this much... You are my son. Make no mistake in that."

"Fine. And if all me being your son ever accomplishes is ending you? Then I accept that. If I need to be like you to destroy you? I'll do that. Get ready to fight. This divorce, and everything that comes after, is going to be uglier than you could have ever imagined."

His father turned and walked out the door and Austin let out a long breath, adrenaline coursing through him. Yes, he knew exactly who he was. What he was. And right now he didn't care.

He was going to win the war by any means necessary.

The only thing that surprised him was how much he was enjoying it.

He walked down the corridor, long strides carrying him out of the building. His body was pumping with adrenaline and all he could think of was Katy.

Of how he wanted her. The ways he wanted her. He wanted to burn all of this away with their passion. He needed to...

You're my son, and you've always been so like me.

You like to dominate her.

Was that all this was? A way for him to enjoy helplessness and exercise control in the guise of a sexual fantasy? Was he just like his father, only so unaware?

No.

He didn't need to do that to her. He didn't need to want it. He curled his shaking hands into fists. If he needed control so badly, he could damn well control himself.

Tonight, he would give Katy something else entirely. Tonight, he would prove that he could.

Katy hummed tunelessly as she reheated last night's takeout. She was poring over new thoughts of revenge, on ways she would put Jason Treffen's head on a pike and parade around with it, put it on display.

Metaphorically, of course. Well, *literally* had its appeal as well, but she wouldn't go there.

Soon, she would be figuring out ways to exploit his newly vulnerable position. With the divorce coming together, since it was certain Lenore Treffen would be filing, Jason would be open to media attacks, and his wealth would start to drain.

The other part of her good mood was Austin. Which was a nice change of pace, to have something other than revenge make her feel happy.

Austin had been gone when she'd woken up. At work on New Year's Day. But then, that was why he was a billionaire, she supposed.

She wished he was home, though.

She snorted. When had she started thinking of Austin's deluxe penthouse in the sky as home? It sure as hell wasn't her home.

Still, the thought made her ache a little bit around her heart.

Grr. Her freaking heart again. Only her body was supposed to be involved. Not her heart.

The front door opened and Austin walked in, his eyes dark, his eyebrows drawn together, his walk purposeful.

She knew, without him saying anything, just what he had on his mind.

"I need you." There was a desperation to his tone, an absence of command. It was disturbing.

She just stood there for a second, totally stunned, because this was coming out of nowhere for her. She'd had nothing but a nice quiet morning. A sex-free shower and the nuking of leftover Chinese food didn't add up to sexy times in her head.

But clearly, he had other ideas.

"Are you asking for permission?"

"Yes, darling. Please."

"Did you hit your head?" she asked.

"No." He approached her, cupped her cheek, his palm warm against her skin. He leaned in and kissed her lightly. Gently. So gently it hurt, and not in a good way. Not in a way she could handle.

Emotion swelled in her chest, rising gently along with his touch, and she wanted to turn and run from it. Wanted to push him away.

She didn't want this sweet, soft side of him. It wasn't enough. It wasn't enough to keep her demons back. She couldn't open herself up to feeling without something to balance it. Without something to help take the pressure away.

The tug of her hair, the firm grip of his hands on her hips, rough words that put a layer of protection over the warm feelings that always poured through her when they touched.

She couldn't do it. It made her want to hold him forever. It made her want to cry. Her stupid heart.

She needed her body back in charge.

"Take me," she said against his lips.

"I am." His fingers drifted beneath her shirt, and for the first time, she noticed he was shaking.

"No," she said, pulling away. "Stop with the tenderness crap. Take me. Hard. Push me down. Make me..."

"No," he said.

"Why not? Why not take what we both want?"

"I don't need it. It was just a game. It's time to...stop with that."

"It wasn't a game to me," she said. "It's not a game. I need it or I can't... I have too many feelings, Austin. Too many... I can't...I can't breathe. I need you to help me breathe."

"No, Katy."

"I'm begging you," she said, leaning in, her lips touching his ear. "Please, please give me what I need. I'm at your mercy. No one else can do this for me. No one. And I'm the only one who can do this for you."

"You have to trust me," he said. "Whether you're down on your knees, or here kissing me. I know what you need. Don't you understand by now?" he asked, drawing his hand over the line of her jaw.

She was trembling, inside and out. Afraid of what he would do next. She wasn't afraid of Austin's intensity. She wasn't afraid to accept his bonds, pain and pleasure at his hand. But this, this care, this...tenderness—*that* was frightening.

She didn't know what to do with it. Didn't know how to process the whisper of his fingertips on her skin, the gentle hold of his palm on her lower back.

It was scarier than bondage, and it was holding her even tighter to him. Something she couldn't turn away from, couldn't deny him. Because no matter what he said, he was the one who needed this, and she couldn't refuse him what he needed.

That was the thing about their relationship. What she needed, he needed the counterpoint. They were all about balance in bed. To some, it would seem like he dominated her, but it had never been true, not really. He needed, she gave. If she didn't give, it would mean nothing to him.

In this moment, he needed. And his needs offered her none of the safety, none of the intensity, of their other interactions. He wasn't asking for her body, or for her submission.

He was asking for something deeper. He was asking her to make decisions. To reach out and give, not simply accept.

She didn't know if she could do it, not without breaking apart.

"Don't make me beg, Austin," she said, her voice shaking.

"I like it when you beg," he said, his eyes intent on hers. "You know I do. But right now, I need you to give me this." He kissed her, his lips light, warm and sweet. "Let me show you I can do this."

"I don't need it."

"*I* need it. And you'll give it," he said, the firm authority in his voice chasing across her skin like a breeze, raising goose bumps on her arms, hitting that place deep within her that responded to Austin. Only to Austin. Wholly and without hesitation.

He pulled her top up, his fingers skimming her stomach, her breasts, as he lifted it over her head. Then he unhooked her bra, let it fall to the floor. He dropped to his knees in front of her and everything in her rebelled, but she held still, held fast. This was what he wanted. He'd given the order; she had to accept. She squeezed her eyes shut, a tear sliding down her cheek.

He leaned in and kissed her stomach, the action reverent. Everything was so slow, so purposeful. And it made her feel desperate. Made her feel like escaping her skin.

But she couldn't. She couldn't leave him, didn't want to leave him, but she wasn't sure she would survive this, either.

He pushed her pants down her hips, her thighs, her underwear going down with them, leaving her bare to him. She'd been naked in front of him so many times, but this was different. It was deeper. She was bare to her soul.

He leaned in, his lips hot on her clit, his tongue sliding unerringly over her, sending a spike of pleasure through her, something intense to hold to. To drown out the thundering of her heart, the swollen feeling in her chest.

Too many feelings. At least with the physical, she could ignore the emotional.

This was what she needed.

He cupped her ass, held her against his mouth as he lavished her with attention, worshipped her with his lips and tongue, pushing her to the edge, pushing her to the brink of sanity.

He pulled back and looked at her, his dark eyes glittering. She looked away and dropped to her knees. "Austin... let me." She struggled with the buttons on his shirt, spread the fabric wide and leaned in, licking his skin, tasting him, relishing him.

She worked his belt, freed his cock from his underwear, squeezing him gently. "Tell me what to do. Tell me," she said, waiting for that hand to tighten in her hair, to force her head down. To demand she suck him.

He didn't.

"Whatever you want."

"Tell me." Because showing was too revealing. It was too much.

He cupped her chin, holding her face steady, forcing her to look at him. "Give me what you want," he said, the command one she couldn't deny. Wouldn't deny.

She lowered her head and drew him deep into her mouth. And she was lost in him. This was what she wanted. Austin. His body. Him. Always.

Her heart sped up. She couldn't have him, though, not

really. Not now. Not ever. It wasn't supposed to be this way. But it was.

He pulled her head away suddenly, his grip in her hair hard. The flash of pain she desperately craved, a momentary reprieve from the pain in her chest.

"Not like that," he said, his breath ragged. "I need you. I need to be in you."

He bent and scooped her into his arms, picking her up and carrying her to the living room.

"I can walk," she said, except she wasn't sure if she could. Her muscles were trembling, her legs boneless. She was on the edge of something. An orgasm, an emotional breakdown. She wasn't sure which. She wasn't sure it mattered which, or if the two were even different things anymore.

"You don't have to." He set her down on the couch and got on his knees in front of her, wrapping her legs around his hips, pausing to pull a condom from his wallet and sheathe himself before pushing inside of her. Slowly. So slowly she felt each inch, felt the full impact of what it was to be filled by him, utterly, completely.

"Oh, yes." He lowered his head and tugged her up against him, forcing himself deeper.

He kissed her then, desperate and wild, not the slow, sensual movements he'd treated her to before. In this, he'd lost his control. But he'd stolen hers right along with it.

She needed to resist. Needed to retreat. But she couldn't. So instead she wrapped her arms around his neck and met his eyes, a feeling so big, so impossible, so painful that at first she tried to push it away as it built in her chest.

She wanted to hide from him, but then his eyes met hers, unveiled emotion in them, and she was caught, transfixed.

Because she could see the desperation in his eyes. The need. For her. She could see how broken he was, way down deep. How he was trying to heal it with this, with the meeting of their bodies. Because the only way they made sense was together. The only way they seemed to make a whole person whose broken edges seemed to be just fine was when they came together.

She understood why he was trying to fix himself this way, because she felt it, too. But she was afraid that when he fixed himself, it might break her to pieces. But she didn't want to hide from him, even if it destroyed her.

This was what she felt, and she hadn't wanted him to be a part of this, because it was too real, too deep to share. But now she saw it in him. Felt it pour out over her. Their pain. Their pleasure. Their need.

And suddenly, she realized she wanted this, whatever had brought him to this point.

She wanted to be there for him. To shoulder it. And it didn't feel like too much. It didn't feel like something she couldn't add to her already immense list of burdens.

This was Austin. And like he'd shouldered her problems, she wanted to take on his. She wanted to catch him when he fell. She wanted to ease the weight that he was carrying with him.

How had she not seen it before? Just how heavy it was inside of him. How had she never realized that he was having just as hard of a time breathing as she was?

So she held him now, because it was what she could do.

He bent and kissed her, fierce and hard, breaking the eye contact. And she kissed him back. Pouring every ounce of that emotion that was building in her chest into him. Because she wasn't sure if she knew what to call it, wasn't sure she would know how to say what it was. Because this was beyond her. Like nothing she'd ever felt before. Like nothing she'd ever imagined she might have.

This man, who managed to touch parts of her she'd thought she'd blocked off from the world. And she wanted him there. She wanted him inside of her. She wanted him to know her. The beauty, the ugliness, the boring. All of it. The poverty-stricken girl she'd been. Whoever she was now. Her anger, her grief, her joy, she wanted it to be his. And she wanted his in return.

Because that was the thing. It was too heavy for him to carry alone. And hers was too heavy for her. But if they could just share it, then they could go on.

She was ready now.

She needed Austin. She needed this. These things she'd never known she wanted, escape she'd never known she could find.

"Katy," he said, his voice rough, his face buried in her neck. "Oh, Katy. I need you. I need you."

"Me, too," she said, kissing his temple. "Me, too, Austin."

"Come for me, baby. I can't last. Come with me."

He put his hand between them, slid his thumb over her clit in time with his thrusts and sent her straight over the edge at the same time he lost it. She could feel him pulsing inside of her, felt his pleasure deep within her, joining with hers, pushing her higher, further than she'd ever thought possible.

She clung to him, her nails digging into his skin as she rode out her orgasm. As she tried to be strong for both of them while he shuddered out his pleasure, his muscles shaking so hard she thought he might break apart.

Not while he was in her arms. Not while she held him.

Slowly, he came back to himself, and when he did, he moved away from her. All too soon. "I can't..." He let out a harsh breath. "I...don't know what happened just now."

"We made love," she said, feeling completely destroyed by the experience. A leveled house after the storm.

"I need to... I have to go back to work."

"Austin?"

"I just need to go."

That was rich. *He* was running now. He'd forced her to lay it all bare, to make love nice and sweet when she was scared to death, and now he was the one trying to cover up.

"What happened?"

"What makes you think anything happened?"

"The fact that you came in and demanded that. The look on your face when you came in... You seemed upset."

He put his hand over his face. He was sitting, naked on the floor, a marble statue in a pose of regret.

"I wasn't upset," he said.

"Really? Is that how you're going to play it? You were totally fine."

"Yes," he growled. "I was fine. I was...happy, for lack of a better word. Do you know where I just came from?"

"No."

"My office. Where I took great pleasure in telling my father that I was going to see him taken for everything he owns." He stood and paced the length of the floor, pushing his hands through his hair. "And he...he said something. And do you know what I did?"

"What?" she asked, feeling hollow. Sick.

"I wrapped my fingers around his throat and it took every

ounce of my control not to squeeze tight and end him then and there. I want to kill him, Katy. Honest to God, I do."

"But you won't."

"No. Because then I wouldn't get to toy with him any-more. Then I wouldn't get the pleasure of watching his life burn around him. Do you know what I discovered today? I am so much more like him than I ever realized."

"What?" she asked. "How can you stand here and say something like that when you just told me you wanted him dead?"

"He likes it, you know? He likes it when he realizes that he has the power. When he can take it and lord it over some-one. See the fear in their eyes. Today, I did that to him. And I liked it. Not a single part of me recoiled from that."

"Because of what he did," she said. "Because of what he's done to countless women. To my sister. Your friend. That's why you enjoyed it. Hell, Austin, I'd wrap my fingers around his throat, too."

"It's not the same. It's not. Do you know how sobering it is to look that man in the eyes and see nothing but myself staring back at me? It's not him I hate. It's me."

"Don't hate yourself, Austin. You haven't done anything."

"I haven't done anything? I let a woman die, Katy. I let her sink into utter despair, because I was too damn comfort-able to look past my own life and into hers. But I have a feel-ing it was even more than that. What if I just didn't care?"

"That's not it."

"Isn't it? That night we met at the hotel? It had nothing to do with you. You were a stranger, and I took you and used you—"

"I used you right back. Don't you dare try to change the story now, Austin Treffen. I will not listen to it."

"The only reason I made love to you just now was to prove that I could," he said, his voice flat. And just like that, he stole it all from her. Everything it meant. Everything she'd thought she'd felt pass between them.

"I didn't need it," she said, angry now, because he'd forced her to give so much, all so he could salve his conscience. "Didn't I tell you I didn't want your guilt? Not in the form of cash, and not from your body."

"So…what? You'd rather I just bend you over the table and force you? Wrap my hands around your throat like I did him?"

"It's not the same. I ask for it. I beg. Look what I begged you for. The first time and every time after."

"As if you even know what you wanted. You were just a virgin."

"Don't you dare try to pull that on me. I don't know why you're spoiling for a fight, but obviously, you have a problem here. And I can also see that you're being an asshole so I'll write you off, since you've clearly written yourself off. But guess what, asshole. I love you."

Her words hung between them in the silence. And no matter how much she wished they would, they just didn't fade. They were so very there. So very raw and true, and she hadn't even realized they were until she'd said them.

"I do," she said again. "I love you."

"You can't…"

"I do. And, you know…I think I have from the beginning, which seems ridiculous, and yet…I knew you. That moment I saw you in your father's office building, I knew you. You're right, Austin. We don't make sense. You said that once. That what we wanted didn't make any sense. And it's true. It doesn't. Not when we're apart. Together we make perfect sense. And it's not just the sex. You're this guy who came from a world where everything glittered and you had to learn the hard way that not everything does. And I never...I never saw anything beautiful until you. You're the one who showed me that sometimes you can trust someone. That there are people who will help. Who will try and carry your burdens with you. You're the first person to ever do anything like that for me. You make me believe in good things and...and for someone like me, from the place I'm from...that's huge."

He laughed. Hollow and bitter. "How can I make you believe in something good when I'm not sure I believe in anything good anymore? How the hell can you stand there and look at me like the sun rises and sets on me when you know what I am? When you know I let your sister die. When you know that I have the same tendencies that that...monster has inside of me. I am not the man to share your burdens with. I can't even be bothered to deal with someone's burdens for five minutes, even if it would keep her from jumping to her death."

"You didn't let her die. You didn't know," she said, her throat tightening. "And you aren't your father."

"Just like you aren't your parents?" he asked, his words a slap across her face. "Like you never hid in a room and got high to escape your life? I'm not my father just like you aren't them, is that it? Let's just face it, Katy. We're fucked up down to our blood and there's no real way to escape that. Did you think we were going to set up a house together and get married or something? Did you think we'd have kids and go to the burbs and pretend none of this ever happened?"

"I...I..." She couldn't speak around the knot in her throat. She felt sucker punched. By the fact that he'd used her confession against her. That he'd betrayed her like that.

No one else knew about the drugs. No one. She'd trusted him with that. It had been a bigger leap of faith than letting him tie her up had ever been, and he'd just used it against her.

"It's not happening. Ever. I don't want that from you. I'm not even capable of it. I might keep you as a sex slave. What do you think about that?"

"Shut up, Austin," she said. "Just shut up."

"Why? Because you built up a fantasy that doesn't exist and now you want to hold on to it? Not my problem. I never promised you a damn thing."

"No, you didn't. But this? This is crap. This isn't you. This is... You're running from something and you're acting like a teenage boy who's afraid and can't admit it. Trying to hide what you want because it scares you. Getting pissed when you can't deny it. You're getting angry when what you really are is terrified. And I want to know why."

"You think you have some sort of insight into my emotions just because you got into my pants? Not even close."

"No, you know what? This isn't you. I have spent every night in your bed, I've told you everything about me, I've held you in some of your lowest moments, and so I think I have a pretty good idea of who you are. And this isn't it. So tell me right now what has you afraid."

"You want to know what has me afraid?" he asked. "I am afraid of turning into a sociopath. I'm afraid I'm halfway there, and the only way to protect anyone in my life is to make sure I cut the head off the source, and do everything I can to right what he's done. Because maybe then I won't have the chance to embrace the ugly inside of me."

"That's not it. You aren't him. You know you aren't. And I love you."

"And so many people love him, you stupid, stupid girl," he said, venom in his every word.

The words hit hard. Mushroomed inside of her chest, blossoming like a bullet, leaving shrapnel behind she didn't think she'd ever dig out.

Of course, to him she was just a stupid, silly girl. A girl from nowhere, with no education. Good for a sex slave and nothing else.

No. He doesn't mean it. He's afraid. It scared him, too. That's all.

"My mother loved him," he continued. "My sister. Me. Sarah. Because you know she probably loved him, too. How do you think she got sucked into it? Why do you think she left Hunter? How do you think all of this started? Love. And all she was willing to do for it. Don't throw those words around like they're a gift that can only be given to the deserving, because that just isn't true."

"So what? That's what scares you? The love thing?"

"No. It's what loving me will do to you. You shouldn't. I don't want it."

"Oh. Well, then. I guess... I really think I should probably go. And I don't know where that leaves this...the stuff with Sarah."

"You can stay here," he said.

"No, idiot, I can't because you just broke my effing heart and I'm not going to let you walk over the pieces. I have pride, or something—I don't really know what—but…I'm done. I'm not staying here and taking half. Or nothing. I'm not going to be your sex slave, even though I know full well you don't want one and you're just being full of crap."

She walked through to the kitchen and started collecting her clothes, putting them on as quickly as possible. Because being naked in front of him now felt stupid.

"You can send my stuff. I'm not waiting around." She clasped her bra and tugged her top over her head.

She headed to the door and paused. "Do you want to know how I know you don't just want me to be your sex slave?" He didn't say anything. "I'll tell you. It's not because you came in here and made love to me. Not because you were gentle and sweet this time. Not because you put my pleasure first, like always. Because you looked into my eyes and I saw myself there. It's because you don't get off on power. You like control. Yeah, you get off on it. But only if I get off on it, too. You don't like my fear. You've never asked for it. So, guess what. I think you're a different sort of beast than your dad. A beast, yes, but a different sort. If you need anything, any information regarding Sarah? Have one of your friends call me. There's still work to do, and I'm not stopping until it's done."

She walked out the door and down the hall, and she didn't start crying until she was safely inside the taxi, with no idea where to tell the driver to go.

Because there was nowhere. There was no one.

No one but Austin. And he didn't want to be there for her anymore.

Chapter Thirteen

"What are we doing here?" Alex asked, curling his lip as he looked at Austin. Austin didn't care about his friend's disapproval. He was too drunk to care about much of anything.

And that was a state of bliss he hadn't been in since before Katy had left.

"Drinking," Austin said, lifting his glass to his lips and knocking back the contents.

"No," Hunter said, "*you're* drinking. I'm pretty sure that was mine. I could have used that, maybe."

Hunter lifted the empty glass and the bartender nodded, sliding a newly filled one over to his end of the bar.

"Your parents' divorce is all over the news," Alex said, looking down at his phone and tapping the screen, pulling up the headlines that were dominating the society pages and entertainment sites. "And it's ugly."

"Yeah, no joke it's ugly," Austin said, his arms resting on the bar, his head starting to droop. He was pretty drunk. There was no denying it. And Alex's voice was a lot more annoying than usual. Not that it was usually annoying. It was just that anyone's voice, anyone's presence, was too much for him right now.

He should have thought of that before he called Alex and Hunter down here for... Hell, he didn't even know what. Advice? An intervention?

"I'm representing my mother in the divorce. So it's going to get uglier. Trust me. Because I'm gonna make damn sure it's ugly."

"And I imagine your father's upcoming honor and interview will be marred by the events," Alex said.

"Here's hoping," Austin said, lifting his glass in salute.

"Is that why you're trying to suck down all the booze on the Upper West Side?" Hunter asked.

"Why the hell else?"

"That's a good question," Alex said, looking down at his phone still, scrolling through the Treffen news, it seemed. "What happened to Sarah's sister? She was staying with you, wasn't she?"

"Yes," he said, grinding his teeth. "But she's not staying with me now."

"I see," Alex said, setting his phone down on the counter. "And is there any reason in particular?"

"Because she loves me," Austin said. "She fucking *loves* me. Have you ever heard anything stupider than that?"

"Other than you saying *stupider?*" Hunter asked. "No."

"Right?" Austin looked at his empty glass and frowned. "I don't know what the hell her problem is. She *loves me*. What the hell is that?"

"It must be your sparkling personality," Hunter said.

"Or your wit," added Alex.

"Your money," Hunter said.

"Your penthouse is nice." This from Alex.

"I don't want her to love me."

Hunter grimaced. "Of course not. I hate when women say they love me. One time both women said they loved me after— Anyway, it was awkward. There was a cat fight. That's...actually not a bad memory." Something about Hunter's humor rang false, and Austin wasn't in the mood to analyze.

"How is that helpful?" Austin growled.

"I don't know. Did you honestly expect me to come here and be helpful about your love issues? Everything I know about love I could write on...well, nothing. I don't know a damn thing about it, and that's not an accident. If you'd like a manual on sexual positions, however, I could work something up real quick."

"I'm good," Austin said, holding up his hand.

"Not anymore, clearly," said Alex.

"We were fine until she said she loved me. What the hell was I supposed to do with that? She's Sarah's sister. There's all this stuff with her sister, being involved with the hooking and my dad and whatever other power games he was playing—is playing—with all these other women. And now here I am, wanting nothing more than to tie Katy up and put her over my knee and spank her. Freud would have a field day with this, you know."

"Dammit, Austin," Alex said, "you should have warned us you were going to be oversharing. I need to be drunker before you start telling us about your sex life."

"I could do details," Hunter said. "If they're on offer."

"No, they are not," Austin said.

"If you change your mind..."

"I don't want her to love me," he said again. "I don't... Why the hell would she love me?"

"You're repeating yourself," Hunter said.

"I know. But I still haven't gotten an answer. I need an answer."

"What did you say when she said she loved you?" Alex asked.

"I told her she was stupid. And she is. I'm... I let Sarah die," he said, something breaking inside of him, something catching in his throat. "I was the closest person to the situation. I should have seen it. Part of me thinks I did, but I didn't want to because...because it would have ruined my life if I'd listened. If I'd let Jason lose his position in society then, what would have happened to my career?"

There was more to the story. But he couldn't say it. Couldn't talk about that last call. That last voice mail. He'd ignored that call. He hadn't listened to it until after she'd jumped.

I really need you. I need to talk to you. I don't think anyone else can help me.

And by then it was too late.

Too damn late.

"You didn't really know, though," Alex said.

"She said...she said, 'Austin, I really need your help. It's about your dad.' And I remember. So clearly her asking me that. For help. To meet up and talk sometime. And I didn't like the way she looked, or the tone in her voice. I knew it was going to be a big deal. I knew it would interrupt my life. I had just gotten into law school and I was so excited about it and I didn't want...problems."

"But you didn't know how it was. I mean, you didn't know what was happening," Hunter said.

"I thought she was having problems at her job. I didn't

think, you know, she was having an issue with my dad having sex with her."

Hunter frowned, deep lines bracketing his mouth. "That's enough. Those are details I don't really need." All of the teasing, the humor, disappeared from his tone.

"It's the truth, though. And that's the thing. I didn't want her details. I was too busy. I was too wrapped up in myself, and...and Katy wants to love me? I don't deserve that," he said, a lump rising in his throat. "I can't accept it."

"Why? Because you need to punish yourself forever?" Alex asked.

"Is Sarah dead forever, Alex?" Alex nodded slowly, his mouth set into a grim line. "Then yeah, forever sounds about right."

Katy walked through the door of the hotel room and unzipped her hoodie and dumped it—and her plastic bag full of cans of spray paint—onto the bed.

Her vengeance effort today had been small, somewhat illegal and a whole lot stupid. And she didn't care.

But what she'd spray-painted on the windows of Treffen, Smith and Howell—Judgment Day Is Coming, Jason—in bold red letters had, perhaps, not been her wisest move.

Though it had been satisfying. It had made her feel active. It had helped soothe some of her pain.

Thank God, most New Yorkers either didn't care what she was up to, or assumed she was involved in performance art. She'd worked in a hurry and scurried back to the hotel as quickly as she could.

But now her high was receding. A petty strike that did

nothing more than give Jason Treffen a slight chill of fore-boding didn't do much to aid her in lasting satisfaction.

Of course, her mood wasn't helped by the fact that she'd never been so miserable. And she was being miserable on Austin's dime, which sucked even more. But she'd remembered some very pertinent details from the vampire brothel room, and she'd managed to get herself installed there by his mysterious friend, whose name she never did catch.

Still, here she was, in this place that was haunted by the ghost of the passion they'd shared, trying to deal with her heartbreak. Trying to deal with what the hell had happened to her since that first party at Treffen's.

Everything in her had changed. Absolutely everything.

Who would have thought she'd find freedom sometime after she let a man tie her hands. Not just any man, though—Austin. With him she'd seen the potential for something, not normal exactly, but something that was right. For him, for her.

Sometime during her affair with him she'd forgotten about running off to the West Coast. She'd forgotten about leaving the Treffens, and New York, behind.

With him, happiness hadn't been a hypothetical thing. A future where her own desires and feelings mattered hadn't been a hypothetical thing. Hadn't been a hazy, gilt-edged fantasy. It had been her reality. It had been grounded in something possible. In a person. In him.

And losing him…

Losing him hurt. It was the kind of pain she'd never endured before without numbing it. With something. Work. Denial. Drugs.

But that was something else she'd learned with him. Not

all pain was bad. Some pain was necessary to experience other feelings. To experience good feelings.

She'd been numb for so long, she hadn't realized that it wasn't just pain she was missing. It was pleasure. It was excitement. Happiness. Aspirations. Hope.

She'd had nothing but black, cold anger. The kind that took, that consumed without giving back.

And now she had…everything. All of the feelings. Even the ones she didn't want, but…she felt human. She felt whole for the first time in…maybe ever. She didn't want to fold in on herself, or blunt it, or hide from it.

Because that was something else. For the first time, she really, really felt like she deserved more than she was getting. She felt like she was worth the love she'd asked for, the love she'd offered, and she was ready to experience all of the negative that came with having it rejected. She was ready to embrace her righteous anger and her heartbreak, and the love she still had for a man who didn't think he deserved it.

A man who was nothing more than a terrified little boy.

And that was something that made her feel proud.

Because she might have been rejected. She might be hurt, heartbroken and, hell yes, afraid, but she'd been brave enough to take a chance.

She was braver than Austin. But maybe someday he'd grow a pair and realize that he loved her, too.

She just hoped it was sooner rather than later because this heartbreak thing sucked so bad.

It wasn't as satisfying to feel emotionally well-adjusted when you had to be adjusted with bad feelings. She would much rather be in love with a man who loved her back while being well-adjusted.

She lay down on the bed and pulled her knees up to her chest. And imagined what it was like to fall asleep next to Austin. To feel like she wasn't alone in the world.

And she let all of the pain, all of the grief, for herself, for Austin, for Sarah, flood over her. All of the tears she hadn't cried when Sarah had died. All of the misery she hadn't allowed herself to feel, all came through now.

She lay there and grieved ten years of loss. Of life. Of love.

And when it was over, for the first time, she felt some light pierce through the darkness inside of her.

She'd spent ten years living for someone's death. And after all that time…she was finally ready, really ready, for life. Without drugs, without self-medication.

She only wished it didn't have to be a life without Austin.

The past week had been hell. And then some. He hated his penthouse because it felt so empty. He hated his chest because it wasn't empty. He hated himself because…because he had for ten years and nothing had changed.

He realized it now, so that was different.

But other than that, nothing had changed.

Except that everything had. Except the entire landscape of his soul was rearranged and felt completely barren without Katy in his life.

Because every breath was a struggle without her.

She was everything he'd never known he needed, and sex wasn't even the half of it.

She loved him. He didn't even love himself. Hell, he didn't *like* himself.

But she loved him.

He'd let her sister die, and she loved him.

He had to see her again. He had to tell her. He had to make her understand. So that she wouldn't love him. Or to see if she still would.

He'd been pissed to find out she was staying at Logan's hotel. Pissed because he didn't want her anywhere near that bastard while she was vulnerable. Logan was a friend, in a strange way, but he wouldn't trust his sister with him, and he certainly wouldn't trust his lover anywhere near the man. Logan had changed in recent years, but that didn't erase his past. There was a reason the rooms of Black Book were brothelesque, after all.

Austin leaned against the elevator wall and waited for it to arrive at the suite. Their suite.

He closed his eyes, erotic images flashing through his mind.

Together we make perfect sense.

Her words caressed his soul, then stabbed his heart.

Because she was right. Apart from her, he didn't make any sense. But with her? He felt like he might find something real in himself. Something that wasn't at all like his father.

He was an idiot. He'd thought because he wanted to tie her hands, that because he enjoyed control in the bedroom, that spoke about deeper, sicker things he had in common with his father.

That because Katy was Sarah's sister the parallel was undeniable.

But that wasn't the thing that scared him most. It was the fact that his father had such disregard for other people. It was the ignored phone call that haunted him, that made him wonder if he were any different.

The elevator doors opened and he walked to the hotel-room door and knocked.

"What are you doing here?" Katy's voice was muffled through the door, but her words were unmistakable.

"I need to tell you something."

"That's too vague," she said. "If you want to tell me more about how stupid I am, you can march on."

"No, that's not it. I need to tell you the truth. I need to figure out if... Just open the door."

The door cracked and he saw one bright blue eye glaring at him. "I opened it."

"Let me in, Katy."

"I already did. And then you rejected me. Give me a good reason."

He pushed the door open and hauled her into his arms, kissing her deep and hard. Because no matter what happened after today, he needed to have kissed her at least one more time. Maybe if he had this one kiss, the rest of his life wouldn't feel so dry and lonely without her.

But he doubted it.

She pushed at his chest, and when they parted, they were both breathing hard.

"What the hell?" she asked.

"I needed that."

"If you're here for more sex you're out of luck. I'm not screwing around with a guy that calls me stupid and tells me he doesn't want my love."

"I lied," he said, the words scraping his throat raw. "You're not stupid. I never thought so. And I *do* want your love, but...I don't deserve it."

"What?"

"Sarah came to me. She told me she wanted to talk to me about some problems she was having with my father. I put her off. I ignored her because I didn't want to deal with her problems. She called me that night. And I ignored the call. What if I would have picked up, Katy? What if I could have just talked to her one more time…?"

"Austin—" Her throat tightened, her stomach twisting tight. "Do you know how many times I wonder the same thing? I hate Jason for driving her to that point. I hate him. I'll never forgive him. Ever. But do you know what? I don't think any of us could have stopped her."

"You don't know that."

"No," she said, tears sliding down her cheeks. "I don't. But she was the one who had the choice. I blame your father. I do, don't get me wrong. But in the end, that choice. The choice to end her life instead of fighting. Fighting for herself."

"What if she just needed someone to tell her to stay," he said.

"You're assuming she would have told you what was happening."

"You should be angry with me," he said. "I'm so angry with me. Why aren't you?"

"Maybe I should be angry with you. But over a decision you made not to answer a call ten years ago? I could waste my life being angry, Austin. And I have. At Hunter for not being a better boyfriend. At my parents for not being the support system parents should be. At Sarah. For jumping. For not fighting harder. At some point, though, I want more for myself than that. I want more than anger as management for all the feelings I don't want to deal with. I want more than a life consumed by ugliness. I love my sister and I always will, but at some point I want my life to be about more than her death. Don't you want that?"

"How?" he asked. "How, when I feel like…no matter what I do, I will hurt people. It's a part of me. I'm part of my father. I wanted to be him from the time I was a kid. And that all changed when I saw the way he responded to Sarah's death, but…part of me wonders if it's just too damn late. If I started down a specific path, and now I'll never be able to change direction."

"You stupid man. That's taking a metaphor way too seriously."

"What?" He felt like he'd been sucker punched.

"Walking on paths. I started my life as the child of junkies, who nearly became a junkie. I spent the last few years fueling my anger. Hell, I've been fueling it the last few days. You may have seen the art added to your father's building in the news."

"I knew that had to be you."

"Naturally." She let out a long breath. "But I don't want it to be my life anymore, because I've found something I want more. I want to be with you. And I don't care that you're a Treffen, because your name doesn't mean anything to me. I didn't know your name when I met you, but I knew you. I wanted you. More than revenge. More than anything."

"That's how I felt the first time I saw you. And the first time we were together…that was the first time I've ever been that…honest with a woman. I'd had sex before, obviously. But that was the first time I'd ever been able to expose what I wanted. But doing that was easier than this."

"Okay, I'm waiting for an example of what 'this' is."

"Telling you how much I blame myself for what happened. And asking…begging you to love me anyway. I don't deserve it. But I need it."

"Why?" she asked. "Just to soothe your conscience, or because you actually love me, too? Because I've had enough giving without getting back. I need more. I need everything. And if you can't give me that then…then it doesn't matter if I love you."

He held her arms tight, held his breath. "It matters."

"Take a chance, Austin. Tell me your secrets before I tell you mine."

He closed his eyes, his need to cling to his control slipping away as he realized that holding on to it would mean losing her. Like giving an order he had to trust she would obey, he had to take a chance now.

"I love you," he said. "Every broken piece of you, with every broken piece of me."

She broke free from his hold and wrapped her arms around his neck. "I love you, too. Still. Always. Even though I didn't know it then, I loved you all the way until I met you. And now I feel everything…so deep and real. And I don't need to run from it. I don't need to handle it by doing drugs. I don't need anything but you."

"I feel the same way. I've been…afraid to want anything for so long because I was afraid I would want the wrong things. That I would turn into him. But…as long as it's you I want, I know it can't be wrong. Because what I want always seems to fit with what you want."

"Except when you broke my heart. Jackass."

"Scared jackass."

"Yeah. That."

"I'm so sorry. But I honestly didn't know what I wanted. Not until I met you. Not until I lost you. And then I was so afraid I pushed you away because…I was afraid if you touched me I would poison you."

"Idiot. You healed me."

"I did?"

"I wouldn't even let myself feel pain, Austin. I was so closed off I didn't feel much of anything. You tore it all open. You made me bleed. And I am so damn thankful."

"You make it sound like it hurt."

"It did. It does. But life hurts sometimes. More than I realized. But it's so much more amazing that I realized, too. And love is so much bigger than the rest of the feelings. Than the anger, and the hate, and the pain. My love for you wins."

"Oh, Katy, my love for you wins, too."

"You have no idea how happy I am to hear that. I don't know how you could ever think you're a man who doesn't care about others. How you could ever think you'd be like Jason. Austin, you care so much it bleeds from you. It bled onto me. You taught me to feel."

"I did that, huh?"

"Yes."

He kissed her. "I do care, Katy. I care so much. I never wanted her to be hurt. I regret so much—"

"And that right there separates you from your father, from men like him."

"I'm going to work to get justice for her, I swear it."

She nodded. "I know you will. But you know, hurting Jason isn't the only thing I'm living for anymore. Fixing things for other people isn't the only thing I have now. I have you. I have us. Life doesn't feel as heavy now, not with you to share it with."

"We could still go to the South. Or California. Whatever you want," he said. "Whatever you need."

"We could stay right here," she said. "I don't feel like I need to run away from myself anymore. Myself is perfectly happy. Right here with you. Engaged in a battle for love, and vigilante justice."

"It will be legal justice," he said.

"I forgot. You're all married to the legal system."

"Yes, I am."

"You aren't going to rat me out for being a vandal, are you?"

"I think there's too much reasonable doubt to take it to trial."

"I love you, Lawyer-man." She leaned in and kissed his nose.

"I'm ready to prosecute you to the fullest extent of the law."

"Maybe you should just stick to giving me commands. I think you're better at that."

"And do you still need to take commands from me?"

"Not any more than you need to give them. I'm not afraid anymore. But it doesn't mean I don't...enjoy the way we are together. The way we've been together. I just...think maybe I don't need it as therapy at this point."

"Well, that is good to hear. I suppose I shouldn't retire those ties I keep by the bed?"

"Not on your life," she said. "I think we'll find use for those for a long time."

"Normally I'd be telling you to get on your knees. But maybe I'll get on mine first." He did, his heart beating heavy, his hands shaking.

Everything he'd asked her to do, everything they'd been through, and somehow, she always made him shake.

"You know me better than anyone else. From the moment I met you I haven't been able to hide anything. I don't have a ring, but I want to ask you this now. Will you marry me? After this is over, will you marry me? Let's make new headlines. Let's make a new history for our family names. For us."

"Yes, Austin," she said. "Yes."

He closed his eyes, his heart full. All of the skeletons had been unearthed. Everything was being brought to light. And for the first time in ten years, he felt unbound.

He felt free.

"Thank God for that. Now, baby…it's your turn. Get on your knees."

Epilogue

*As a Lifetime Achievement Award Looms,
Treffen's Life Begins to Crumble!*

Shock waves went through Manhattan social circles when
Lenore Treffen, wife of Jason Treffen for more than thirty
years, demanded a divorce during Treffen's celebrated
New Year's bash. What's even more scandalous? The couple's son has taken his mother's case, and will be representing her during court proceedings.

The reconciliation we all hoped for barely lasted from
"Have Yourself a Merry Little Christmas" to "Auld Lang
Syne."

With court documents being kept under wraps, and
tempers turning ugly on both sides, we wonder what this
means both for the future of the family and for Jason
Treffen's illustrious career.

The pristine Treffen legacy is certainly showing some
wear and tear...and we wonder if this will make the Jason
Treffen Special all that much more interesting! We know
one thing for certain—we'll be watching as the drama
unfolds.

"You finally spent the money."

"Charitable donations hardly count as spending money," Katy said, giving her fiancé the evil eye.

Her fiancé. She really could get used to that. About the time she did, though, she imagined he'd be her husband.

That sounded even better.

She'd just come into his office, flushed and excited over gaining nonprofit status, her enjoyment of organization and planning put to far better use now than planning parties for Jason Treffen.

"True," Austin said, wrapping his arm around her. "The Sarah Michaels Foundation is something I'd gladly sink my life savings into. And I'm very happy it's where you put my dad's blood money."

"Me, too," she said.

The foundation would provide career, financial and personal counseling for women in difficult situations, with a focus on women who wanted to leave the sex industry. They were still working toward ultimate justice for Sarah, but at least in this there was some closure.

At least with the foundation there was some action that wasn't purely destructive. With this, she could create something with Sarah's legacy. Help other people, not just tear down Jason Treffen.

"I don't ever want anyone to feel so hopeless, so ashamed, that they do what she did," Katy continued. "I want them to know that there's always a future."

Austin smiled at her, bent down and kissed her on the lips. "That seems to be the lesson you're out to teach everyone."

"Oh, yeah?"

"Yes. It's what you taught me. That there's light at the end of the tunnel. More than that, that I deserved to step out into it. That there was a future past the pain."

"What do you know? You taught me the same thing." She wrapped her arms around his waist and buried her face in his chest, taking in his scent. It was such a wonderful thing to stand there with him. To know that even on this side of revenge there was happiness. New life.

"You'll redeem your name, Austin Treffen. I firmly believe that you'll do the world much more good than he did harm."

"With your help, Katy."

"It's true. I will be a Treffen in about eight months."

"You will. And you'll have almost single-handedly redeemed both names. Sarah's name, and mine."

"It's fair, because I feel like you saved me."

"I think we saved each other, love," he said.

"You know, I think you're right about that. We're two halves of a whole. We make a lot more sense when we're together."

"Good thing we're going to be together forever, then."

Katy laughed and looked out at the sun shining on the skyline, drenching everything in light. "It's a good thing, Austin. It's a very good thing."

★ ★ ★ ★ ★

IT wasn't the first time a man had propositioned her. But it was the
first time she'd felt a burst of flame lick over her when he did, and
she was terribly afraid he knew that, too. That he felt the same
slap of heat.

She couldn't let that happen, it was impossible, so she shoved
it aside.

"Is that caveman code for 'sleep with me so I can put you back
in your proper place'?" she asked, cool and challenging and back
on familiar ground, because she knew this routine. She could
handle this. Jason Treffen had taught her well, one painful lesson
at a time. "Because you should know before you try, dragging
me off by my hair somewhere won't end the way you think it
will. I can promise you that."

Hunter looked intrigued and his head canted slightly to one
side, but that wolfish regard of his never wavered—bright and
hot and knowing. Reaching much too far inside her.

"I don't want to drag you off somewhere by your hair and have my way with you, Ms. Brook."

The smile on her lips turned mocking, but she was more concerned with the sudden long, slow thump of her heart and the heavy, wet heat low in her belly. "Because you're not that kind of guy?"

There was something more than predatory in his eyes then, hard and hot, a dark knowing in the curve of his mouth that connected with that deep drumroll inside her, making it her pulse, her breath, her worst fear come true.

"I'm absolutely that kind of guy. But I told you. You have to ask me nicely."

He smiled, as if he was the one in control. And she couldn't allow it.

"No," she said, furious that it came out like a whisper, thin and uncertain. His smile deepened for a moment, like a promise.

"Your loss," he murmured, and that aching fire swelled inside her, nearly bursting.

And then he laughed again, dismissing her, and turned to go. Again. For good this time, she understood, and she couldn't let that happen.

Zoe had no choice.

"I wouldn't do that, Mr. Grant." She didn't know why the dryness in her mouth seemed to translate into something like trembling everywhere else when she'd known before she'd approached him that it would probably come to this. She made herself smile. "I know about Sarah."

* * *

*The second step to revenge in the **Fifth Avenue** trilogy.*
Hunter has the money...
July 2014

EXP430383TR

"You sound like you hate the man."

"*Hate* isn't the right word. But I'd like to see what he does
with an interview. What you do with it." He raised his beer bottle
to his lips, his eyes hard.

She straightened, flashed him one of her glittering smiles.
"Well, stay tuned, then. It airs live on March twentieth." And
without waiting for a response, she turned and walked away from
him, her shoulders thrown back, her chin held high.

Alex watched her leave. For a moment there he'd considered
telling her the truth about Jason Treffen, but then he'd thankfully
thought better of it. It was hardly cocktail party chitchat, and
he didn't know her well enough to trust her with that particular
powder keg. Not yet, anyway.

She was ambitious, he got that, and tough. He was pretty sure
she had the balls to bring down Treffen on live television if she
wanted to.

The question was, did she? Could he convince her? He possessed a savage need to see Treffen with his world crumbling around him while everyone else saw it, too. No longer would the man fool everyone into believing he was such a damned saint. They would know him not just as a sinner, but as a devil.

Austin had already exposed Treffen to his family with the help of Sarah's sister, Katy. Hunter was working on ousting Treffen from his law firm. And Alex had been charged with showing the world what he really was: a monster who used the women he claimed to be saving. Who damned them to lives of shame, scandal and sin. Everything in Alex ached to see Jason publicly exposed—and he would do whatever it took to make it happen.

Including use Chelsea in whatever way he could. The woman was cold. He didn't feel so much as a flicker of guilt for using her. But he did feel a certain amount of frustration. *Sexual* frustration. He wanted Chelsea Maxwell in bed, beneath him, those gray-green eyes turned to molten-silver with desire. He wanted her haughty little smile to become a desperate begging kiss, to turn her tinkling laugh into a breathy sigh of pleasure and need.

He wanted to be the one to do it. To shatter her icy control and make her melt. For him.

* * *

The third and final step to revenge in the **Fifth Avenue** *trilogy.*
Alex has the power...
August 2014

HARLEQUIN®

Presents®

Revenge and seduction intertwine...

Behind the Scenes of *Fifth Avenue:*
Read on for an exclusive interview with Maisey Yates!

It's such an exciting world to create. Did you discuss it with the other writers?
There was a lot of discussion! Thankfully we live in a world of Skype and FaceTime and we were able to spend time not just emailing, but having face-to-face discussions, in spite of the fact that we're in different states and countries. I love technology.

How does writing a trilogy with other authors differ from when you are writing your own stories?
Kate and Caitlin are not just fantastic writers, but they're friends as well, which made collaboration and communication so much easier. There's a fine balance to constructing a series that will have different elements executed by different authors. I'm used to focusing on an individual book, but in this case a broader awareness was required.

What was the biggest challenge? And what did you most enjoy about it?
I think the biggest challenge was pinpointing which series elements needed to happen in which book. There has to be excitement and new revelations in every installment of the series, and making those decisions was tricky! I think what I most enjoyed was brainstorming as a group. Watching this germ of an idea expand and grow. We each brought a unique perspective to the overall series, which created something I'm not sure would have been possible if we'd simply tackled it as individuals.

As you wrote your hero and heroine was there anything about them that surprised you?
I think Austin surprised me the most. He has such a huge amount of decency, and so many ideas about what it means to be a good man. Which is why he's so conflicted by what he sees as "dark desires." They don't mesh with who he thinks he should be. But even I was surprised by the full intensity that he had hidden beneath his suit!

What was your favourite part of creating the world of *Fifth Avenue*?
I love the idea that such a beautiful world, insulated by money and power, could be hiding something so dark. I think digging in and exposing all the ugliness beneath the glitter, and really going for the scandal, was so much fun!

If you could have given your heroine one piece of advice before the opening pages of the book, what would it be?
Probably DON'T sleep with your mortal enemy's son. (Katy says: But he's superhot and good with a tie. Me: I retract my advice.)

What was your hero's biggest secret?
A lot of the secrets in the book belong to other people. Austin is, in many ways, kind of a normal guy (for a billionaire philanthropist). But I think his biggest secret is what he really craves from a sexual partner. He was even lying to himself about it! Until Katy.

What does your hero love most about your heroine?
Her strength. She's been through hell and never stops pushing, never stops pursuing justice for her sister, and a better life for her brother.

What does your heroine love most about your hero?
I think Austin restored her faith in people. And in love.

Which of your *Fifth Avenue* characters would you most like to meet and why?
I'll be very simple and say Austin. Who doesn't love a hot man in a suit?

HPQA0614TR

HARLEQUIN®

Presents®

Glamorous international settings…
powerful men… passionate romances

Harlequin Presents stories are all about romance and escape—glamorous settings, gorgeous women and the passionate, sinfully tempting men who want them.

From brooding billionaires to untamed sheikhs and forbidden royals, Harlequin Presents offers you the world!

Eight new passionate reads available every month wherever books and ebooks are sold.

HPBPA2014TR

Harlequin Presents welcomes you to
the world of **The Chatsfield;**

Synonymous with style, spectacle…and scandal!

SHEIKH'S SCANDAL by *Lucy Monroe* (May 2014)

PLAYBOY'S LESSON by *Melanie Milburne* (June 2014)

SOCIALITE'S GAMBLE by *Michelle Conder* (July 2014)

BILLIONAIRE'S SECRET by *Chantelle Shaw* (August 2014)

TYCOON'S TEMPTATION by *Trish Morey* (September 2014)

RIVAL'S CHALLENGE by *Abby Green* (October 2014)

REBEL'S BARGAIN by *Annie West* (November 2014)

HEIRESS'S DEFIANCE by *Lynn Raye Harris* (December 2014)

Step into the gilded world of **The Chatsfield!**
Where secrets and scandal lurk behind every door…

Reserve your room!
June 2014

Love the book you just read?

Your opinion matters.

Review this book on your favorite
book site, review site, blog or your own
social media properties and share
your opinion with other readers!

HREVIEWSTR